D1706982

ARRIVAL

(KYRON INVASION BOOK 1)

(1st Edition)

by Jasper T. Scott

JasperTscott.com
@JasperTscott

Cover Art by Tom Edwards
TomEdwardsDesign.com

CONTENT RATING: PG-13

Swearing: Brief instances of strong language
Sexual Content: Mild
Violence: Moderate

Author's Guarantee: If you find anything you consider inappropriate for this rating, please e-mail me at JasperTscott@gmail.com and I will either remove the content or change the rating accordingly.

ACKNOWLEDGMENTS

My thanks go out to my editor, Aaron Sikes and to my proofreader, Dani J. Caile. And a big thanks to my family. I never could have finished this book on time without your support.

Also, I owe another big thank-you to my advance readers who saved me from a great deal of embarrassment by finding the remaining typos in this book. My heartfelt gratitude goes out to: Ray Burt, Gwen Collins, Michael Madsen, Bob Sirrine, Harry Huyler, Jackie Gartside, Howard Cohen, Gaylon Overton, William Dellaway, Mary Whitehead, George Geodecke, and Mary Kastle.

Finally, many thanks to the Muse.

To John Bowlzer, who said he wished I'd write another book in the Ascension Wars Series. Here it is, John, with another two to come. Thanks for the great idea.

DAY ONE

CHAPTER 1

I pull into the employee parking lot around back of the Pearson family estate and kill the rumbling V8 of my antique gas-powered F150. The engine takes a few seconds to actually shut off, rumbling and wheezing even after I've stabbed the ignition button.

Popping the door open, I step out and straighten my suit and activate my Augmented Reality Contacts (ARCs). They detect the degree of sunlight and automatically tint themselves to my preferred setting. Colorful icons appear, crowding the edges of my vision. An envelope for messages. A telephone for incoming calls. The ubiquitous gear icon for settings. A miniature map in the top right with me in the center, three green dots up ahead, which are the Pearson family, sans Mr. Pearson, and a few blue dots to mark their domestic bots, shuffling about doing chores.

I feel a sigh building in my chest, but it dies

before it reaches my lips. I'm lucky to have this job. I have to remember that.

But I hate mixed reality overlays, just like I hate self-driving electric vehicles and smart guns, and a dozen other trappings of the modern world. But I'm on the job now, and Mrs. Pearson insists that I use my ARCs.

"You don't have eyes in the back of your head, Mr. Randall! That's what ARCs are for. To warn you of potential threats before you even see them coming."

I had to bite my tongue to keep from telling her that most criminals have found a way to deactivate or block the signals from their ID chips, so ARCs *won't* see them coming. ARCs are just fancy comms without the audio, controlled mentally via neural implants. They're talking constantly to the Satnet, sharing what I see and where I am with AI-driven supercomputers to help me identify, highlight, and interact with bits and pieces of the world around me. Whatever happened to using our own damned brains? Pretty soon we won't actually have any knowledge or ideas of our own, only what Big Data and Big AI feed to us.

Twisting around, I ignore the mixed reality overlays and scan the expansive grounds of the Pearson Estate with my real eyes. Bright green grass and hedges speak to an excessive use of water in an otherwise dry and parched landscape.

A cloud of dust is still settling in the wake of my truck. The employee lot is gravel, not paved. Mrs. Pearson keeps nagging Mr. Pearson about that, but he has other priorities. Golf mostly, and sailing around the world on his yacht—or buying more diamond-studded bags and jewelry for his wife to apologize for spending so much time away from home. Diamond studded problems for diamond studded people. Must be nice.

I cross the parking lot briskly, my boots crunching on the gravel. Within seconds I'm melting beneath my layers. It's mid-January, but today is shaping up to be a hot day, and San Bernardino is never really cold. Doesn't help that the air conditioner in my truck was blasting tepidly on the way over. Yet another damned thing to fix.

I reach the asphalt driveway and see it sparkling with flecks of silica and quartz even through my sunglasses. As I jog up the marble steps to the front door, I self-consciously pat my hip to check that my sidearm is there. Of course, it is. I wouldn't forget that. Then again, I have been more scattered than usual lately.

Money troubles have split my focus in a thousand different directions. The car needs repairs; the house has a leaky roof; my wife's student loan payments are going up, not down. Some months we have to choose between feeding our kids and paying the minimums, and damn it if food isn't getting more expensive by the day.

My wife, Bree, and I have been over the

budget a hundred times; on her salary as a hostess, and mine as a bodyguard, there's no other way to fix our downward spiral unless one of us starts making more money—and fast.

So, I'm going to try asking my bosses for a raise. I'm really not sure which way that's going to go. They spend more money on a Saturday afternoon than they pay me in a month to be their bodyguard-slash-driver, but that doesn't mean much. Rich people, I've learned, can be both cheap and lavish at the same time.

I reach the top of eight onyx steps leading to the columned portico and stand patiently in front of an extra-wide, frosted and stylized glass door with a gold inlay that might actually be real. This is the entrance of the Pearsons' boxy mansion. There's no need to knock or touch the holocomm. By now the security system has already recognized and announced me.

Plodding footsteps approach the door, followed by the sound of locking bolts *thunking* aside. Then the door pivots open from its center, and I'm greeted by Emily, the Pearsons' head domestic bot. She's all gleaming white plastic and rubberized padding, with a vaguely human face and rubbery expressions that make her look more frightening than friendly. And those fiercely glowing blue eyes have always looked far too human for my taste.

"Hello, Mr. Randall," Emily says.

"Call me, Chris." We have this conversation

every damn day.

"Of course, Mr. Chris Randall. Mrs. Pearson is waiting for you in the parlor. Please follow me."

My brow furrows as I follow the robot inside. Mrs. Pearson is rarely up this early, and what is she doing *waiting* for me? Maybe she had some business to attend to for a change.

Emily's pace is ambling at best, a fact which leaves me with the urge to breeze by her to the parlor, but I hold myself back. I'm not going to go barging around like I own the place. Not today.

I distract myself by taking in the details of the home as we walk through the entrance hall. White marble floors gleam under sloping skylights. Sweeping glass and chrome stairs rise to either side of the entrance hall to a balcony supported by square columns paneled with brushed steel and more onyx. We walk under that balcony and emerge in the great room. Twenty-four-foot ceilings soar above an austerely decorated space. Massive windows look down on the city of San Bernardino below.

Emily leads me to one side, to the parlor. A pair of glass and chrome doors slide open ahead of our approach, and we pass into a large sitting room with sofas, a poker table, a pool table, and a wet bar. Floor-to-ceiling windows overlook a pristine patch of bright green grass and a rose garden that's been trimmed into a maze. Mrs. Pearson is sitting on a white sofa, sipping what might be a mimosa from a fluted glass.

She smiles tightly as I come in, and the glowing displays vanish from her ARCs, leaving cold blue eyes in their wake.

Jessica Pearson is a gracefully aging, blonde former model, turned socialite, with a sharply-angled face that actually looks airbrushed. That face once adorned dozens of holomags and earned her minor roles in at least as many holovids. At forty-one she's twelve years Mr. Pearson's junior and five years younger than me, but she could pass for thirty-one in a heartbeat.

And yet, my wife makes her look like a horse's ass. That thought makes me smile. There's no love lost between me and Mrs. Pearson, but I hide my side of it well.

I stop in front of Jessica with my hands folded in front of me. "Good morning, ma'am," I say, inclining my head to her in a shallow nod.

"Sit please, Mr. Randall." She gestures off-handedly to a matching couch opposite hers. I glance at the sofa. It's white. My suit is black. For some reason, I'm worried that the color will rub off. That's probably because Mrs. Pearson once mentioned in passing to me that these sofas cost forty thousand credits each.

I take my seat reluctantly, but sit perched on the edge of it rather than leaning back as she does.

Mrs. Pearson regards me steadily over the rim of her champagne glass, her blue eyes like ice chips. She's frowning, but her face doesn't crease or wrinkle the way it should. The skin is too thin from her diet of alcohol, fat-burner pills, and plastic surgery. There's nothing left to wrinkle up.

Something is wrong. I can feel it. *Shit. What did I do?* Whatever it is, it's going to make asking for a raise a lot harder.

I clear my throat to get the ball rolling. "Ma'am, is there something you wanted to ask me?"

"No, not ask. This is more of something you tell." She takes another sip of her drink. "Would you like one?"

Before I can remind her that it's nine in the morning and that I'm on duty, she snaps her fingers at Emily and says. "Another mimosa, please."

"Of course, ma'am." The robot goes whirring off toward the bar.

Mrs. Pearson obviously doesn't remember that I hate fruity drinks, but I'll take a sip just to be polite.

"I don't know how to put this, Mr. Randall." She cradles her glass in her lap and peers into it, as if looking for inspiration. "I want you to know that this hasn't been an easy decision."

What hasn't? Spit it out already, I want to say.

She takes a breath. "We will no longer be re-quiring your services."

I blink in shock and my jaw drops. I'm left shaking my head slowly. Emily sidles up with my mimosa and passes it to me. "Here you are, sir."

I snatch the drink from her and gulp down half the glass before I remember what it is. It goes down with a grimace. "Can I ask why?"

"Of course—Jeremy, come in here please."

I hear more whirring of motors and robotic joints, muffled by the distance, but approaching fast. A blue dot comes inching toward me on the map in the top right corner of my ARCs.

I turn toward the sound just in time to see the glass doors of the parlor swinging open, and a gleaming black version of Emily stepping in. He walks up to us. He's wearing two weapons, one holstered on each hip. A stun gun on the left, and smart-locked M91 on the right. It's a civilian version of the M99 that the Union Army and Space Marines currently use. I handled weapons like those back in the days when I was an Army grunt, and again when I transferred to Space Force, but these days my guns are all old school, just like my truck.

"You bought a bodyguard bot." I turn back to Mrs. Pearson and stare hard at her. "What happened to not trusting machines to protect your family?"

"Civil defense units have come a long way since we hired you, Mr. Randall. Omicron Delta is revolutionizing the business. Their programming is state-of-the-art, as are their bots. I'm told they're impossible to hack."

"Impossible is a big word, ma'am. Even if it's

true, they still can't respond to threats with lethal force if the need arises, whereas I'm fully licensed to do so."

"They can use lethal force after a remote pilot takes control, and Omicron has pilots standing by 24/7 for just that purpose. One call, or even just uttering our code word, and they'll connect immediately."

"What about driving? You may as well leave your cars on autopilot if you're going to let a bot take the wheel. It's the same damn thing."

"Again, autopilot is much better than it used to be, but a remote pilot can also take manual control of any of our vehicles if the need arises, just the same as you could."

"Mr. Pearson can't be okay with this," I insist.

"He was the one who suggested it."

I knock back the remainder of my mimosa and set it down on the priceless designer coffee table between us. Emily swoops in to remove the fluted glass before it can make a ring. Not that it would. It's a champagne glass. *Stupid bot...*

"Did I do something wrong?" I ask. "I realize I've been distracted lately, but I promise I've got my head in the game now. Would you consider keeping me on? Double the protection wouldn't hurt. This city is only getting more dangerous, and it would be good to have someone to go with you or your husband when you travel. The bot could stay and look after the kids when you're out."

Mrs. Pearson chews briefly on her bottom lip, revealing blindingly white teeth. She looks sheepish, like there's something else she wants to say. And then she says it: "Paul, would you come in here, please?"

Another whirring sound starts up, approaching fast from the distant recesses of the mansion. I'm on my feet before it comes gliding in. I've worked for the Pearson family for almost a decade, and this is how they repay me? So much for a raise.

A second gleaming black machine appears and stops beside the first. Both look identical. I wonder how the Pearsons can tell them apart. Jeremy and Paul. May as well just call them CDU One and CDU Two.

"You'll be paid a generous severance, of course," Mrs. Pearson says.

"Yeah, of course," I say, and nod stiffly to her. In this economy, it won't last long. "Well, I guess this is goodbye," I say. "Tell the kids I said *adios,* would you?"

Mrs. Pearson rises to her feet now, setting her glass aside. "I am truly sorry about this, Chris. You're welcome to come by and visit anytime."

Ten years of *Mr. Randall,* and *now* she calls me Chris. "Yeah, I'm sorry, too," I say, already turning to go.

"Maybe you should apply to be a remote operator with Omicron," Mrs. Pearson says. "We would give you a glowing reference."

I smirk at that. "Maybe, yeah." It's an old joke. I got out of the military when they started replacing us with remote-piloted units. My simulator scores were too low. Those damn VR helmets make me dizzy as hell. SpaceComm was going to ground me and make me a trainer at the academy, but I checked out instead. Something tells me my VR scores will be too low for Omicron, too.

"Let me show you out," Mrs. Pearson says, wringing her hands awkwardly. At least she feels bad.

I wave my hand dismissively at her and send her half of a smile. "Don't bother. I know the way." And then I'm turning and striding past my mechanical replacements with my pulse singing in my ears. My boots strike the marble floor like hammers.

Plenty of people have been replaced by cheap robotic labor over the years, but somehow, I'd lulled myself into thinking that I couldn't be replaced, that after all of these years the Pearsons felt some kind of loyalty toward me. Hell, their kids knew me from the cradle up. I was like family.

Or so I'd thought, but I should have known better. You don't call family by their last name.

CHAPTER 2

Streetlights strobe through the windows of my truck like golden lasers as I drive down the Foothill Freeway on the outskirts of San Bernardino. Glowing lines of air car traffic trace grid patterns in the sky. I take Exit 79 and hook a right past the Taco Cabana. I'm on my way to pick up my wife from The Pines, the fancy steakhouse where she works.

Since Mrs. Pearson fired me this morning, I've spent the whole day visiting security companies and sending out resumes. I even squeezed in a few interviews and visited the local branch of Omicron Delta to take a run at their simulator room. My scores were crap, but I already knew they would be. I'm a dinosaur in the modern era—obsolete just like my antique gas-powered truck.

As if to rub it in, I pass a supercharger station full of Teslas, but nary a gas station in sight. I have to lug gas around in jerry cans and order it special-delivered to my house. Old, refurbished gas and diesel vehicles from the 21st-Century are a niche market, mostly old-schoolers like me who don't trust a car that will pull itself over for the authorities and drive at 59 miles an hour when sixty is the limit.

I breathe out a sigh and smack the steering wheel with the heel of my hand. What am I going to tell Bree? My mind turns to that severance Mrs. Pearson mentioned. Maybe it will be enough to tide us over until I can land a new gig. There has to be something I can do besides security. Some job market that the machines haven't already taken over.

And that's the other reason these old gas and diesel cars are still around—backlash against the rise of the machines. They're not smarter than us, thank God, but that hardly matters. As it turns out, most of our jobs were repetitive half-witted affairs to begin with. All that's left is the complicated shit. Like programming the machines. It's one big damn vicious circle. My wife's lucky. She got her job as a hostess because it turns out that pretty women are still a valuable commodity. A groundswell of hot robots will probably replace her one day, but for now they're too dumb to bat their eyes at assholes' innuendos while their wives are in the ladies' room. I guess having to flirt with a robot takes all the fun out of it.

I smirk dryly at that. What I wouldn't give to sit through one of Bree's shifts with my Glock and cap them all below the waist. I'd be doing the world a favor, taking out the next generation of assholes before they can be born.

Before I know it, I'm pulling into the lot outside the old San Manuel Casino. The Pines has always catered to the money crowd, another reason the place is still in business and able to employ real people. An air car hovers down a few spaces over from me. I watch as a young couple emerges from the vehicle, all smiles in their expensive, designer clothes. They're probably out for a night of gambling at the casino. Living it up, while I'm barely getting by. It's hard not to feel resentful of that. At their ages, what are the odds that they actually worked for any of their money? Probably spoiled brats with trust funds. Their air car alone is worth as much as my house.

Opening my door, I jump down and slam it behind me with a *bang* that makes the young woman flinch. Her boyfriend turns a disdainful look my way.

"Sorry," I say through a smile.

He looks away and I hear them muttering about me under their breath as they lead the way to the casino.

The night air is warm and dry. I take a deep breath to calm myself.

Soon I'm walking past the colorful lights and electronic beeps and bleeps of slot machines, watching scantily clad human waitresses cruising around with trays full of complimentary drinks. Funny how the seedy underbelly of society is still more human than not.

I reach the end of the casino and walk down a marble-lined corridor to the restaurant. The flashing lights and sounds of the casino fade away as the door of The Pines swings open for me. A male host is on the other side of the door, holding it open, while his female counterpart, Julie, is standing ready with a smile at the welcome stand behind the doors. She's the girl who takes over for my wife when her shift ends. Her eyes light with recognition upon seeing me, and she says, "I'll let Bree know you're here."

"Thanks," I say.

I glance around the waiting area, consider sitting on one of those sticky wooden benches, but then think better of it.

Julie hasn't moved from her position; that's what comms and ARCs are for, but I didn't hear her speaking into her ear piece, either. Maybe she used her neural implant for a text message.

Probably.

The door swings open behind me and I turn to see a *handsome* couple walking in—a man of at least seventy who's all wrinkles and beer belly, and a girl of eighteen or twenty who could be a model or a hooker, hard to say which. The man's arm is wrapped around her bare shoulders like a scarf, but that does nothing to cover up her substantial cleavage. His lilting gait suggests that his arm might be there because he's using her instead of his cane tonight.

I step out of the way and watch with a frown as they walk by. My ARCs would give me their names and ages if I cared to activate them, but I don't. My eyes are good enough, and I don't care to know the names of people I'm never going to talk to.

The man is obviously drunk, and smiling insouciantly. That's the word. Damn it if my law degree didn't turn out to be a pile of horse shit. The system is mostly automated these days, so only the best get to practice. Smiling. Not a lot of guys come out of a casino with a smile. He must be a lucky winner. That, or he's so damned rich that he doesn't care if he wins or loses. Maybe the girl is his prize tonight.

I snort at that, and cross my arms over my chest, turning away from the spectacle to peer out the glass doors at the gleaming marble corridor I came from. Colorful reflections from the flashing neon lights of the casino are the only sign that it's there. On this side of the doors, all I can hear is the crystal melodies of classical piano music mingling with the hushed conversations of late-night diners and knives and forks sawing on expensive china.

Bree and I are barely paying for rent and groceries and there are guys out there buying dinners that cost half of my monthly paycheck— or the paycheck I used to get, I remind myself. It doesn't seem to matter how bad things get, there's always going to be someone standing on top of the garbage heap.

"Chris!"

I spin around and my wife is all but running to reach me. My mood immediately brightens with the sight of her. She's smiling and smelling of the cheap perfume I bought her for our anniversary. She crashes into me and wraps her arms around my neck. Guava-scented shampoo fills my nostrils as I bury my face in her dark brown hair. She pulls away and kisses me quickly on the lips, leaving me with the taste of strawberry lip gloss. Her hand slides into mine, and I catch Julie looking on with a wistful smile as Bree peels away from me.

"Get a room," Julie mutters wryly.

"That's the plan!" Bree answers with a grin. She grabs onto my arm as we leave the restaurant.

The sounds of slots and roulette wheels and of dealers' repetitive announcements come fading back into range of hearing as we stride down the marble corridor. If I had my ARCs on, those glowing displays would all be leaping out at me in a desperate attempt to suck me dry.

"I'm *so* tired," Bree whispers beside my ear; then she adds, "These heels are killing me!" I notice her batting her eyes at me. "My feet *need* your hands."

"Just your feet, huh?" I ask with one eyebrow raised.

Bree   punches   my   arm   and   withdraws

sharply, pretending to be annoyed. I reel her back in. "I was just kidding."

She smiles, gleaming like the jewel she is, and then we're gliding through the casino like we own the place. Poor as dirt, but rich in all the ways that count.

Back outside, a cool night breeze makes Bree shiver and throws her hair in front of her face. She reaches up to tuck dark strands behind her ears. Scattered couples are leaving the casino with us. Most of them are drunk and stumbling. That's one good thing auto-piloted electric cars did for us: no more drunk drivers. I steer Bree around them to our truck and open the door for her.

"Always such a gentleman," she says as I help her up.

I slam the door behind her with a *boom*, because that's the only way to shut the door of an antique like mine.

Then I'm climbing in on the driver's side and stabbing the glowing blue ignition button to start the truck. The engine turns over a few too many times, then clicks sullenly, waiting for me to try again.

"Shit," I mutter under my breath.

"What's wrong?" Bree asks, rubbing her bare arms to keep warm. I guess I didn't notice when the desert went from warm to cold. That's the beauty of deserts; after the sun goes down, it just takes a stiff wind to blast the heat away.

I scan the dash, hoping for my relic of a truck to give me a clue. The engine light is on, but it's always on, so that doesn't mean much. I try the ignition again. More impotent crackling from the spark plugs as the engine sputters.

My breath comes out in a sigh. "Damn it! Not today old girl. Come on." I whisper a prayer and try to start the vehicle one last time.

This time something wheezes like an old man on oxygen, followed by a *boom* that could have come from a shotgun.

Bree jumps a few inches out of her seat with the noise.

I spare a grin for her as I shift down into reverse. "Just some bad gas," I say.

Bree glares at me. "We need a new car."

With what money? I think, but I nod agreeably as I twist around to look where I'm going as I back out.

There's a gleaming black machine standing right behind the truck with both hands raised.

"Halt!" I hear the booming robotic voice and stomp on the brakes to avoid running the thing over.

The machine glows crimson in the brake lights as it lowers its hands and comes clanking up to my window. It raps gently on the glass with a metal fist. *Clink clink clink.*

I lower the window. "Something wrong, bolts?"

"My designation is CDU-TR4479, but the

proper colloquial term is simply *bot*. And yes, there is a problem. A high decibel noise erupted from your location a moment ago. Pattern-matching suggests a 99.9% likelihood that the sound resulted from the illegal discharge of a firearm. The authorities have been notified. I'm here to inform you that you are strictly prohibited from leaving the premises until this matter has been resolved."

I'm too shocked to reply. My jaw is hanging open.

Bree leans over me with a smile to say, "It was just the car. It's not electric. It backfired."

The bot glances back at the rear of my truck, as if to check for evidence of what she's saying. "I am afraid I cannot verify those claims. You will still have to explain yourself to the police before you can leave. Please turn off the vehicle."

I grit my teeth. If I turn it off now, I probably won't get it to start again. The old gal needs a few hours of quality time with me under the hood. If that sounds dirty, it's because it is; she's turned half a dozen of my t-shirts to grease-stained rags.

"Am I talking to a human operator?" I ask.

"No, sir."

"Then get me one."

"All operators are currently engaged. Please hold."

"Holy shit... you've got to be kidding me. This is what we get for replacing ourselves."

Bree pulls me back from the open window before I can add vandalism to the specious charge of firing a weapon that I don't even have in my truck. To be fair, I do have my Glock in the glove box, but it doesn't sound like a shotgun when it goes off.

"How long before the authorities arrive?" I ask. "You're wasting my gas."

"Typical response time is five to ten minutes, sir."

"And how long before I can speak to a human operator?"

"Ten to fifteen minutes, sir."

This must be a joke. Or maybe a nightmare. That's it. I'm face down at the bar I went to after passing out all my resumes, and Bree is pissed as hell that I forgot to pick her up.

"Just let it go," she whispers to me. "Tell me about your day. How did it go with the Pearsons?"

I stare blankly at her for a second. Her clear, amber brown eyes are aglow in the bluish light of her ARCs. I find myself staring at the reversed images of tiny icons clustered around the edges of her irises. Such pretty eyes to hide with all that clutter.

"The raise...?" Bree prompts me.

Somehow, in the time between arriving and Bree pouncing on me with a hug, I forgot that I'm the bearer of bad news.

Her eyebrows are hopefully raised, lips ever so slightly parted, as if she's getting ready to scream for joy and kiss me. Bree's always been the optimist.

"I didn't get it," I say.

Her face falls. "What? But did you explain, did you tell the Pearsons that we're—"

I cut her off with a shake of my head. "I didn't even get that far. Mrs. Pearson fired me before I could ask."

The color drains from Bree's face, and something inside of me withers and dies.

"But... why? Did you do something to upset them?"

"That's what I asked. No, they decided to upgrade with two matching boltheads like slick over here." I jerk a thumb at it.

Bree is speechless. Her eyes are wide and unblinking. She and I both know what could be next. We've driven past the lines at the UBI offices and ration counters more times than we can count. You lose your job these days and it's not like you can just go out and get yourself another one. Unemployment is a one-way street, and it usually leads to another one: union housing projects. Ghettos by any other name.

"Hey, it'll be okay. I'm getting a nice severance."

Bree just nods.

We have two kids and my mother at home. That makes five mouths to feed. One job as a hostess and a dwindling severance check aren't going to cut it for long.

"I could pick up some extra shifts on the weekends," she says slowly, her voice as dull as a rusty knife as she stares sightlessly out the windshield at the flashing lights of the casino.

"Hello, sir, I am Operator 917 of the Ophram Security Group. I see here that you've been detained on negligent discharge of a firearm, pending investigation by the police. Is that correct?"

My head turns and lands on the gleaming black bot standing beside my truck. He's wearing a human face now, projected a few millimeters under his vaguely human features. The man tries on a tight smile.

I glare back at him. "As I told your bot, it was my truck backfiring."

"Yes, I have record of that conversation here. The trouble is, we don't know for sure that is the case, and I can't legally search your vehicle for weapons, so we still need to wait for the authorities to arrive."

A distant *boom* thunders through the night, and I'm expecting a flash of lightning to follow, but I should know better. Lightning doesn't *follow* thunder.

Half a dozen more claps of thunder rumble through the air in quick succession, and then I'm staring up at the grid patterns of traffic in the sky. Glowing orange contrails slice between the flowing lines of traffic. A squadron of scimitar starfighters is streaking down from space at a forty-five-degree angle between the air cars.

Sonic booms. That's what the sound was. Those glowing tails of fire vanish into thick clouds soaked black with the night, and then emerald lightning illuminates the clouds from within, and I hear more thunder—followed by flaming chunks of debris raining out over the valley.

CHAPTER 3

The operator controlling that security bot is gawking at the sky as I roar out of the parking space. As soon as we're clear, I ram the gas pedal to the floor.

"Look out!" Bree says as I almost slam into a Tesla that's busy reversing out of another space in front of us. The autopilot sees us coming and stops immediately.

We roar past it, leave the lot, and fishtail onto the street. I'm going flat out, weaving between auto-driving cars to get home faster. They're all driving the limit and keeping to their lanes, but their human passengers are hanging out the windows and staring up at the sky. A flash of light dazzles my eyes and then another boom *rattles* through the windows of the truck. More fiery debris blossoms in the sky.

"Chris, what's happening?" Bree screams as she yanks out her seatbelt. It locks up at the speed we're going, and she has to try again.

"The hell if I know," I say. A wall of red taillights appears up ahead, and I see the traffic light where all those cars have stopped. Cursing under my breath, I stomp on the brakes and sit leaning over the steering wheel, my eyes darting among the clouds and the air traffic above us. Air cars are streaming away to all sides, some coming down for emergency landings, others fleeing for the mountains.

A distant, roaring chorus of ion thrusters screams, followed by the rattling cry of fifty cal. cannons, and the *booming* of missiles striking their targets. Flashes of light precede those concussive blasts, but I can't see what they're hitting. Tracer fire slashes out in crisscrossing golden lines to targets unseen. The chemical rockets of missiles flare bright orange then shriek away on thin gray lines of vapor.

Finally, as if someone was asleep at the switch, the whooping cry of the civil defense sirens starts up.

"Is it a war?" Bree asks. The traffic light flicks green and I'm gritting my teeth in frustration as the mob of electric cars ahead of me rolls leisurely through the intersection.

"With who?" I ask, shaking my head. "The UNE is it. There's just one government for the whole damn solar system."

"Then it's terrorists," Bree suggests.

A stuttering flash of emerald fire turns the sky into a laser light show and more explosions pepper the night. A chill courses down my spine. "Who the hell fires lasers in atmosphere?" I ask, forgetting that Bree doesn't know about these things.

"Why not?" she asks slowly, her voice a shaky whisper as she stares up at the sky.

"Because water vapor splits the beams, making them less effective. You don't use lasers in a dogfight any more than you'd use a knife in a gunfight. They're space-to-space ordnance not air-to-air. We use them to punch holes in enemy hulls from extreme range. As far as I know, we don't even have lasers on our fighters, which means those have to be coming from orbital ships. Except..." I'm watching the next volley as it lights up the night.

The beams are all horizontal, which puts the source somewhere in atmosphere, not orbital. This time I see what I missed before. It looks like a cloud, but it's not. It's a giant wall of shadows cruising along the horizon at about 5,000 feet —an aircraft carrier in the sky. But we don't have anything like that, certainly nothing that big that can fly in atmosphere. It's like the thing is just floating there, which of course, is impossible. A light bulb blinks on in my brain.

"It's not terrorists," I say.

"Then what is it?" Bree asks, not having seen the wall of shadows.

"It's an invasion."

"An invasion? From where?"

"Call home. Tell Mom to start packing. Clothes, food, jackets, gloves—make sure she has the kids ready to go. We need to bug out as soon as we get there."

Bree nods woodenly and pulls out a comm piece from her bag. She slots it into her left ear and says, "Call home."

I'm still weaving through traffic. At least these auto-piloted cars are good for something: they're all leaving a perfect following distance. They may as well be orange cones in a parking lot, or trees in a slalom race.

"Well?" I ask.

"It's ringing..." Before I can say anything else, Bree says, "Mom! Start packing. We're on our way... yes, I know we've seen it... The news is saying *what?*" Bree's hand flies up to her mouth and she looks to me with terrified eyes. "That's not... who... what are they?"

I spare a hand from the wheel and make a cutting gesture. "It doesn't matter. She needs to get packing, now!" I veer into oncoming traffic to avoid hitting a car that stopped to let someone out of their driveway. The oncoming vehicle blinds me briefly with its lights, and then I duck back into my lane. We're almost home now. Houses are flashing by on either side. Cars are backing out of their driveways everywhere I look. People are making a run for it, just like I'm planning to. More explosions echo in my ears, farther away now. The battle is drifting toward LA. I almost breathe a sigh of relief with that, but it catches in my throat. There are millions more people in LA than San Bernardino.

I turn onto our street and roar down to the end. We're in the cul-de-sac, right next to the mansion at the end. I barrel up the driveway to my parents' old house, stop in front of the two-car garage, and leave the engine running. I turn to look at Bree as I unbuckle and crack my door. She's looking at me with glazed eyes. Shock is settling in.

"Snap out of it!" I bark at her.

She flinches at the sudden volume of my voice, but her eyes swim back into focus. "We don't have long before things get really bad. If we want to live through this, we need to get ahead of it."

"Get ahead of it?" Bree is shaking her head. "Get ahead of it *where?* They're invading *Earth,* Chris, not California. It doesn't matter where we go!"

"Wrong. We go somewhere far from other people, as remote as we can get. If the goal is to wipe us out, we need to be as far from population centers as possible. And if the goal is something else... same thing. Now let's go!"

I jump out of the truck and run up the walkway to the front entrance. Then I'm leaping straight up the short flight of stairs to the front porch. Old wooden beams creak and sag with my weight. My wife's footsteps come racing up behind me as I fumble with my keys to find the one for the house.

Bree starts repeatedly stabbing the old vidcomm buzzer before I can find the key. The front door swings open, and we're greeted by my mother and our two kids, Zach and Gaby. My mom's face is pale and drawn, more wrinkled than I remember it. She waves us through, wincing as another series of explosions shatters the sky with tongues of fire.

"I packed clothes for everyone," my mom says breathlessly as we rush inside. She shuts and locks the door behind us, as if that will keep what's out there from getting in.

Our son and daughter crowd in before we can make it two steps from the door. Both look terrified, their eyes wide and glowing with displays from their ARCs. Gaby wraps her arms around my waist and says, "What's going on, Daddy?" She's six years old with her mother's dark hair and pink lips, but my blue eyes.

Zachary is twelve with a thick mop of blond hair like me, but light, amber brown eyes like his mom. He's trying to look brave, but the act crumbles as another explosion rattles the windows of the sitting room where we're all standing. Zachary's forehead wrinkles and pinches together as he cringes away from the door. His eyes dart up to the ceiling as if he's expecting it to cave in.

"Where are we going?" he asks, swallowing a lump of fear. Bree pulls him into a hug, but his arms stay flat at his sides. He's at that awkward age where he doesn't want to act like a kid, but doesn't know how to be a man.

"Away from the city," I say. My gaze lands on the top of Gaby's head. "Honey, I need to get something, okay?"

She shakes her head.

"It's important," I insist, and gently peel Gaby's arms away from me. On my way down the hall to the basement, I see the pile of backpacks and luggage lying on couches and chairs in the sitting room. I hesitate briefly before glancing back at Bree. She has both Gaby and Zach wrapped up in her arms now. My mother is standing beside them, wringing her hands.

"Bree, make sure they have enough clothes packed. Winter ones especially. And food. The more rations we take with us, the longer we'll last out there."

Bree's eyes flare wide and slide down to Gaby, who I can hear sobbing against her mother's sweater. I grimace at that and turn away, shaking my head. There's no time to sugarcoat this, and frankly, we shouldn't. I'm scared that if my kids don't grow up fast, they're not going to make it through what's to come.

CHAPTER 4

Civil defense sirens are whooping as I load up the back of the truck with the suitcases and backpacks. Zach comes running out with a bag that I missed.

"Thanks. Get back inside with your mother," I say.

Zachary nods and runs back inside.

My eyes flick up to the sky as I bend down to pick up the duffel bag that I packed with guns from the basement. In there are two shotguns, a hunting rifle with a scope, a pair of compact Glock 26 Gen 15's, tac-lights, flashlights, flares, a flare gun, spare batteries, and loads of ammo for all.

I use bungee cords to secure everything, along with a five-gallon tank of fresh water from the dispenser. Bree convinced me to buy it after one of the neighbor's kids got stomach cancer. She was convinced there had to be contamination in the water. Maybe she was right. The hell if it matters now. I pack it all under a blue tarp, leaving plenty of space behind the tailgate for my final addition. Fuel. I look up from my work to scan the sky warily. If you don't count the distant whooping of the civil defense sirens, it's as quiet as a church on a Monday.

I peer due west, down my driveway and over the sycamore trees that line our street. We're slightly up the hills from the city, giving me a peeking view over the scraggly tree-lined suburbs to the blazing streetlights of downtown and empty hills beyond that. Flickers and flashes of light pepper the horizon in the direction of LA, but the booming roar of battle has faded to inaudible whispers with the distance, and I can no longer pick out the jagged mystery bulk of something-that-isn't-a-cloud.

It's almost enough to fool me into believing that those flashes of light are just lightning. I shake my head and suck in a breath of the cool desert air. Snapping out of it, I run around to the driver's side of the truck. She's still idling, snoring in her sleep.

Yanking the door open, I pull the sun visor down and touch the remote for the garage door. I hear the chain rattle to life and the door start clattering up. Before it's even halfway, I'm ducking under and hurrying over to the gasoline drums that line the other side of the two-car garage. We only have one car these days, so I use the second half of the garage for spare fuel. I don't walk straight to the drums, though. They weigh 60 pounds when they're empty, let alone full.

In one dusty corner of the garage, I find what looks vaguely like a metal skeleton standing on a pedestal that's plugged into the wall. A skeleton is exactly what this is. Well, almost.

In one of my more idiotic attempts to keep up with the wave of cheap robotic labor sweeping the globe, I spent a fortune on an exoskeleton. Lining myself up, I step into the boots and clamp them around my own, and adjust the straps for a tight fit. Next, I cinch padded ratchet-clamps around my thighs, then slip into bulky metal gloves and adjust more clamps for my arms. Finally, I close the rib-like metal cage around my chest and shoulders. I test my range of movement by taking a few swings at an invisible punching bag. The exo-skeleton whirs to life with my movements.

A deep female voice says: "Power levels optimal. Warning: joint degradation detected. Please report to the nearest service—"

"Be quiet, Mara," I say, and she shuts up. That's my name for this beasty—the Hindu Goddess of death. She was supposed to make me into superman, or at least Batman. Then a year later, a group of enterprising criminals used suits just like it to pull off a bank heist, and they became illegal for civilian use.

Silence rings loud in the dusty garage, and then a muffled pop reaches my ears. That could have been a thunderous explosion over LA. The noise jolts me into action. I hurry off the charging pedestal, metal legs whirring and buoying my steps to make them unnaturally fast. I feel like I've just stepped off a treadmill at the gym after running for five miles.

Waltzing over to the fuel drums, I bend with the suit's legs, tip the drum up, and work my metal fingers underneath. I let the drum fall back on those fingers, don't even feel the squeeze, and then grab it on the other side and *lift.*

The drum glides up as I straighten. I feel some measure of the weight, but it's not breaking my back or dislocating my shoulders the way it should. Walking out and around to the back of the truck, I ease the drum in past the lowered tailgate. The F150 sags to one side with the weight. I slide it in right behind the wheel well, gouging fresh furrows out of the hardened plastic bottom of the truck bed. I go back for a second drum and then ease it in on the other side and slide it down. That done, I flip the tailgate up and secure both drums with ratchet clamps before hurrying back for the siphon tube and hand pump. The tube connects directly to the spout of the pump so I can gas up without even using the jerry can as a go-between. Stepping back from the truck, I check the sky again. Nothing up there, but a Tesla goes whirring by the driveway. That's the neighbors at the end of the cul-de-sac. We need to hurry.

I run back inside, almost breaking the door as I hammer on it with my hardened fist and the suit's enhanced strength.

A ruffled curtain flies away from one of the slat windows beside the door, and my wife's angry face appears. She opens the door a second later. "You almost gave me a heart attack!" she hisses at me. "I thought—" she breaks off, shaking her head.

"We need to leave. *Now.*"

I hear Gaby crying and my mother trying to soothe her.

Bree turns from the door and yells, "Kids! Mom! Let's go!"

Commotion sounds from the living room, followed by booted feet clodding on the old, creaky pine wood floors. Bree already has her winter coat on, but not zipped—a shiny red jacket that anything with eyes could see for a mile in all directions. Gaby and Zach come into view, wearing piss-yellow and puke-green jackets respectively. My mom is wearing Barbie pink. I grimace at that and shake my head. We're going to stand out like road signs against the snow. My coat is camo-patterned white. Old habits. Speaking of... I'm looking around. My eyes land on Bree just as she's bending to grab something behind the door.

"Here," she says to me, hoisting a heavy duffel bag up and handing it to me. "Clothes and food. Jacket, gloves, and tuque."

I nod at that and step aside to usher everyone out ahead of me. It's been at least twenty minutes since we arrived. We need to hurry. My eyes are drawn back to the flickering flashes of light coming from LA. The battle is still raging there, but nothing catastrophic yet. How long before they break out the heavy artillery?

I take a breath and shut the door, not even bothering to lock it before tearing off after my family.

CHAPTER 5

I yank open the driver's side door and pass a shotgun and box of ammo over to Bree. She accepts them with wide eyes.

"Just in case," I say. Having all our kit in the back is a bad idea if we run into trouble on our way out. I've already snapped a tac-light to the barrel, and there's a spare flashlight in the glove box with my sidearm and holster from work.

I slide into the driver's seat. It's a bit snug with my exosuit on, but I can't afford to leave it behind. No telling yet if I'll need it to move debris off the road. I also have the tow bar and chains for that.

I yank the door shut with a *bang* and Bree flinches with the sound. Then we're rolling down the driveway. I twist around to look behind us, catching sight of the pale, frightened faces of my children huddled on either side of the ghostly statue that is my mother. She's staring dead-ahead with glassy blue eyes, her head blocking the view out the back window. "Belt up, every-one," I say, noticing that they're not wearing their seat belts yet.

Then we're bouncing heavily through the depression formed by the rain gutter at the entrance of the driveway, and I'm shifting into drive and roaring down the street. A couple of RVs and sports cars litter either side of the road, narrowing the usable lanes down to one. A few sedans are there, too, and I estimate that fully half of our neighbors are hunkering in their basements and praying for a miracle, while the other half have already fled for the hills. Streetlights strobe orange through the windows as we race by, picking up speed. So far, this could be any other night on our street.

"Where are we going?" Bree whispers, then glances around, as if someone, or *something,* might be listening.

Before I can answer her, the sound of car horns rises swiftly into hearing and a snarled intersection appears at the T between our street and the main drag through the suburbs.

"Shit," I mutter, and crank the wheel to get around the gathering knot of EVs. They're supposed to be on autopilot. People are obviously taking manual control and screwing everything up. I jump the curb onto the sidewalk and roll slowly down it with my wheels kicking up dirt and grass to either side of the pavement. A gleaming black Tesla kicks up onto the curb in front of us and honks its horn at the last minute. Too late, and I'm not stopping.

"Hold on!" I say.

Our front ends slam into each other at just ten miles per hour, and the Sedan goes skidding out from under our bumper. I wince at the sound of shrieking metal and shattering glass. The glass is all from the Tesla, though. The driver leaps out of his car, shaking his fist at us as we rumble past. *Sorry bud. Family first.*

I'm coming up on the intersection. The lights are blinking orange just as they always do this time of night—not that people would have paid any attention to them if they'd been blazing red.

I have to scrape through someone's hedge to make it off the sidewalk. Branches scream and leaves rustle against Bree's window; then we're bouncing off the sidewalk and onto gleaming blacktop. The intersection isn't clear enough to get through, and half of the drivers are out of their cars, yelling and pumping their fists at one another, while the other half have their tail lights firing as they bump and scrape around, trying to squiggle free. I'm aiming for a gap of about five feet between two crumpled cars that's just big enough for me to force my way through. Slowing to a crawl, I stick the truck down into four-wheel-low and cruise into the back end of the nearest vehicle. We jerk hard into our seatbelts and then the car's wheels are screaming and skidding on pavement as the other vehicle gives way to my truck and etches out the first fifteen degrees of a donut.

We break free just as the driver of the car hops out. This time I'm in trouble. I see a pistol flash into view, and he's aiming for my window.

"Everybody down!" I cry just as the bullet shatters my window in a pebbly rain of safety glass. I floor it to get away and hear two more parting shots go crunching into the truck.

A few more echo after us, but no impacts register. Then we're racing down North Palm to East Highland.

"Everyone okay?"

A chorus of shaky acknowledgments answers me. Gaby doesn't say anything, so I glance back. She's sobbing, but my mom bobs her head. "Yes. Just drive," she says.

I nod back and check Bree. She's visibly shaken but still breathing and not bleeding, so we're good.

The avenue is four fat lanes wide, and mostly clear. Thank God for that. I weave around a few knots of crashed vehicles coming out of rural side streets along the way. Then we reach the 7-Eleven at the intersection between East Highland and North Palm. It's snarled with crashed vehicles again, but this time it looks like people have made a path. Traffic is snaking steadily through. I join the stream, heading East toward state route 330.

People start banging on the sides of our truck as we slither through, testing the door handles. Rapping on windows.

"Chris..." Bree trails off with her voice rising in alarm.

"Hand me my gun!"

She starts to hand over the shotgun.

"No! In the glove box!"

One of the back windows shatters and Gaby screams.

Bree snags the holster out of the glove box and throws it into my lap. I fumble for a minute with my armored hands. The exosuit is awkward, but my trigger fingers are slimmed down and tapered to fit.

I pull the pistol free and hold it left-handed out the driver's side window, aiming in sweeping arcs. "Get back or I shoot!" I bellow. The crowds stop and hesitate. I catch the glint of someone else's gun swinging into line, and instinct takes over. I fire my Glock at it, and the gun vanishes. The crowd screams and scatters. Then we're through the clog and fanning out with the rest of the traffic.

I pull my gun back in and stow it between my legs before grabbing the wheel two-handed and roaring into the empty oncoming lane. A set of oncoming vehicles barrel around a corner and flash their brights at me. I weave back into my lane between a pair of economy-sized EVs. Within minutes, we're passing the shopping center and flying across the overpass of route 330. I veer left onto a down ramp with a chugging line of vehicles, all heading for the shadowy rise of the San Bernardino Mountains.

In another minute, we're cruising North up the highway with traffic spreading out around us. The city lights and the whooping cry of the civil defense sirens are fading fast behind us.

Cold air hammers in through the two broken windows on my side, and before long I can't feel the left side of my face or hear much out of that ear.

"Chris, where are you taking us?!" Bree asks for the umpteenth time, but this time she has to shout to be heard over the thundering wind.

I jerk my chin to the rising swell of the mountains. "The Pearsons' cabin up in Big Bear," I say.

"But that's not ours! What are we going to do, break in?"

I just look at her, and Bree's eyes sharpen on mine.

"What if they're already there, and they took their bots with them to guard the place?"

I shrug casually. In all honesty, I've been hoping that the Pearsons are among the ones who've decided to hide in their basements. If not—

"I'm like family to them," I say. "I'm sure they'll let us in."

My wife glares darkly for a moment, a look that says I've screwed up. She crosses her arms over her chest and turns her head away, staring out of her window.

A small voice pipes up from the back, all-but stolen by the wind. "Do you think there'll be snow up there?" Gaby asks.

A crooked smile tugs at the corner of my mouth, and I glance at her in the rear-view mirror. Her face is tear-streaked and eyes wide, but innocence is making a swift comeback.

"Maybe, kiddo," I say.

"Good. I like snow," she says.

"Me, too," I reply.

And then a dazzling flash of light tears through the night, and I'm flash-blinded. Our tires squeal as I swerve. A rumbling explosion echoes to my ears, and I'm blinking fast, trying to recover. A faded-green after-image peels away from my eyes to reveal a pitch-black river of asphalt, but nothing else in sight. No street lights. No cars. Not even the reassuring white cones of my own headlights.

I jerk the wheel back over to get us off the shoulder and stare in horror at the fading glory of a massive explosion that just ripped through the sky behind us. As that light fades, the night crowds in and steals away our surroundings.

"Chris! Lookout!" Bree screams, and then I'm slamming on the brakes and swerving again to avoid the sloping, wraith-like curves of a black Tesla with no brake lights. But it's not enough. My brakes have seized up, and the steering wheel is harder and slower to turn than I'm expecting.

The front right corner of our truck slams into the back left of the Tesla, and I fly into my seatbelt. Airbags deploy, and I slam into mine with a loud *slap!* The sound of metal crumpling and glass shattering mingles with my family's screams, and then another blinding flash of light explodes around us, followed by a rumbling *boom.*

CHAPTER 6

The truck comes to a grinding halt, the wheels spitting out tufts of grass and gravel. The airbags have deflated already. Moonlight makes the clouds of dust we've kicked up sparkle around us.

I notice that my dash is dead along with everything else. Even Bree's eyes are dark. I test my ARCs to be sure. Not so much as a flicker of colored icons appears. The familiar rumble of my F150's engine is also gone. No sign of lights along the highway or from the cars now frozen in the middle of it.

And my exosuit has turned to a whole lot of dead weight. I can still move, but my movements are slowed by the weight and friction from the mechanical joints.

"Shit," I mutter.

"What is it?" Bree asks.

I flick the headlights on and off to no effect, then try the turn signal indicators.

Still nothing.

Stabbing the engine start button, I hold my

breath.

Silence. Not even a click.

I stare hard at the wall of shadows behind the steering wheel. Every electrical system was knocked out in an instant. Put that together with the fact that all of the streetlights and the other cars driving around us also lost power, and I know what I'm dealing with.

This was an EMP. Either theirs or ours. An unfortunate side effect of those bright flashes that blinded me in the rear-view. SpaceComm might have decided to nuke the bastards from orbit. High-altitude nuclear blasts would certainly generate a nasty electromagnetic pulse...

Is that what happened?

My thoughts are interrupted by this loud whistling sound coming through the broken window beside me. It sounds like... Missiles. Hundreds of them.

Leaning over the steering wheel, I can't see anything but stars. My brain puts the pieces together a split second before something hits the ground about a hundred meters from us and explodes in a raging fireball. My whole family screams, and I flinch. A shock wave rushes by, briefly warming the frozen side of my face.

"What was that?" my mother cries amidst the whistling roar of a hundred more impending fireballs.

And then they hit and I can actually feel the impacts thumping through the truck and the ground.

"Air cars!" I scream into the deafening roar of explosions.

I briefly consider abandoning the truck with my family, but running around haplessly won't be any safer than sitting tight.

My stomach does a sickening flip as the rumbling roar of explosions rages on, echoing steadily as fireballs pepper both sides of the highway, lighting candles for the dead. Hundreds of cars. Thousands. All falling from the sky, knocked out by that EMP. I hope the president knew what she was doing before she fired those nukes.

Gaby is still crying and screaming even after the cracking thunder of the explosions fades. Her hands are clapped over her ears.

My mother looks equally terrified, cringing as she peers up at the roof of the truck.

"What if one of them falls on us?" she shrieks to be heard above the barrage of crashing vehicles.

Another one crashes about a hundred feet away, and Bree yelps with fright. She turns to me with a tear-streaked face and slowly shakes her head. "All those people..."

My mind flashes back to the bitter envy I experienced when I went to pick up Bree and that young couple landed beside me in their shiny new air car. In hindsight, we're lucky we're not rich like them. Having or not having money doesn't matter anymore. The new haves and have-nots will be determined by a simple binary equation: alive or dead. Survival is the only thing that matters now.

With that in mind, I try to snap armored fingers at my wife, but they grind together soundlessly, so I gesture hurriedly to the glove box instead. "Get the flashlight out."

"The..." Bree is giving me a doe-eyed stare that tells me she hasn't really heard what I just said. Maybe because her ears are still ringing in the wake of those explosions. The booming crashes are distant and sporadic now. Just the high-flying supersonic cars are left.

Rather than ask again, I reach over Bree's lap to pop the glove box open for myself. The flashlight is sitting on top of a heap of tools and old junk. I grab the textured-steel cylinder and flick it on with a welcome wash of clear white light. At least that's working.

"What happened?" my mother breathes shakily from the back. "Why aren't we moving?"

"Daddy, I'm scared!" Gaby adds.

I pop my door open and twist around to look at them. My son, Zach, is quietly staring out his window, watching the flames flicker from hundreds of wrecks.

"Don't be scared, honey," I say to Gaby, and then I reach under the steering column and pop the hood with an audible *clunk* of the catch releasing. "I'll have this fixed in a second."

As I jump out, I notice my wife staring after

me, her eyebrows raised in question. I wave for her to follow. "Bring the shotgun."

It has a second flashlight clipped under the barrel, but that's not why I want her there. If—hopefully *when*—our vehicle starts back up, and all of the others on the highway remain frozen, suddenly we're going to become really popular as the people with the only working vehicle for a hundred klicks in any direction.

I walk around to the front of the truck, reaching in once more to release the safety catch and lift the hood. It's a bit awkward to manage that with my exosuit's armored gloves, but my trigger finger is skinny enough to find the catch and release the hood.

It feels like I'm wearing a lead suit and drowning in molasses. I wonder if I should ditch the suit, but if I can get the truck to start, maybe I can do it for the exosuit, too.

My wife's boots touch down on the other side of the truck with a loud *crunch.* "What caused this?" she asks, her eyes darting around as she stalks over to join me. She has the shotgun in a two-handed grip, and the tac-light on, but keeps the barrel down and pointed away from me. I'm glad she remembers muzzle discipline from the shooting lessons I gave her. The last thing I need right now is for her to blow my foot off. Or her own. "Even my ARCs stopped working," Bree adds.

"Mine too," I say, but don't waste any breath

on further explanations. I'm saving all of my attention for the problem—not the cause.

As I'm shining the flashlight around inside the engine, looking for any obvious issues, the beam flickers over the terminals of the battery, and I sweep it back. No sign of fluids leaking. That's a good sign, but the car wouldn't start when I hit the ignition. Not even a whisper or a chuckle from the engine.

My frown deepens as memories seep back in. I went through EMP training when I was with the Army. They taught us how to reboot equipment. If the exposure wasn't too bad, all it really took to get things running again was to remove or disconnect the batteries and put them back in. That was the technique they taught for getting smart weapons, tracking systems, and gear back online. Maybe it will work for my truck, too.

"Stay here and guard the truck," I say to Bree. "I need to get my tools."

"Guard it?" she asks. "From *what?*" Her voice is small and shivery. It's cold out here, but that's not why. She's shivering from spent adrenaline. I can feel the same thing wobbling in my knees, but I drive it off with a fresh dose of reality. If I can't get this working, we're in big fucking trouble.

I stomp around to the truck bed and reach under the tarp for my tool chest. It's been a permanent fixture in the back of my truck ever since this beauty turned into a beast about six months ago. I kept putting off a visit to my mechanic for a lack of funds. In hindsight, that was probably one of the stupider places to economize.

I yank the tool chest out from under the tarp with a grunt of effort and carry it to the front. It takes me about a minute to loosen the nuts and remove the battery terminals. I count to five—not really sure why—and then re-attach the terminals. By now I'm really doubting that any of this will work, but I don't have any better ideas, and hiking all the way to Big Bear with two kids and my aging mother is simply not an option. Hell, even I would struggle with that, and there's no way we'd be able to bring all of our gear.

"This had better work," I mutter to myself.

"I thought you said you could fix it?" Bree asks, her voice rising to a panicky register.

By now I can hear commotion out on the highway. People are getting out of their useless electric cars and trading equally useless theories about what the hell is going on.

"Hey!" a man says. I whirl toward the voice and see him standing beside the nearest vehicle. It's the black Tesla we smashed into, its rear right fender smashed in from where we hit it.

"What?" I snap.

"You hit my car!" he cries.

Really? That's what he's worried about? I shine my flashlight in his eyes and Bree does the same. He throws up an arm to shield his gaze, then appears to notice the shotgun, curses, and dashes back into his vehicle.

"Yeah, you stay there," I growl.

"Chris... Can you fix this or not?" Bree asks. She flicks a glance over her shoulder to regard me with one of those *don't-you-dare-try-to-bull-shit-me* looks. Her aim is still on the driver's side of the Tesla where that man was standing a moment ago. Good. We don't want him getting twitchy.

"I think I *did* just fix it," is my reply. "Wait here and keep us covered. I'm going to crank it."

Bree's cheeks bulge out with an objection that misses my ears as I run around to the driver's side and hop in. I whisper a prayer before I try the engine start button once more.

This time the lights on the dash flicker on. Headlights blaze to life, and I hear the engine turning over—and over...

She's struggling, same as she was when I picked Bree up from the restaurant.

"Come on, baby... You can do it..."

Sweet-talking doesn't work, so I ease off to give the starter motor a rest, count to three, and then crank it again.

This time she lights up with a throaty roar and another *bang.* "Hell, yeah!" I crow, and slap the steering wheel with my armored palm. The column shudders. Jumping back out, I pack up my tools, then remember why my limbs feel so heavy. Turning my back to Bree, I say, "I need you to eject the battery pack and put it back in.

No tools needed for that. The batteries were designed to swap out with spares while on the job."

"Wh-where?" Bree asks.

"See the red lever just below the big black rectangle?"

"Yes."

"Push it down with your thumb until it clicks."

She does, and I feel the protective casing pop open.

"Good. Now put down the shotgun, and pull the battery out. Careful, it weighs about thirty pounds."

"Okay..."

I feel Bree tugging on my back, then a heavy weight leaves my back, and she grunts. "Now what?"

"Now plug it back in."

Bree puts the battery back, and I raise one gauntlet to flip open the control panel and try the power button.

The suit whirs to life, and I feel about 50 pounds lighter. The automated female voice nags me about servicing the suit. A sigh escapes my lips. Thank God, it worked.

"Pick up the gun. Let's go," I say to Bree.

She nods quickly as I drop the hood with a bang. I lug the tool chest around to the back, and hear Bree's door slam as she returns to the vehicle.

Once I'm climbing back in behind the wheel,

I hear, "Nice work, Dad."

This is from Zach. He sounds genuinely impressed. It's hard to impress him these days, and that brings a smile to my lips.

"Thanks," I say as I shift into drive and crank the wheel around to get back onto the highway. As soon as we're facing the other way, I see the reaction from the other travelers. They're all swarming toward us, waving their arms in the air.

"Chris... w-what do I do?"

She could lower her window and aim the shotgun at them, but I don't think that's a good idea. It's a bluff, and if someone calls it, they might grab the barrel and wrestle the gun away from her.

"Nothing. Just hang on—"

I hit the gas and the V8 roars as we skip up onto the highway and race down the shoulder toward the encroaching crowds. They scatter before us just as I expected they would, but a few of them bend down to throw handfuls of rocks and sand. I hear the debris *skrishing* and *thunking* off the sides of the truck.

Gaby screams, and terrors claws inside of me. Her window is out. If one of those fuckers hit her in the head with a rock—

"Gaby, are you okay?!" Bree cries before I can ask.

"She's fine!" my mom replies.

I gun it down the highway at sixty miles an

hour with the needle edging steadily upward. I'm riding the shoulder the whole way to avoid colliding with the staggered lines of stalled-out EVs. More rocks fly at us, and a soda can splashes off the windshield, leaving a smear of sugar water and a forking crack in its wake.

But then we're through. A collective sigh escapes from all of us. No more cars in sight. No angry mobs. Just open road and Big Bear ahead.

"We're going to make it," I say as I wheel us back onto the highway.

A quick look in the rear-view mirror shows relief cracking through the fear in my kids' eyes, but I can also see flickering pulses of light tearing through the sky above LA, and that adds worry to my mental stack.

What happens when the dust settles? What do these invaders want with us? Who are they? And how am I going to feed my kids in the middle of winter after our hastily-packed stash of rations runs out?

"We need to know what's going on," I say, and start fumbling with the radio to scan for stations. I'm surprised it's taken me this long to think of that.

Before long, a static-filled voice crackles through the speakers:

"*Krsshhh...* —rived with hundreds of ships, now hovering over all of our major cities... *sshhhhrrr...* —'ve lost contact with the colonies on Mars and Europa, and the Fifth Fleet is currently engaged in the Belt. There are widespread reports of landing craft and fighters coming from these vessels... Enemy soldiers are *kshhhh...* Military action...*ksss*—ongoing. Civilians are advised to stay in their homes and stay hidden. *Krsshh...* —do not know what... *kkssshh...* —or where they came from, and we do not know what they want. All we know is that they fired the first—"

My wife kills the radio with a twist of her fingers and gives her head a quick shake. "We know as much as they do," she says.

I can hear Gaby whimpering in the back, and my mother whispering reassurances that sound more frantic than calming. Bree's right. Based on that broadcast, we know as much as anybody else does right now, and there's no sense breathing extra life into our fears by having someone speak them aloud.

Right now, the only good news is that we're still alive, and we have a plan to stay that way.

CHAPTER 7

The winding road up the San Bernardino Mountains steals away the flashing lights of fighters and ordnance exploding over LA. The drive is quiet but for the thunder of wind roaring through the broken windows on my side. My mom and kids are all three asleep in the back, resting on each other's shoulders and laps. It's a good thing they're already wearing their winter coats, because I can see blankets of snow carpeting the sides of the road and weighing down the branches of the pine trees flashing by. My entire face is frozen at this point, and I can't feel my nose, but that's the least of my worries right now.

There haven't been any other cars around us on the way up. I wonder if that's because we left them all behind at the exit from San Bernardino. Did the EMP cut off all of the evacuees? If so, we'll have Big Bear mostly to ourselves. It's not a weekend, so the usual crowds won't be here yet. Just the full-timers, and there aren't that many of them. I'm guessing that the Pearsons didn't make it up here, either. Their mansion is farther from the mountains than our house and all of their vehicles are electric.

I should be happy that we won't have to fight for their cabin, but the thought of them stranded on the side of a road somewhere with two disabled bots and a useless car leaves me with a painful ache in my chest. Sure, they fired me, but I've spent as much time with their kids as I have with my own. Little Haley Pearson reminds me of Gaby, and Sean, A.K.A. Mr. Cool, is only a few years younger than Zach. I still remember both of them crawling into my lap during a particularly rough thunderstorm a couple of years back. Their parents were out, and I was on babysitting duty. They were scared to death in that big echoing mansion, all cold marble and nothing warm...

I shake my head to clear it.

I notice my wife looking at me and biting her lower lip.

"What is it?" I ask her.

"I'm just thinking. If they're so advanced, why aren't they using some kind of advanced weapons on us?"

"Like what?"

"We have nuclear weapons, so they must have something worse," Bree suggests.

I nod along. "Probably."

"So why haven't they used it?"

She makes a good point. Apart from those nuclear blasts that knocked everything electrical out, we haven't seen any serious firepower brought to bear yet, but maybe that's because we're too far from LA to really see what they're doing.

We drive on in silence for a while. The road has leveled out, and Big Bear Lake is coming into view. I can see a few lights glittering between the dark, scraggly cutouts of the pine trees.

"There's still power here," Bree says. "How is that possible?"

"Backup generators," I reply. "People have to have them up here. But they really shouldn't have turned them on."

"They'll freeze without them," Bree says.

"So make a fire. The glow won't be visible from LA. But *lights* can be seen for hundreds of miles from the air. They're going to draw whatever the hell is out there straight to us."

Worry flashes through Bree's eyes as she rubs her hands together and blows into them.

I glance over at her. "Where are your gloves?" My hands are kept warm by the armored gauntlets of the exosuit.

"In the back," Bree says, and I frown unhappily.

"Tuck your hands under your arms."

She does exactly that, and then jerks her chin to the snaking ribbon of gleaming asphalt ahead of us. A dusting of snow is fluttering down and tracing out the cones of our headlights.

"Where is the Pearsons' cabin?" Bree asks.

"Do they have neighbors?"

"They're right on the lake, and they do have neighbors. But these are all vacation homes, so none of those people should be here. We'll avoid drawing attention to ourselves if we keep the lights off."

Bree nods absently with that. There's a wall of tension and fear between us. This feels like a dream, something you see in the holovids, but not for real. Not something that could actually happen.

None of the streetlights are on, but the touristy town of Big Bear is as quaint as ever. A chocolate shop has the lights on, and I can see kids' faces pressed up against the glass, watching us as we roll by. I'm tempted to stop and tell them to turn off the damn lights.

But I don't. I've got my family to think about, too. Realizing that I'm also a beacon with my headlights on, I slow right down and flick them off.

"Did we just—" Bree glances sharply at me, checking that the dash lights are still on.

"I turned them off on purpose." My breath fogs between us as I speak.

The street has plunged into darkness, and I'm barely going ten miles an hour now. Our surroundings gradually swirl back into focus. White snow gleams bright beneath a sparkling dome of stars as I wind slowly through town to the Pearsons' cabin.

* * *

I stop at the driveway around back of the Pearsons' 'cabin.' My truck grinds to a halt in the snow and I search the area for any sign of activity. I notice the driveway isn't plowed, and there are no tire tracks to indicate the Pearson family might have beat us here. The house is unoccupied as far as I can tell.

It's a sprawling two-story log mansion that is going to be impossible to heat without electricity, but at least there are plenty of fireplaces. There's also an attached four-car garage. Two electric SUVs are parked in there, as well as a snow blower and a snowmobile.

"Looks like we have the place to ourselves," I say. Twisting around, I find my family still asleep in the back seat. "Wake up," I whisper loudly. My mom stirs awake, blinking bleary eyes at me, but the kids remain asleep. "Gaby, Zach!" I reach back and shake Zach by his shoulder. He's the deepest sleeper of the two.

He rubs his eyes. "Wha...?"

"We're here."

I pop my door open, tuck my Glock into the waistband of my jeans, and take a few crunching steps in the snow to yank open the back door.

Gaby reaches for me with both arms and I lift her out. She gloms on like an octopus—all arms and legs.

"It's very big, isn't it?" my mom says, staring at the house as she slides out of the back seat.

"Too big," I reply. It's going to be hell to secure this place. Too many possible points of entry. Too much perimeter for so small a force.

Bree walks around to join us at the top of the driveway, blowing clouds of steam into her frozen hands. I glance back to the truck, realizing she's left the shotgun behind.

"Get the shotgun, Bree," I tell her.

She looks around quickly, as if only now realizing that we're not out of danger, then nods, and runs back for the gun.

The truck is still on and rumbling beside us. I'm afraid to turn it off, because I might not get it started again—especially in this weather, but I guess I'd better save what fuel I can.

Reaching in, I hit the engine start/stop button. The idling rumble of the V8 dies, and a heavy quiet crowds in, pressing hard on my eardrums. There's no sign of any invasion up here: no screams or shouts, explosions, gunshots, or sirens. No electricity. Just the still, frozen air and the brittle silence of an icy winter's night.

"Let's get inside," I whisper, and lead the way down the driveway. I parked in front of it for a reason. Two reasons actually. One, to block the driveway from other vehicles, and two, just in case I get stuck. Four-wheel drive might not be enough to deal with a foot of unplowed snow on a steep incline.

Once we reach the back porch, my mother says, "Stomp off the snow. We don't want to make a mess inside."

We diligently stomp off the clumps of snow from our boots and jeans, as if that's a priority right now. I set Gaby down beside me and spend a moment studying the pair of wood-painted steel security doors in front of us. I'm trying to decide on the best way to get in. There's a security system, too, but without power, it's not going to bother us. I happen to know that it's not on a backup power system, because the Pearsons forgot to replace those batteries the last time they were up here.

"Do you have a key?" Bree asks.

I arch an eyebrow at her. "No..."

"So how are we getting in?"

My gaze pans away from her and past the doors to a big double-glazed window beside them. I hesitate as I consider smashing it. Any entrance we make for ourselves is one we'll have to guard later.

Walking over to the window, I press my face to the glass and peer in. It's one of the bedrooms. We can bar or block the door to it after we get in. Good enough. I make a fist and thrust the steel plated-gauntlet of my exosuit through the window with a loud crash. It breaks into jagged chunks that fall to the deck and shatter into smaller pieces. Not a peep from the alarm; so far so good. Larger bits of glass are still clinging to the window frame. I knock them out carefully and clear a space wide enough for us to get through. Turning to my family, I nod for them to come, and then start lifting them through one by one.

Soon we're all inside and walking through the bedroom into the entry hall. I open the back doors from the inside and look back to my wife. "Take everyone through to the living room. Stay warm and wait for me. I'm going to get our bags."

"I can help," Zach says, straightening and stepping out from under my mother's arm.

"No," Bree replies, grabbing him and pulling him back. "It's too dangerous. We don't know what's out there."

Zach frowns at that.

"Your mother's right. Let me handle it for now, buddy." I take the shotgun from Bree, and then I'm clomping out and back up the snowy line of footprints trailing down from our truck.

Before I'm even halfway up to the top of the driveway, I hear a high-pitched shrieking noise shatter the rhythmic crunching of my boots and the rasping of my breath. The sound is quickly rising in pitch and volume—

My eyes snap up to the sky just as something I can't see goes screaming by, heading for the town. A missile? A fighter?

Then comes a blinding flash of light and the world-cracking *boom* of an explosion. Orange fire blooms above the trees, and they're cast into sharp relief, painting jagged silhouettes against the night.

It takes me a split-second to recover from shock, and then I'm sprinting the rest of the way to the truck, the shotgun in both hands, tac-light bobbing steadily. I rip off the tarp at the back to get at the duffel bag with the rest of our guns and ammo. The other supplies can wait. I go hurtling back down the driveway with the guns weighing me down and bouncing noisily in the bag. My boots hit the porch just as another shrieking shadow darts by overhead to draw more thunder from the town.

My mind flashes back to the handful of stores we passed with their lights on—the chocolate shop with the kids pressing their faces against the windows—and I hope to God that they're okay.

CHAPTER 8

The five of us huddle together on the floor of a walk-in closet in the master bedroom. We've collected all the pillows and bedding from around the house to make a kind of giant futon bed. The blankets help to keep us warm. The closet was the only place I could find that didn't have a direct line of sight to any of the cabin's many windows. We don't know if the invaders' weapons are homing in on heat signatures, but I suggested hiding in here just to be safe.

"If they're looking for heat signatures, can't they just see us anyway?" Zachary asks.

"Not if we're tucked out of sight," I tell him. "Staying away from the windows where our signatures might register is just as important as not lighting any fires or starting up the generator to get the lights and heat on. I figure we can wait until morning, at least, before we risk turning anything on."

Zachary nods and goes back to his usual quiet self.

I'm sitting with my back against a rack full of

ARRIVAL

Mrs. Pearson's expensive shoes. Stiletto heels jab into places that I'd rather not have them, but I'll live. My shotgun is balanced in my lap.

"How long are we supposed to hide like this?" my mom whispers.

"As long as we have to," I say.

"I need to use the bathroom," Gaby adds.

I glance at her. The en-suite is around the corner from the closet, but we'll have to walk by in plain sight of the bedroom's picture windows to get there.

"I'll take her," Bree says.

"I've got it," I say. "Come on, Gaby."

I hold the shotgun in a one-handed grip as I lead the way to the bathroom. I turn with my back to the door, planning to keep a watch from here, but Gaby stops on the threshold and peers into the shadowy bathroom. "It's dark," she says. "What if something is in there and waiting to get me?"

I hold back a sigh, and walk in with her. "There's nothing. See?"

I turn to leave but she catches me by the arm and says, "No, you have to stay."

"Okay." I turn my back to her and watch the open door. On the other side of the bedroom the picture windows give a clear view over the rippled carpet of shadows that is Big Bear Lake. There haven't been any more explosions after those first few, but for all we know, there are enemy soldiers on the ground going door to door in the town right now and shooting everyone in the head.

Enemy soldiers. That's wrong. *Alien soldiers.* But that doesn't sound right either. This still feels like a dream. Where did they come from? How did they find us? Why now?

I can't help thinking that this has something to do with the Forerunners. The first one left more than ninety years ago, headed for Trappist-1. The UNE sent three more within the same decade, all headed for different star systems. They were exploratory ships with colonists, scientists, and soldiers on board. So far, we've only heard back from Forerunners Two and Three, but they didn't report any kind of first contact. Forerunners One and Four might have encountered something, but it's too soon to expect a report from them. Lightspeed comms are damn slow over interstellar distances.

"Done," Gaby whispers.

I hear the toilet flush and wince at that. I forgot to tell her. "Don't do that again," I say.

"Do what?"

"Flush. Unless it's number two. We need to save water."

"Sorry," Gaby says.

"It's okay. Come on." I lead her back to our futon bed in the closet, and we snuggle under the covers once more.

I check my smart watch out of habit, but it doesn't flick on with the movement. The EMP took it out along with everything else. I have to go with my gut. And my gut says that it's about one or two in the morning. We're all still awake. Adrenaline is better than caffeine.

Ten minutes later, though, I hear that everyone's breathing has slowed right down, and I can see eyes sinking shut.

I settle in to a more comfortable position and blink to clear my eyes. Someone has to stay up and keep watch.

I'm listening for sounds in the house and staring out the doorless entrance of the closet to the windows in the master bedroom, checking for signs of movement. Nothing so far.

A shaky sigh escapes my lips, and I glance at each member of my family. Bree is fast asleep with one kid tucked under each arm. My mom is curled up next to Zach, and Gaby is sandwiched between me and Bree.

A tight smile twitches onto my lips and then I'm back to watching and listening. The minutes tick by with agonizing slowness.

It's going to be a long night.

* * *

By morning I'm sitting on the master bed, watching the sun come up over the lake. After an uneventful night, I'm less concerned about heat-seeking weapons spotting me through the windows.

Clouds, bright crimson with the sunrise, cast shimmering reflections on the glassy water. Snow-covered trees frame the scene and line the far side of the lake. A scattered group of five birds flies over. It's almost peaceful, but my mind jumps to wondering what the town looks like after those explosions tore through it last night.

Maybe I don't want to know.

"Hey," Bree says. She's whispering, but the sound still makes me jump. I turn to see her stepping around to my side of the bed. She's blowing steam into her hands again, and her lips are actually blue. "You think we can risk lighting a fire now? It's freezing in here."

I frown at that. A smoking chimney is another heat source to home in on. But if we don't do something soon, we could freeze to death.

"I'll get our bags from the truck. You can put on gloves and something for your head. We'll be okay without a fire for a while longer."

"Okay." Bree is watching me as I rise from the edge of the bed and stretch out my cramping muscles. "Were you up all night?"

"Someone had to be."

"Then you should sleep now. I'll take over."

"I'm okay," I insist. But that's a lie. My head feels like cotton and my eyelids have turned to sandpaper. I'm too old for this shit.

Bree steps in front of me to block my exit. "After you get the bags, we'll all eat something and then you're going to rest."

"Later," I try.

"No, now," Bree insists.

"Okay. Go back to the closet and stay out of sight. I'll be back in a few minutes."

"Be careful," Bree replies.

I nod as I walk past her, heading for the door. I ease it open, then shut, and hurry down the stairs to the first floor.

I emerge in the great room at the bottom of the stairs and see another flock of birds flying over the lake. At least a dozen of them this time. I stop and look on with a deepening frown. What are they running from?

Maybe it's nothing. Snapping out of it, I hurry down the entry hall to the back doors. The downstairs bedroom door where we broke through a window is still barred with a heavy wardrobe. My exoskeleton is sitting beside the back doors. It takes just a few minutes to strap in and power it up. The battery level is down to forty-nine percent after yesterday, but that's more than enough to get the truck unloaded and save my back from all the heavy lifting.

As soon as I'm done strapping into the exosuit, I go stomping back up the driveway, following our footprints from the night before. I have the shotgun in a two-handed grip, my eyes scanning the trees that flank the driveway, checking for threats.

A group of birds swoops by overhead, casting long shadows over me. I glance up, and see them diving down on the other side of the house, maybe for a landing on the beach—

And then I freeze, staring hard after them and blinking in shock. Those weren't birds. They were far too big. But also too small to be aircraft.

Unless they were missiles with wings, but I didn't hear the telltale roar of chemical rockets, and they were moving too slow.

I run back down to the house, my head spinning with conflicting thoughts. I'm half-expecting the place to explode with a burst of searing light before I can reach it, but that doesn't happen.

I'm storming up the back steps and in through the door, racing down the entry hall to the stairs in the great room. Still no explosions. I stop and stare hard through the picture windows, but there's no sign of anything flying over the lake. *Where the hell did they go?*

My heart is hammering in my chest. The silence is ominous. Images are repeating through my mind's eye. What the hell were those things?

I don't have long to wonder. One of them swoops down onto the front deck and lands with a muffled *thump*. It's a hunching creature on two short legs that are bent at the knee. A pair of skinny arms are protruding directly from its chest and curled up against its body. It's wearing a matte black suit with a faint fish scale pattern to it, a pointed, triangular helmet that's as glossy and black as an oil slick, and a pair of translucent wings that shimmer like rainbows are now folding up against its back. It's only slightly bigger than Gaby, but frail-looking.

Before I can recover from my shock and hide, the creature's head turns to me, and one of those skinny arms snaps straight, holding a small, slender black weapon.

I hit the floor just as a flash of emerald light tears through the space where I was standing. That laser missed, but it leaves a molten hole in the window between us.

I drag the shotgun out from under me and take hasty aim before pulling the trigger with a deafening *boom!*

The picture window shatters loudly, and I hear my family screaming upstairs.

The creature's matte black suit flashes with pocks of white light, and then its wings spread and it leaps into the air, soaring out of sight.

I scramble off the floor and race upstairs to my family.

"Bree!" I cry as I reach the top of the stairs.

She has the master bedroom door cracked open and a Glock sticking out, but then she recognizes me and yanks the door open. "Chris, what's going—"

"They're here," I say, gasping as much from fear as exertion. I push past her to get inside.

"Who is here?!"

I tread quietly over to the master bedroom windows, my eyes warily scanning the sky—

And see the creature that I shot flying in circles above the lake. We're in trouble. I start backing away from the window. "Get back in the closet, Bree."

"But—"

"GO!"

She flinches and turns to run, but before she's even made it two steps, emerald fire slashes through the windows and hits me in the thigh with a blinding flash of pain. The exosuit holds me up, but I'm seeing stars. I can see a smoking hole in the padded armor of the exosuit. That laser beam sliced through my armor like butter.

"Chris!" Bree lunges toward me as I'm staggering around to return fire.

"Dad?" Zach's voice. I can hear my mom and Gaby crying, but I don't have time to deal with them. I pump the action of the shotgun just as that creature comes swooping toward us. It folds its wings to make a smaller target—a black bullet streaking toward the windows. Is it going to ram them? I hope it snaps its neck.

I take aim and squeeze the trigger with another *boom.* The window shatters and more pocks of white light flicker over the creature's helmet. Beside me, Bree has planted her feet in a wide stance and she's firing repeatedly with my Glock.

One of those shots hit the creature's helmet at the last second before it reaches us—

And flashes off with a sound like water hissing on a hotplate.

"Bree get the hell back, damn it!"

But she just keeps firing.

I pump the shotgun again and pull the trigger once more before that thing careens through the broken window. Sprinkling flashes of light ripple over its armor and more hissing fills the air. It spreads its wings at the last second and knocks us both over with its momentum.

Bree screams as she falls. I'm scrambling back up and whirling around to face our adversary.

It's standing on the other side of the room, right by the entrance of the closet. Everything feels like it's happening in slow motion. I see its wings folding against its back and then watch as it stands there, peering in at my children and my mom. Gaby screams and my mother, too. Zach lunges for the gun bag. I can't shoot without risking that I hit one of them, so I toss the shotgun aside and charge.

It hears me coming and spins around. That slender-barreled weapon is swinging into line with my chest. Too slow.

I grab it and yank it away as hard as I can. The alien staggers back with a hissing sound as I toss the gun away. Then I'm wrapping steel-plated fists around its skinny throat and squeezing as hard as the exosuit will allow.

I can feel something pushing back. A force-field of some kind. Slender arms snake out to pry mine away with three-fingered hands, but this creature, whatever it is, isn't nearly as strong as I am. A glowing radiance is leaking out around my hands. A foot flashes up with gleaming black daggers for toes. Fire rakes through my left side, but the tide of adrenaline surging through me dulls the pain. One of the three-fingered alien hands leaves mine, reaches for something on its belt. A black cylinder appears between us. I realize it might be some type of grenade. A threat. If I kill it, it kills me. Maybe my whole family.

Too late. The sensation of something pushing against my hands abruptly stops. A loud *pop* sounds, and the bright light slipping through my fingers vanishes. There comes a sickening crunch as my armored hands crush the alien's throat, and it sags lifelessly in my arms.

The grenade goes off a split second later with a *bang* and a blinding flash of light.

DAY TWO

CHAPTER 9

Awareness trickles back in. A roaring, crackling sound drifts into hearing along with chattering voices. A groan escapes my lips, and then I'm blinking bleary eyes up at a sloping ceiling with darkly-stained wooden beams and golden pot lights shining between them. I struggle to move.

"Don't," Bree breathes beside my ear. "You don't want to open up those gashes in your side again."

"What..." My tongue is stuck to the roof of my mouth. I try to work in some moisture, but my lips are dry and cracked. "What happened?" I can see that I'm zipped into a sleeping bag. There's a fire roaring in the fireplace in the corner of the room, and the windows are dark with the night. I recognize this as Sean Pearson's room, just down the hall from the master. "How am I alive? The grenade..." I ask, remembering that it went off just as I killed the alien who was holding it.

"It released a bright flash of light and a loud noise. It didn't hurt you, but it knocked you out cold," Bree explains. She and my mom are kneeling on the floor on either side of me. Gaby and Zach come padding over, their faces pale and eyes shining with unshed tears. "Your mom and I managed to stop the bleeding. We found a first aid kit and cleaned the wound first, as best we could," Bree says, cracking a shaky smile. "But you've been asleep since this morning. We thought..." Bree just shakes her head, and tears pitter patter to the carpet beside me.

"We thought you might be in a coma," my mom explains.

"Some kind of stun grenade," I decide. The Union has those, too, but the effect doesn't last for hours—usually only a few minutes. "What is that sound?" I ask, meaning the chattering voices. "It sounds like a holoscreen. And how are the lights on?" I'm guessing that Bree fired up the Pearsons' backup generator. It's not hard to get it going—just have to flick the ignition switch and the expensive LP generator roars to life.

Bree wipes away her tears and smiles more steadily, but that expression never reaches her eyes. "It's over," she says.

"Over?" I struggle inside of the sleeping bag, again trying to sit up. "What do you mean *over?*"

"Stop it! You'll hurt yourself," Bree says.

"Then let me out, damn it!"

Bree gives in with a nod and unzips me. I see blood-soaked sheets tied around my side. I'm naked besides a pair of boxer briefs. There's another sheet-bandage tied around my thigh. It looks like that one was cut with a pair of scissors.

"We couldn't find any bandages," Bree explains. "Just band-aids."

My thigh. I probe it experimentally with one finger. Hurts, but not too bad. That's where the laser pieced me, but there's no sign of blood soaking through. The heat of the beam must have cauterized the wound.

I grimace and struggle to sit up. Pain flares in my side. My mom and Bree help me, and soon I'm sitting with my back against the foot of the bed and my eyes pinned to the holoscreen on the wall.

The volume is turned down low, so the voices of news anchors are still indistinct, but I can see clips of smoking ruins and raging fires playing on repeat. LA is pocked with flaming craters, and fires are raging out of control through the suburbs. A dark, teardrop-shaped hulk is hovering above it all, clouded by drifting walls of smoke. Small black specks are flitting to and from the gargantuan bulk of it—alien fighters or shuttles, maybe.

The scene cuts to a new clip: New York. Manhattan is a flaming crater with another one of those teardrop-shaped vessels hovering over it. Central Park is a blazing orange square of flames amidst shattered and leaning skyscrapers.

Then DC: it's burning out of control. Fires frame the Whitehouse, licking and blackening its sides as people flee the building only to get cut down by the slashing green lines of lasers.

More cities appear, and each time the ruins and wreckage are the same: Tokyo, Beijing, London, Paris, Berlin, Rome... Dubai... My jaw drops a few centimeters with each additional scene of destruction.

"They didn't leave," I croak. "You said it was over..."

Bree doesn't answer. I turn to look at her. "Well?"

Her amber eyes are haunted and drifting out of focus.

"We surrendered," my mom explains, her voice rasping with emotion.

"How do we have power if LA is in ruins?" I ask.

"The generator," my mom explains. "I found it and turned it on."

"We need to turn it off," I say, even as I try to push off the floor. "They could be homing in on the heat radiating from this place."

Bree snaps out of it and pushes me back down by my shoulder. I wince with another blinding wave of pain. "You're not listening, Chris!" She twists around to look at Zach. "Turn up the volume. Your father needs to hear what they're saying."

He darts out of view, and a second later I hear the droning, indistinct voices of news anchors snapping into focus. It's just one voice, female, and it has an odd sing-song quality to it.

"Do not resist. Do not fight back. Your government has surrendered."

I'm gaping in shock, glancing back and forth between my wife and mother. "How do they know our language?"

Bree just points to the screen, her face contorting with horror and disgust. "Watch."

The ruins of the Kremlin vanish, and a short, pale, bony-faced thing with bright red eyes appears. I can see black veins snaking beneath its skin in the same fish scale pattern as the black suit that it's wearing. Instead of the glossy black helmet that I remember, this one is wearing a boxy black mask with a grille where a human's mouth and nose would be. Four snakelike tentacles are waving around above its head, each of them ending in a cone-shaped tip that makes me think they might be for hearing.

The camera zooms out, and something far more shocking appears standing beside this creature. It's the president of the UNE: Carmen Romero. Her blue eyes are flared wide and staring, bloodshot and leaking actual blood from the corners. She has a glossy black helmet on *her* head with a bundle of wires snaking from it to some unseen location. She's also wearing a torn and blood-stained white pantsuit.

The sing-song voice continues, and I see that the president's mouth is moving. The voice is *hers.*

Revulsion lances sharply through me.

"We will help you to rebuild, and we will look after you as if you were our own children. Welcome to the Kyron Federation."

The broadcast lingers on the blazing red eyes of the alien, then vanishes and returns to panning over the ruins of major cities around the world. The president's sing-song voice comes back after just a few seconds, saying, "Do not be afraid! The war is over! Your people fought valiantly, but the Kyra have won. If you fight us, we will kill you. If you yield, you will live. Heed my words before more of you must die."

"Zach, turn it off," Bree says. "We don't need to see it again."

The holoscreen blanks and fades to a transparent rectangle that blends against the wall.

"That's not our broadcast," I realize.

"No, it's not," Bree says.

Gaby comes over and crawls into my lap. I wince as her weight presses into my injured side. "They hacked into our network?" I ask.

"Or we helped them," Bree replies.

"Shit."

"Shit's a bad word, Daddy," Gaby says. "You're supposed to say sugar."

"You're right, sweetheart," I reply while absently stroking her hair. This is a lot to take in. "How did you know it was safe to turn on the generator?" I ask my mother.

"There were Union drones flying around the

lake earlier," Bree answers for her, jerking her chin to the windows. "They were ordering everyone to surrender, telling us that we would be spared as long as we didn't resist the invaders."

It takes a few seconds for me to process that. A heavy frown settles onto my face as I think about these developments. Bree eases in under my arm on the side that Gaby hasn't already taken. Zach walks around to the foot of the bed and curls up next to his mother, while my mom sits on her haunches, staring into the fire that's roaring in the corner of the room. Before long we're staring into it with her. It strikes me that it's symbolic. Our entire civilization is ablaze right now.

For a long moment, nobody speaks, we just sit there, staring into the flames. My throat is parched, but I have bigger concerns than dehydration. "What did you do with the body?" I ask.

"We hid it in the yard between some pine trees and shoveled snow over it," Bree replies.

I nod slowly. "We're going to have to do better than that. If they find out we killed one of theirs, they might not care that it happened before the surrender—or believe that it was self-defense. They'll probably just kill us."

Gaby whimpers, and I wince at my own candor. "Don't worry, honey, I won't let that happen. We'll bury it."

"But what if they find it, anyway?" Gaby asks.

I shake my head. "They won't."

"But what if!"

"Trust me, kiddo. We're going to be okay. We just have to keep our heads down and do whatever they say from here on out, okay?"

Gaby sniffles, and her voice is muffled against my bare chest. "Okay."

Time drifts by. The heat and the mesmerizing dance of the fire is lulling me to sleep.

"Don't do that," Bree says, and shakes me awake by my shoulder. "You've slept enough."

"Okay... Well, I'm thirsty. Do you think you can—"

"I'll get you some water," my mom says, and jumps up from the floor, as if desperate to have something useful to do.

"Thanks," I reply as she dashes out of the bedroom. A wash of cold air gushes in as she opens and shuts the door. I guess this is the only warm spot in the house. We should probably fix that by turning on the heat at the nearest thermostat.

My eyes slide away from the door and I notice my wife and kids looking up at me, their eyes wide and blinking. Even Bree looks like a child in that moment, and I realize they're all waiting for me to reassure them that this somehow isn't as bad as it seems.

"What do they want from us?" Bree asks.

And it's then that I realize that president Romero, A.K.A *the alien hand puppet*, didn't mention why the Krya came here. "Maybe they like our planet and they didn't think we'd agree to share if they asked nicely."

Zach nods slowly with that, as if it makes sense, but I can see the naïveté retreating from Bree's eyes. That moment of youthful innocence and vulnerability is gone. She's too old for fairy-tales, and she's right to be skeptical.

If the Kyra are so advanced, why bother with Earth? It's a polluted, over-populated, resource-depleted rock. I'm pretty sure they could find a dozen other places to colonize that are all much better than this. So what do we have that all those other planets don't?

Only one answer comes to mind: those other planets don't have *us*. That would also explain why they didn't wipe us out. They smashed all of our biggest cities and broke our spirits. Now we're ready for the bit and saddle. But what do they want with billions of human slaves?

My mom returns with a glass of water. She holds it shakily to my lips and I drink greedily. Icy liquid leaks from my mouth and snakes down my throat.

"Thanks," I gasp as the glass drains dry.

"Anything else?" my mom asks. "Food?"

I shake my head and ease it back against the foot of the bed. "Later."

My mom flashes a brittle smile and then sits beside Bree and me. The crackling fire pops loudly, drawing our eyes to it, and soon we're sucked back into the mesmerizing flicker and swirl of the flames.

My gaze drifts out of focus and horror seeps in. I push it down with positive thoughts: All of us are alive, and the fighting is over. The worst of this nightmare is already behind us just twenty-four hours after it began.

Another *pop* sounds and the fire roars with sparks. There's just one problem with all that positive thinking—

Bree's the optimist, not me, and I'm also too old for fairytales. I can't fool myself. The worst isn't behind us.

The worst is yet to come.

CHAPTER 10

An hour later, I'm sitting under the covers in Sean Pearson's bed, dressed in pajama bottoms and a black hoodie sweater, which is one of the only things that fits over the sheet tied around my injured left side. The night has almost fully fallen now.

My wife is tucked under my arm on my right side, and we're both staring fixedly into the crackling fire. There are three empty granola bar wrappers on the nightstand beside me—my dinner. My mom and Zach ran a quick supply run to the truck a few hours ago, before dusk fully fell. After that Bree had the kids shower and change in Haley Pearson's room. That bedroom is right across the hall, and my mother drew the blinds to give them at least the illusion of safety. Bree also drew the blinds in here, so hopefully no one —alien or otherwise—can see us too clearly. Supposedly, the fighting is over, but I'm not expecting a peaceful transition.

Forget the invaders, what are our own people going to do? I can only imagine the chaos out there: looting and rioting. Rape and murder. It's going to be utterly lawless. Basic services have been disrupted, and much of our infrastructure destroyed. Will the invaders reestablish law and order? If so, what do they consider a crime? Maybe they won't even get involved in our petty disputes. Or maybe murder is okay to them so long as we're not killing any of their people.

Yesterday morning my biggest problem was finding a new job to avoid sinking below the poverty line. Now, Earth is occupied by an alien species that calls itself the Kyra. Tens or hundreds of millions are dead. The aliens are promising peaceful co-existence, but I know better than to believe a word of that. I can't get this image out of my head; of the way they turned our president into a mouthpiece to communicate the terms of their occupation and our surrender.

That isn't the act of a peaceful species.

Bree finally breaks the silence, her voice a whisper. "What are we going to do? Do we go home?"

I shake my head. "No."

"But this isn't our house. We can't just stay here like squatters. For all we know, the Pearsons could be on their way here right now."

"I don't think they made it," I say, remembering the air cars we saw falling from the sky when that EMP hit. If the Pearsons fled the city, they would have taken their air car to get away faster. And if they'd made it away in time, then they would have been here already.

"Well, still... it's illegal. They must have surviving heirs."

"Maybe, maybe not, but right now I don't think there are any laws still in effect—at least, not our laws. It's the law of the jungle right now: kill or be killed. Eat or be eaten. Survival of the fittest."

Bree nods along mutely with that.

I'm just glad I brought so many guns, because I have a bad feeling we're going to need them. Glancing away from the fire, my gaze finds the shotgun and the Glock that Bree and I used to fight off that creature in the master bedroom. Those weapons are sitting atop the duffel bag with the rest of our guns and ammo.

"So we stay here. Until when?" Bree asks. "What happens when our food runs out?"

"Then we check the surrounding houses. Most of them are probably empty, but their pantries should be full."

This multi-million-dollar neighborhood was a vacation getaway for the rich and famous. Now LA is a smoking crater, and all the rich people in their air cars were hit by the EMP.

So Big Bear will likely remain vacant until vagrants and squatters like us make it up here.

"We should start scavenging for supplies in the morning," I say, realizing that we need to get ahead of the wave of refugees from the valley.

"You mean breaking into people's homes and

stealing their stuff?"

I glance at Bree. Her honey brown eyes are wide with shock, her pretty pink lips twisted in disgust.

I can see that it's going to be hard for Bree to adjust. She's still clinging to the rules and laws of a civilized society that no longer exists.

"Can't we just go to the town and buy whatever supplies we need?"

"With what? Digital payments won't work without power to scan our ID chips, and UNE credits are probably worthless now, anyway."

"Well..." Bree trails off uncertainly.

"I get it. It feels wrong."

"It *is* wrong," Bree argues.

"Would you rather die with a clean conscience or live with a bit of guilt? I'm not talking about killing anyone. Just stealing food to survive. Food that will get stolen anyway when more refugees find their way here."

Bree doesn't reply. Maybe she doesn't like the thought that we are all refugees now. Or maybe it's still her conscience eating away at her. I can tell she doesn't approve of my suggestion, but she'll just have to get used to making moral compromises. We all will.

A sound pricks through the crackling of the fire at the foot of the bed—a familiar whirring and a crunching of tires through snow. It abruptly stops.

"What was that?" Bree asks.

"A car," I say as I carefully crawl out of bed to peek through the roller shades at the window. There's a vehicle parked in the driveway, right below us. It's a big, black electric Suburban. The headlights are on, the taillights glowing crimson on the snow-covered driveway. I can guess who it is, but I'm shocked to see them here. Apparently, my assumptions were wrong.

"Who is it?" Bree asks as she comes to join me by the window.

"The Pearsons," I reply.

CHAPTER 11

"**T**he Pearsons? They survived?" A mixture of relief and concern flashes across Bree's face.

My own feelings mirror hers, but relief wins. I'd hate to think of the Pearson kids among the casualties.

Somehow, they must have gotten one of their vehicles working. Maybe Niles Pearson figured out that trick with disconnecting and reconnecting the terminals from the battery. Or maybe he didn't need to. EMPs don't typically take out electronics when they're turned off. Maybe they waited until the fighting was over to leave the city.

"We'd better go down and say hello. They're going to want an explanation for what we're doing in their home."

"Yeah, in a minute..." I trail off, waiting to see the headlights wink off and the doors of the Suburban open. Two people get out, followed by two more, but I can't make out anything in the dark. It's their vehicle, but that doesn't mean that it's them. Maybe one of their neighbors stole their car and came up here to take their vacation house, too.

"Wait here, I'm going to go see if it's them."

"What do you mean *if* it's them?" Bree asks, blinking rapidly in confusion.

I shrug and cross the room to our gun bag. Snatching my shotgun off the floor pulls a wince from my lips. My side hurts. Probably needs stitches. I drop down to my haunches beside the duffel bag. As I do so, a sharp stab of pain erupts from my injured thigh, nearly making me fall over. I stifle a cry, and Bree hurries over to steady me. At least the laser burn is a clean, small-bore wound. Hurts, but it won't do much to hinder my movements.

"Let me help you," Bree says.

"I'm fine," I insist as I begin awkwardly re-loading the Mossberg from a box of spare shells in the bag. My injured side and the sheet tied around it makes using my left arm awkward, but I finish loading and pump the action to chamber a shell.

"Who else could it be?" Bree whispers.

"I'm sure it's them," I reply to avoid a longer conversation.

"Then why are you taking a gun?" Bree asks as I straighten with a groan and head for the door.

"Because they might have been followed."

Bree nods slowly. "You want me to go down with you?"

"No, go over to the kids' room and let Mom know what's going on."

"Okay. Be careful."

"Always." I lean in for a kiss and then limp to the door. My leg is feeling a bit better. Maybe I just needed to get the blood pumping again. Finding my boots at the door, I set the shotgun down and attempt stepping into them to avoid bending down again. Bree rushes over and helps me pull the boots on.

"Thanks," I say.

She nods and follows me out with a Glock gleaming in her hands. I raise my eyebrows at that, but don't risk raising my voice to ask about it. She knows how to handle a gun. I wait for Bree to enter the other bedroom and shut the door behind her before proceeding down the hall to the stairs.

The air is much colder out here, and an icy wind whistles in through the window that I shot out this morning.

That broken window gives me pause. I stop at the railing overlooking the great room to check for any signs of trouble on the main floor below. Anyone or any*thing* could have crept in through that window while we've been hiding upstairs in the bedrooms.

But there are no signs of intruders, or of the Pearsons. Yet.

I switch to a one-handed grip on the shotgun and grab the railing to support my injured leg as

I descend the staircase. Broken glass reflects scattered fragments of the full moon and night's sky above the lake.

At the bottom of the stairs, I hear voices coming from the back entrance. I pause, straining to identify them.

I recognize Jessica Pearson's imperious voice as it hits a shrill note. Her words are muffled, but her tone is indignant, which makes me suspect that she's just noticed the window I broke to get in. Niles says something in a lower, more cautious volume.

Turning the corner at the bottom of the stairs, I limp hurriedly down the entry hall to the back entrance. Niles and Jessica are arguing in hushed voices on the back steps. I open the door, and both of them turn to me with widening eyes.

Their two bodyguard bots are there with them. They raise their stun guns and aim them at my chest.

"Halt!" one of the CDUs says in a strident voice. "Hands in the air and drop your weapon."

I oblige by raising my hands, but one of them is still holding the shotgun. The moonlight is just enough to see the enraged look on Jessica Pearson's face. She crosses her arms over her chest. She's wearing a glossy black ski jacket with a fur-lined hood.

"What are you doing here, Mr. Randall?" she demands.

One of the two bodyguards tries to step in

front of her to shield her from me.

"Paul, Jeremy! Stand down," she snaps.

"Understood," one of them says, and then both units step aside.

I lower my hands and hold the shotgun across my chest, my eyes checking the sky and the street at the top of the driveway to make sure that we haven't attracted any unwanted attention to ourselves with all of the noise we're making. No sign of anything yet, but that doesn't mean we're not being watched.

"You should get inside," I say. "We're too exposed out here."

Mrs. Pearson concedes my point with a grudging sigh. "Fine. Come help us with our luggage."

Niles Pearson greets me with a shallow nod, orders one of the CDUs to watch the door, and then the three of us turn and trudge through half a foot of snow to reach their vehicle. The back of the Suburban is already open, and Emily, the Pearson's domestic bot is standing there, guarding their luggage. I see Haley's and Sean's heads peeking above the headrests, still seated inside. I reach for a backpack before Niles stops me with a hand on my arm and a shake of his head.

"Let Emily take care of the bags. You can help the CDUs watch our backs."

"Yes, sir."

"Just call me Niles," Mr. Pearson says. "My wife did fire you, after all."

I acknowledge that with a nod as Jessica opens one of the side doors to get her kids out. Niles leaves my side to help his wife while their domestic bot grabs heavy suitcases from the back.

Haley is the first one out. Her cherubic face lights up when she sees me. It's hard to tell in the dark, but she has long blonde hair and green eyes, just like her mother. But thank God, her personality is more like her dad's.

"Chris!" Haley cries as Niles picks her up. She squiggles in his arms, waving at me over his shoulder.

"Hey there, Hales," I reply.

Then Sean jumps down. His face is sharply angled like his mother's, but he has his father's jet-black hair and brown eyes.

Jessica reaches in for a designer handbag that she left on the front seat.

"Hurry up, Jess. Let's go," Niles says, glancing worriedly at the sky.

Jessica leads the way to the back steps and the open door of the house. She makes an irritated sound as she pauses to stomp off the snow from her boots.

"I hope you're prepared to pay for the damages, Mr. Randall," she says, pointing to the broken window.

A muscle jerks in Niles' cheek, but I can't tell if it's because he's annoyed with me or with his wife. She breezes through the open door with

Sean. Then Niles sets Haley down and ushers her through next. He holds the door and waits for Emily to follow. The bot has to turn sideways to fit through the door. She's tottering back and forth under what must be a couple hundred pounds of luggage. Once the bot is through, Niles makes a sweeping gesture to me to indicate the open door.

"You first," I say.

"I insist," Niles replies.

I step through the open door in time to hear Jessica exclaim: "Another broken window!" She's reached the great room and seen the glittering pool of shattered glass from the window that I shot out.

Niles waits for the CDUs to follow me and then shuts and locks the door. He and I join the others in the living area. Mrs. Pearson rounds on me with her arms crossed over her chest once more. "What exactly are you *doing* here, Mr. Randall? I think you owe us an explanation."

"I'm here for the same reason as you, Jessica," I say, working hard to keep an even tone of voice. Her attitude is getting on my nerves.

Mrs. Pearson's expression darkens, probably because I addressed her by her first name. That gives me some small, petty satisfaction.

"It's *our* house!" she adds, as if I didn't already know.

"How did you break that window?" Niles asks, looking at the one in the great room.

"One of the invaders found us this morning. It attacked me. I managed to kill it—barely."

"You killed one of them?" Sean asks in a hushed voice.

I'm about to reply, but Niles interrupts me, asking, "Us?"

"My family. They're upstairs." I explain, jerking my chin to the stairs.

"Ah, of course," Niles nods.

Jessica waves impatiently at her husband, like she's shooing a fly. Her eyes pinch into slits and she glares at me. "Well, you can't stay. I expect you to get your family and your things and leave immediately."

"My truck won't start," I point out.

"That's not my problem," Jessica counters.

"Hold on, darling." Niles steps over to his wife, who is two inches taller than him by virtue of the heels on her utterly impractical winter boots.

He pushes his augmented reality glasses up higher on his nose—they're also corrective lenses, but I've always wondered why he doesn't use augmented reality contacts instead. Maybe he thinks the old-fashioned version is a fashion statement. Niles draws himself up to confront his wife. He's an average height and build, slightly out of shape, with a weak chin that he hides under a carefully trimmed beard that he takes the time to dye to hide the gray. His thick black hair is also dyed and sticking up at odd angles, a hairstyle that's at odds with his fifty-three years of age.

He and Jessica make an oddly matched pair that leaves no doubt as to why they're together. Trading her beauty for his money must have seemed like a good deal at the time. Maybe not so much now that the whole world is being turned upside down. I wonder if she'll claim *force majeure* and glom onto the first man she finds who's better equipped to protect her when the shit really starts to hit the fan.

"We're better off sticking together right now," Niles explains as he places a hand on his wife's arm.

"Really?" she counters. "With limited resources you want to have another four mouths to feed?"

"Actually, we're five. My mother is here, too."

"Even better!" Jessica exclaims.

"Food is going to be easier to provide than security," Niles says. Glancing at me, he adds, "We're happy to have you here, Chris."

"*Excuse* me?" Jessica turns a glowering look on her husband, and he visibly shrinks beneath her gaze.

"He's obviously brought guns," Niles explains, gesturing helplessly to me and the shotgun that I'm holding. "The more firepower we have, the better. The CDUs can't use proper weapons without human operators, and there aren't any human operators right now."

I jerk my chin to one of the security bots. "Can they use lethal force on the invaders?"

Niles grimaces and looks at the nearest of the two rubber-faced sentinels—the one standing between them and the broken window in the great room. The other one is behind, watching the door where we came in. They've silently identified the best places to keep watch without having to be told. "I don't know," Niles admits. "Thankfully, we haven't had a chance to test that, but I doubt it."

"Yeah." I nod knowingly. "They'll make good lookouts at least."

Niles brightens. "Yes, that they will. They can see perfectly in the dark—even through walls if they can get close enough."

I nod absently as if that's news to me. Bots like these two replaced me in the Army long before they took my job with the Pearson family.

"What do you know about the invaders?" I ask, switching topics.

Mrs. Pearson turns away, calling to Emily and her two children, who are sitting together on the living room couch. She tells them to go upstairs and pack their things away in their rooms.

They obediently leave the couch and run upstairs, their boots clomping noisily as they go.

"Shoes by the door!" she calls after them, and they come trudging back down. Both kids look tired and scared, not unlike my own.

Niles watches them go to the door. He seems

to be waiting for them to leave before answering my question.

I wait with him, wondering how Mrs. Pearson will react when she sees yet another broken window in the master suite.

Once everyone has gone upstairs, Niles pulls me aside, heading for a wet bar to one side of the main living area. He ducks behind the bar and pulls out two tumblers and a bottle of an expensive eighteen-year-old scotch.

He holds out one of the glasses to me, but I shake my head. "No, thank you."

He shrugs and pours half a glass for himself, which he promptly downs in one gulp.

"Well? What happened in the valley?" I ask.

"We were watching the news until the power went out," he says. "I saw their carrier ship flying over LA and raining waves of green fire on the city. There were lots of smaller vessels buzzing all around it, sleek black things engaging with our starfighters. And then these big, square landers came raining down all over the valley. Troop transports, or some kind of landers, I guess. They had six cylindrical engines, all glowing blue and facing down, radiating from a central hull."

I nod for him to continue, wondering why he waited for his family to go upstairs before telling me things that they must already know.

"I went to get a better look from the terrace on the roof. That was when I saw one of the landers coming down right on top of us. It set down on the street, over by the Garcias' place. They were busy pulling out of their driveway in their Cadillac when it landed. I thought maybe it was going to shoot their car with one of those green lasers, but Sienna and Javier got out of the car and ran screaming down the street.

My eyebrows inch upward as I imagine Mr. and Mrs. Garcia running for their lives. They were a young couple, both of them successful actors. "What happened to them?"

"The center of the lander opened up, and these pale, hairless creatures came running out on four legs. They ran Sienna and Javier down like dogs and tore them apart with these thick, muscular arms that extend right from their chests. They actually pulled arms and legs right out of their sockets, Chris. The sounds those poor people made as they died... You have no idea." Niles looks like he's about to be sick.

"Don't be too sure," I reply. "I saw some hairy shit go down in the Army. What happened next?"

Niles swallows visibly. "They—they ate them."

"You said they had four legs and two arms?"

Niles nods.

"Then there's more than one species of aliens here."

"At least two," Niles confirms. "But those flying ones seem to be in charge."

A word jumps to mind from the holonews

broadcast that I saw when I came to in Sean's room a few hours ago: *federation.* That thing speaking through President Romero said, *welcome to the Kyron Federation.*

"What did you do?" I ask.

"I ran back inside, of course. I didn't want those monsters to see me and tear me apart next."

"So how come they didn't find any of you? You were hiding in your place all night?"

"We hid in the panic room and only came out in the morning. One of the windows was broken, but that was the only sign that any of them might have come in."

"What about the lander?" I ask.

"Gone. There was no sign of any of them in the morning. I guess the fighting was concentrated around LA. We were getting ready to go when we heard Union drones flying around and ordering us to surrender. We heard the rest on the radio as we drove up here. What do you think they want?" Niles asks as he pours himself another glass of Scotch with a shaking hand.

"I was about to ask *you* the same question."

CHAPTER 12

What do the invaders want? That question rattles around inside my head for the umpteenth time as I consider next steps. Niles scratches the side of his jaw, staring absently up the stairs where his family disappeared a moment ago. I wonder if my wife and Jessica are getting ready to claw each other's eyes out. I don't hear any raised voices coming from upstairs, so that's a good sign. Maybe Jessica has finally learned to bite her tongue.

"If the Kyra have already been here, then we should probably leave," Niles says. "Besides, we'll never be able to heat this place with that window broken."

"I shot out the one in the master, too."

Niles heaves a weary sigh and shakes his head.

"Any ideas about where else we can go?"

Niles appears to think about it. "Maybe. The Willards' place. It's bigger than ours, with a guest house and an LP generator."

"And the owners?"

"They're from LA and they're almost never up here, so..."

"They probably didn't make it."

Niles nods gravely with that assessment.

"Let's get our families back in our cars and go."

"You said your truck won't start?" Niles asks.

"I can try."

"If it doesn't work, you can take the Tesla in the garage," Niles says.

"Great."

He leads the way up the stairs to fetch his family, rather than calling up to them. I'm right behind him, limping and pulling myself up the stairs with one arm on the railing. I appreciate Niles' discretion. We don't know if there are hostiles nearby. I hear boots thumping around upstairs, followed by the sound of raised voices. Bree's and Jessica's. I grimace at that. Maybe they were talking more quietly a moment ago.

We follow the sound of the confrontation to Haley Pearson's room. Niles opens the door, and a swath of light pools in the hallway. I see Jessica, her two kids, and Emily all standing on one side of the bed while my family faces off with them on the other side.

"There are only five bedrooms, and your husband broke the windows in the master *and* the guest suite downstairs," Jessica Pearson is saying as we step in. "You can stay in either of those two rooms." Jessica turns a scowl on Niles and me as

JASPER T. SCOTT

we go to stand beside our respective families on opposite sides of the room.

"We'll freeze," Bree objects.

"Please," my mother adds with her hands pressed in front of her as if praying for Jessica Pearson's heart to thaw.

"There's more than enough room in here and the other bedroom for us to lay out sleeping bags on the floor," Bree says. "In fact, we could probably all fit in just this one room."

"And what about privacy?" Jessica asks, her voice rising precipitously. "You're suggesting that we all sleep together on the floor like cavemen?"

"I think we have more important priorities than privacy, don't you?" Bree counters. "If we split up in different rooms, it will be harder to defend ourselves, and harder to stay warm, too." Bree looks to me for support. "Chris, tell her."

Jessica snorts at that. "I'll keep my own counsel, thank you. I think it would be better if you and your family left. There simply isn't enough space for all of us to stay here, and this is not your home."

"Darling..." Niles trails off in a shrinking voice.

"What?" Jessica demands as she rounds on him.

"We can't stay here, either."

"What do you mean *we* can't stay? This is our home! Where else would you have us go? We can't go back to the valley!"

"No. To another house on the lake."

"What house?"

"I know a place. It's bigger than ours, so space won't be a problem. It even has a guest house."

"Niles Wallace Pearson, are you suggesting that we break into someone else's home and squat in it?"

"They won't be home," he says. "And I'm almost positive that they didn't survive the attacks, so we won't run into them later on."

"That doesn't make it right!"

I take a moment to appreciate the irony that both Jessica and Bree have made similar arguments against staying in other people's homes.

"Chris killed one of the Kyra here," Niles reminds his wife. "They could come back here looking for it. Or they might have a way to track the body. Either way, we know for sure that they've already been here, which means they could come back."

Jessica turns a glare my way. "I hope you realize this is your fault."

"My fault?"

"You broke in, and obviously drew their attention to our home. Now we have to leave because you led them here."

"Darling." Niles gives his head a slight shake. "It's not Christopher's fault."

"Then whose is it?" Jessica demands.

A thin smile twitches onto my lips. "It's okay,

I'll accept the blame." Inside I'm boiling, but what else can I say to shut her up? We have more important battles to fight, and right now we're wasting too much time by arguing. "We should go."

Jessica huffs and storms out, saying, "Sean, Haley, let's go downstairs."

Emily is carrying their luggage again as she trails behind them. A fuzzy white sweater sleeve is peeking out of one of the two backpacks she's wearing, and she has a heavy suitcase in each hand.

It takes my family ten minutes to gather our belongings back into our two duffel bags and backpacks. My exosuit is in the master bedroom, lying discarded on the floor in a sticky pool of my own blood. A quick look at the control panel on the suit's gauntlet tells me that it's only got five percent charge left. No point in trying to take it with us.

"All packed?" I ask quietly.

My kids nod their heads.

"I think so," my mom replies while glancing around the master suite. We all have our jackets and gloves back on now, but my legs are frozen through my sweatpants, and my ears are growing numb.

"Let's go." I balance the shotgun in my left arm and heave the gun bag off the foot of the bed with my right, wincing as the weight of it pulls at my injured side. I feel blood leaking hotly through my improvised bandage, but there's nothing I can do about it right now. Bree grabs the other duffel with our spare clothes and food. The kids each have their backpacks, and my mom has a small suitcase.

Leading the way downstairs, I find the living area empty, and the doors at the end of the entry hall both standing open.

The Surburan is humming quietly, and the headlights are on again. Niles stands beside it with a bodyguard on either side, blowing steam into his hands. He's obviously feeling the cold even through his leather driving gloves.

The Pearsons are seven with their three bots. That leaves just one seat empty. There's no space for my family and our luggage, and I seriously doubt my truck will start, but it's worth a shot.

"I'm going to check my truck," I say.

Niles nods and turns to pull open the driver's side door of his SUV. "Hurry up."

I run over to my aging F150 and yank the door open. Jumping in behind the wheel I give the start button a stab. The engine turns over and over about a dozen times before giving up with a gasp.

"Come on, girl..." I whisper under my breath.

Waiting a beat, I try the ignition button again.

The starter motor whirrs and spark plugs click fruitlessly. Lights flicker all over the dash—

Then die.

I'm wasting time. Pushing my door open, I jog back over to Niles' Suburban and rap on the window with my knuckles.

"No luck?" he asks before I can say anything.

I shake my head. "Dead. You mentioned that the Tesla in the garage is charged?"

"Should be," Niles says.

Jessica leans past him. "What's the delay? Let's go! We can meet them there."

"Just a minute, darling. I'll be right back," Niles says. He pops his door open and jumps out of the Suburban. One of the bodyguard units moves to follow him, but he orders it to stay.

Niles leads the way down to the house and through the back door. The first door to the right off the foyer leads to the garage. He opens it and points to the nearest vehicle, a sleek black electric SUV with the stylized Tesla logo branded across the front.

He grabs a key fob off a wooden rack shaped like a pine tree beside the garage door. He unlocks the doors and turns on the engine. Headlights blaze to life, and I hurry down a short flight of steps to the garage. Going around the back of the SUV I set down the gun bag and open the trunk to put it inside. Bree comes over, struggling under the weight of the other duffel, holding it with both arms in front of her like a kettle bell. I take the bag from her and pack it in beside the guns.

"Chris, heads up!" Niles says.

I look to him. He tosses me the fob. I barely

manage to spare a hand from my shotgun to catch the key. "Thanks," I breathe, now feeling the exertion from carrying heavy bags.

"You can open the garage from the holo display, but if it doesn't work, there's a garage opener in the glove box."

I nod to him and he vanishes from the open door. Bree is busy getting the kids inside. My mom goes last.

Heading for the driver's side, I pull the door open and climb in. My injured leg aches as I do so, but it's more of a nuisance than a disability at this point. The gashes in my side are another matter. I can feel them throbbing, and the hot, wet sensation of blood trickling down my torso.

Once we're all inside the vehicle, I pass my shotgun over to Bree and drop the key fob in one of the cup holders in the central console. I find myself staring at the oversized touchscreen between Bree and I, my eyes drifting out of focus as I take a second to catch my breath and calm my racing heart.

"Are you okay?" Bree asks in a whisper.

Rather than worry her with the truth, I nod and say, "I'm fine." Not bothering to try the garage controls from the vehicle's touchscreen, I reach over to the glove box, find the old-fashioned remote, and touch the button. The door rattles to life, rumbling as it rolls up.

I select the vehicle's all-wheel drive option from the touchscreen and then gently hit the accelerator, remembering that it's much more sensitive than my gas-powered truck.

The SUV rolls quietly and smoothly up the snow-covered driveway, not struggling at all. Headlights reflect brightly off the snow. At the top of the driveway, I just barely manage to squeeze between the back end of my truck and a snow-covered pine tree. The branches scrape and scratch noisily against the side of the vehicle, probably doing thousands of credits worth of damage.

Then I'm clear.

Niles already has their Suburban on the street, waiting for me. He rolls forward as soon as my headlights flash off the back of his vehicle.

In moments we're breezing down Eagle Drive, headed for Eagle Point at the tip of the peninsula. Quaint cottages and sprawling mansions flash by on either side of us. I can't see any sign of people, but there are tire tracks on the street, and some of the driveways have cars in them. The bigger houses tend to be to our left, built on lakefront properties.

We continue driving for several minutes. I'm starting to feel nervous. Ours are the only two cars on the street, and our headlights and taillights are making us clear targets.

"Chris..." Bree says slowly. "Should we be driving around like this right now?"

"No," I say through a scowl. "Niles said it was close."

My scalp is beginning to itch and my neck is prickling with that feeling like I'm being watched.

Counting out the seconds in my head as much to save my patience as to keep track of how long we're spending out in the open, I reach twenty-six before I finally see the Suburban's taillights blaze crimson. An open lakefront lot appears to our left, followed by a massive log house all on one level. There's a decorative wood fence across the back with a metal gate barring the driveway.

I put my vehicle into park and take back my shotgun from Bree. Climbing out, I do my best to keep to the tire tracks to avoid making extra footprints as I head over to Niles. He hasn't taken the same care to watch where he steps.

I watch Niles walk right up to the gate and rattle it to see if it's open. The gate isn't chained or padlocked, but it doesn't give when Niles shakes it.

"Motorized," he says. "We'll have to climb over."

It's a fair walk to the house from the street. Maybe fifty meters. There's a detached garage with two sets of double doors and one single. The building looks like it might be deep enough to hold seven or eight cars rather than just five. An external staircase leads to a second floor above and that guest house Niles mentioned. Beyond that, at the end of the snow-covered driveway is the house itself, a sprawling mansion with a roof that peaks in at least three different places. To the left, the neighbors have a more modest home. Then comes an empty lot. And on the right, another mansion.

"What do you think?" Niles asks.

I'm frowning. The place is big, but not particularly defensible. Lots of windows at the back. No doubt it will have even more facing the lake, and it's all on one level, so we'll be sleeping next to those windows.

It's obvious that Niles picked this place because he secretly wishes it was his, or maybe because he always wanted to get a look inside, and breaking in now is his chance to do that.

Who knows. Whatever the hell his reasons are, he's not doing us any favors.

But we can't just keep driving around forever. We've been out in the open too long as it is.

"It'll have to do," I say. "Let's get everyone inside."

Niles nods and begins turning back to his vehicle. I catch him by the arm before he gets more than two steps.

I've just spotted something.

Niles sends me a questioning look.

I point to the other side of the fence. "Are those footprints?"

Niles squints to where I'm pointing. The prints cross over the fence beside us and go meandering through the trees to the main entrance.

"It looks like someone beat us here," I say.

CHAPTER 13

"**M**aybe it's the owners?" Niles wonders aloud.

A darker possibility crosses my mind. What if it's one of *them?*

I walk down the fence to the place where the footprints begin and drop to my haunches to examine them. No claws or weird alien shapes, thank God. They just look like ordinary boot prints to me. Only one set, and the prints are on both sides of the fence, which means whoever it was climbed over. The toes are pointing toward the house. I straighten and examine where the prints came from. They're running all the way down one side of Eagle Drive, disappearing in the direction that we just came from. It could be one of the neighbors. Niles can't be the only one hoping to upgrade to the nicest place on the block. Or maybe it's just someone scavenging for supplies.

Either way, they could be armed, and if that's the case, we definitely don't want to surprise them.

"Wait here," I say. "Tell your CDUs to get out

and scan for signs of trouble."

"Where are you going?"

"To introduce myself," I say as I duck through the fence and start following the footprints through a line of towering pine trees that partially obscure the house from the street. Still only one set of prints, so whoever this is, they're either inside, or else they left by another route.

Keeping my shotgun across my chest in a firm two-handed grip, I follow the prints to a porte-cochère in front of the main entrance. One of the two wood and glass doors is cracked open. The glass window in the top half is smashed, leaving no doubt about whether this could be the owner of the home.

I step carefully to one side of the door and peer in through the broken window. Announcing myself could be a good idea—or a very bad one. But I decide that surprising the intruder would be worse.

"Hello?" I call into the house.

No answer.

Sticking to cover behind the other door, I push the open one a few inches wider. It creaks loudly, and I try again, "I don't want any trouble, and I don't care that you broke in. I was about to do the same." Then I add, "I've got my kids outside." A family man should seem less threatening than a lone vagrant. "We're just looking for a place to lie low for a while. Maybe we can help each other out?"

I wait for a handful of seconds, but my only reply is an icy wind creaking through the trees. Maybe the intruder already left. Grimacing, I step out of cover and peek around the open door.

No sign of anyone, but I can see clumps of snow melting to water on the tiled floor. The water follows the grout lines to the right, toward the main living area, and I can feel heat radiating from inside. The air is warm, but I can't see any lights. Maybe one of the fireplaces is lit.

Waiting another beat, I step through the open door.

"Put it down—slowly."

I turn my head to the voice, and come face to muzzle with a hunting rifle. The bearer of the weapon is standing ten feet away in a cozy sitting room with an unlit fireplace, a book shelf, and an upright piano.

My heart is hammering in my chest, and I curse myself for not being more careful. I should have expected an ambush.

Slowly bending down to place the shotgun at my feet, I take the time to size up my adversary. The lights are out, but there's enough moonlight coming in through the windows to get a clear look at him.

He's an average height, neither skinny nor overweight. Pale, with the craggy weather-worn features of a man who has spent his life out-doors. I estimate that he could be in his mid-forties to early fifties. There's a hard, unfriendly look in his black eyes, and I get the impression that he's a man who's had a tough life and developed a crusty personality to match. A thick, unkempt salt and pepper beard covers the lower half of his face and neck. Matching, overgrown black hair with streaks of silver is peeking out from under a classic black watch cap. His faded gray boots look long overdue for a replacement, but he's wearing a shiny black ski jacket, and a clean pair of blue jeans. The fact that he came here on foot, combined with his unkempt appearance makes me wonder if he's a vagrant, but maybe he was worried about attracting too much attention with a vehicle. Or maybe his vehicle broke down or got stuck like mine.

"What are you doing here?" the man asks in a deep, gravelly voice as I straighten with my hands in the air.

"We came from the valley. We're just looking for a place to hide."

"We?"

"My wife and kids," I deliberately don't tell him about the Pearsons and their bodyguard bots. If I don't come back out, Niles might have the sense to send one or both of the CDUs looking for me. They're practically bullet-proof, and their stun guns should be more than enough to take this guy down.

"Look, we can stay here together," I suggest.

"I wasn't plannin' to stay," the man replies, but a speculative look enters his gaze that tells me he's thinking about it now. Good. Maybe I can talk him down.

"You know what's going on out there?" I ask.

He nods. "Aliens, right? We surrendered. That about sum it up?"

"More or less, yeah."

I take a moment to think about what I'm going to say next. The guy is wearing a ski boot bag on his back—black with reflective orange piping—but he doesn't look like the skiing type, which makes me think that he stole the bag from this home—along with whatever he's stashed inside of it. There's also a big black canvas bag sitting on the floor by his feet. He was definitely here scavenging for supplies. That, or stealing valuables. But who cares about money at a time like this?

I try a different approach. "Look, we're not here to cause you any trouble. You can leave. We won't try to stop you. I don't care that you broke in. I was about to do the same."

"Hmmm," the man replies. "Maybe *you* should leave. I was here first."

"That's true, but there's a third option. We could all stay. If we work together, we can keep watches all through the night. You won't be able to do that by yourself." Even as I suggest the idea, I wonder if it's a good one. I don't know this guy. For all I know, he could be a complete psycho.

The barrel of the rifle wavers and then drops a few inches. His finger ducks out of the trigger guard to rest beside it, which tells me that he's had some experience with guns. An Army background like mine, maybe? I wasn't the only one who got booted out and replaced by robots.

The man's brow tenses and his eyes narrow once more. "How do I know I can trust you?" he asks.

"You don't, but we don't know if we can trust you, either."

A grunt. "Fair enough." He lowers his rifle the rest of the way, and I drop my hands.

"Thank you," I say. "Do you mind if I pick up my shotgun now?"

There comes a long pause before the man inclines his head to me in a shallow nod.

"What's your name?" I ask as I pick up the weapon.

"Bret," he says.

"I'm Chris. You live around here, Bret?"

"Uh-huh," he says. His eyes slide away from mine to the open door behind me. "You gonna go get your family?"

"Yes."

"I'll wait here for ya."

I send Bret a tight smile before ducking back outside and running down the driveway to the gate and the two waiting vehicles. The CDU bots track my approach from where they stand guarding Niles' Suburban. Their stun guns are drawn and ready for action, while their smart-locked Glocks remain holstered.

The driver's side window of the suburban rolls down. "We all good?" Niles asks.

I climb over the gate and walk up to his door. "I met the guy inside. He's armed, but he seems..." I trail off. "I don't know. He's agreed to share the place with us. He got the drop on me with a hunting rifle, but I talked him down by suggesting that we stay in the house together and watch each other's backs."

Niles blows out a breath that steams the air between us. "Great, so he could be dangerous, and you've invited him to join us."

"Or he could be an asset. He looks like he knows how to handle that rifle, and we outnumber him pretty handily, so the risk is manageable. Think about it—what's his incentive to turn on us? There's nothing he could gain."

"Not yet. That could change. He could also get us into trouble through sheer negligence."

"He didn't look like the negligent type to me."

"You'd trust your kids around him?" Niles counters.

"I don't know," I admit.

Jessica is frowning at us from the passenger's seat. She has her arms crossed over her chest and she starts shaking her head. "We should go somewhere else."

"We could..." I say slowly. My eyes dart up to the moonlit clouds. "But the longer we spend driving around, the more likely it is that we'll attract attention from the invaders." My gaze comes back down to Niles. The haunted look in his eyes tells me he's thinking about whatever the hell he saw eating his neighbors last night.

"You know of any other places close to here that might work?"

Niles shakes his head. "Not with propane generators, and we're going to need that until the electricity comes back. The CDUs can watch our backs," Niles says. "If that guy makes a move, they'll put him down."

"Fair enough. Let's get everyone inside," I say.

Jessica doesn't look happy with the decision, but I'm not sure if she's ever really happy about anything.

I leave Niles to get his family out, and hurry over to the SUV he loaned us. As I open the door, Bree asks me what happened, and I repeat the explanations that I gave to Niles.

My mother looks horrified. "What was he doing in there? Is he a thief?"

"You could have gotten yourself killed!" Bree hisses at me.

"Relax," I reply, waving away both of their concerns. "He doesn't seem dangerous." That's a lie. "He was just being cautious," I add in my next breath.

"And obviously you weren't," Bree adds.

Rather than continue the argument, I reach in for the key fob and turn off the car. "Let's go." Reaching for the back door on my side, I pull it open. Gaby holds out her arms to me, wanting me to pick her up.

"I can't. I have a gun. You need to walk on your own, okay?"

She makes a pouty face, but does as she's asked and climbs out of the car by herself. Zach crawls out on her side, and my mother follows. She sends me a reproachful look as she does so. "You need to be more careful."

I nod in agreement as I go to grab our supplies. She's not wrong. I still can't believe that I let that guy get the drop on me. It's a wake-up call. I'm rusty and making sloppy mistakes.

Realizing that another mistake would be weighing myself down with bags when I should really have my hands free for the shotgun, I wave to my mother and Bree. They come over, and I point to the bags.

Bree arches an eyebrow at me, as if to ask me what happened to chivalry. "I need to have my hands free for the gun, and my side is bleeding."

Concern briefly replaces accusation in my wife's gaze, and then the accusation is back as she reaches past me for the bag with our clothes and food in it. "Why didn't you say something earlier?"

"Because we didn't have time to stop and re-dress my wounds."

"Well, we do now."

"Once we get inside, sure."

My mother takes Gaby's backpack and her carry-on luggage, and then Zach comes to take his backpack. That only leaves the gun bag for me. I loop the shoulder strap over my head, and moments later we're climbing over the fence and following Bret's footprints to the house. I lead the way with Niles and one of his two bodyguard bots, while the other one brings up the rear.

As we draw near to the house, I see a light flick on in the sitting room where Bret surprised me a moment ago.

"Looks like the propane generator is already running," I say.

"They turn on automatically when the power goes out," Niles explains. "Keeps the food in fridges and freezers from going off while people are away."

Sounds like a rich man's problem to me—I've never owned more than one fridge, and there's usually not enough food in it to worry about it going off even if the power does go out.

Passing under the roof of the covered parking area in front of the doors, I stomp off my boots on the back step to let Bret know we're here.

I see his craggy face appear in one of the windows. His eyes widen fractionally at the sight of the extra people—and bots—that I didn't mention when we first met.

Bracing myself for trouble, I step up to the doors and knock lightly on one of them.

"Bret?"

CHAPTER 14

"**B**ig family you have, there," Bret says, stepping into view behind the open door of the house.

Once again, I can feel the heat radiating out from the open door. But since we know the generator is supplying electricity, that's less mysterious. It means the furnace is probably running.

"We're actually two families—and three bots."

I wait outside the doors, listening to the silence as Bret processes that.

"The more the merrier, right?" I add. "More eyes, more guns."

Glancing over my shoulder, I take in the worried looks on my mother's and Bree's faces, the unhappy scowl on Jessica's, and the fidgety look on her husband's. The kids are all staring blankly ahead.

"And more liabilities," Bret says.

"It's not going to be a problem, is it?" I ask. "Because if it is, we can go somewhere else."

"No problem. But you shoulda mentioned it."

"Sorry," I say through a tight smile. "Mind if we come in now? It's freezing out here."

"Go right ahead."

I lead the way, pushing through the open door with my shotgun held casually. The others follow me in, and we all stand quietly eying the unkempt man standing between us and the rest of the house. He's leaning on his rifle like a cane— the butt under one arm, barrel facing down.

Bret clears his throat. "You gonna make the introductions, or what?"

I make the rounds, telling him everyone's names. I'm watching his reaction carefully as he studies each of us, but there's no flicker or flash of anything to betray malign intent.

"Good to meet you all," Bret says when I'm finished. "So how's this gonna work?"

"What do you mean?" Niles replies.

Bret nods to me. "He mentioned setting up watches so we can all get some sleep. What he didn't mention was those two *clankers*. Seems like we can let them do all the watching and just have them wake us if they detect anything."

"It's a big house," I say.

"But they have sensors, right? Radar, infra-red, night vision."

"Yes," Niles confirms.

"Then they've got us covered." Bret stops leaning on his rifle and loops the shoulder strap over his head while he goes to pick up the canvas bag he left in the sitting area. "If you'll all excuse me, I'm going to go wash up and get some rest. Feel free to take any of the empty rooms. I'm in the master." He jerks a thumb over his shoulder to a hallway at the back of the sitting room.

"We should probably keep the lights off—at least at night," I say.

"Fair enough."

Bret takes his things and flicks off the light he turned on as he heads for the hallway. Watching him take his things and leave without causing any type of trouble releases some of the tension in my chest. Exhaustion hits me fully, and I remember that I was up all night last night. Getting some sleep has just jumped to the top of my priority list.

But first, we need to secure this place. I turn to Niles and find him staring fixedly after the scraggly man in the watch cap as he shuffles down the hallway at the back of the sitting room.

"Well, I'd better go get the kids settled in," Jessica says. "Sean, Haley, let's go find a room. Emily, Paul, follow us, please."

"Of course, ma'am," the bots reply in unison. Emily totters after them with all of their luggage, and Paul hurries by with whirring steps to keep pace with Jessica as they head deeper into the house.

"We should find a room, too," Bree says quietly beside me. Her blue eyes linger on mine, as if waiting for me to say I'll go with her. I can tell she doesn't like sharing a place with a stranger, much less an armed stranger, but she's trusting my judgment.

I nod to her. "I'll come and find you in a minute."

"Okay..." Bree picks up the duffel bag, struggling under its weight once more, and then Zach, Gaby, and my mother follow her deeper into the house, heading for what looks like the main living area.

Bret went in the opposite direction to my family, so I don't feel the immediate need to chase after them. Besides, one of the CDUs went with Jessica, and they're leading the way.

Turning to Niles, I say, "We need to identify all of the entrances, exits, and windows, then figure out where best to position the CDUs," I say.

"Yeah..." Niles sounds distant. He's still staring at the hallway where Bret disappeared.

"I'm sure he's harmless," I say.

"Probably," Niles agrees.

I head down the hall from the foyer, following my family as they disappear through a door to the left. The soft whirring of the other CDU echoes after us.

Immediately after the sitting room is a formal dining area with a ten-seater table. Then comes the great room with an open kitchen. The walls are all made of exposed logs. The peaked ceiling is also wood and supported by more log beams. The great room has a stone fireplace with a deer's head mounted above the mantle.

It occurs to me that Bret might not have brought that hunting rifle with him. He might have stolen it from this house.

A wall of windows and sliding glass doors lead to a deck that faces the moonlit lake. There's a dock down there with a small motor boat at the end.

Open doorways lead away to both sides of the great room. To the left, where our families went, we find a games room with a bar, and doors to two bedrooms at the back. I can see my wife and kids through one door and Niles' family through the other. They've picked adjacent rooms on the same side of the house. Smart move. It keeps us separated from Bret, and makes it easier to defend ourselves from external threats, too.

Leaving my bag of guns on the pool table, Niles and I go back through the great room to check the other side of the house. The doorway from the great room leads us down a short hall lined with photos of a big family—kids, grandkids and grandparents. They're all posing in snowy scenes with colorful ski jackets, snowboards, and skis. The solitary wooden door at the end of the hall is shut.

This must be the master suite where Bret went. I try the handle. It's locked, so I knock twice, softly. "Bret? You in there?"

Footsteps approach the door. It cracks open to reveal Bret's craggy face. "What?" He has his rifle balanced across one arm, and he's shielding his body behind the door. I catch a glimpse of a spacious bedroom behind him.

"Can we come in to check for possible points of entry?"

"No need," Bret says. "I've got it covered."

"What happens when you're asleep?" I ask.

"The bots will see trouble coming a mile away. Wake me up if they detect anything."

I frown at that, wanting to argue further, but Bret shuts the door in my face before I can say anything else. Heavy footsteps retreat from the door.

"Come on," Niles whispers, pulling me away by one arm. "Leave him."

"What's he hiding in there?" I whisper back as we cross the great room on our way to the other side of the house.

"Maybe nothing," Niles says.

"Or maybe something," I reply.

"Such as?"

I hesitate, trying to come up with a theory, but at this point anything I suggest will only be wild speculation. We reach the bar and pool table.

Niles fixes me with a troubled look. "It's not too late for us to leave."

But I'm tired of hopping from place to place, and at this point, there's more risk to us moving around outside in plain sight than staying here with an unknown variable like Bret.

"Let's just station one of the CDUs here so it

can watch the door to this side of the house. It can also watch the deck from here." I point past the bar to another sitting area that leads to the deck we saw earlier. It seems to run the whole length of the house.

Niles nods his agreement. "And the other bot?"

"Outside, at the back doors where we came in."

"That leaves Bret's side exposed," Niles points out.

"He said he had it covered, didn't he?"

"Well, yeah, but that doesn't mean he can stop those things if they decide to get in."

"Bret's right. The sensors in the CDUs should see trouble coming for miles. If the aliens find us, we'll know where they are approaching from in time to defend ourselves."

"What about that broken door?" Niles asks. I grab the duffel with the guns in it and head for the room where I saw my wife and kids a moment ago. The door is shut now.

"Block it with some furniture," I suggest. "Get Emily or one of the CDUs to drag something heavy in front of the doors."

"Okay..."

Reaching the door to the bedroom, I call through it. "Bree?"

She opens the door, and I walk in sideways. There are two double beds, a rear-facing bay window, and an armchair with an ottoman beside it.

The curtains are drawn across the window. My kids and my mother are sitting on the bed closest to the door, the three of them huddled under the covers to keep warm. The heat is on, but it's still chilly in here. A bearskin rug hangs like a tapestry at the top of the wall, between the two beds and below the exposed logs that support the ceiling.

There's another stone fireplace in here with a deer's head mounted above the hearth. Whoever owned this place was definitely a hunter.

Owned. Past tense. I realize I'm assuming that the owners died in the initial attacks, but what if they didn't?

They could be on their way up here right now to get away from the chaos in the cities.

And here we are, squatting in their home. I set the duffel bag beside the fireplace, and turn to Bree with a weary sigh.

"Everything okay?" she asks, her eyes dark with shadows as she shuts and locks the bedroom door behind me.

I nod. "He's on the other side of the house, so we have this end all to ourselves."

A muscle jerks in Bree's cheek. "He looks homeless. What if he's on drugs?"

That's a fair question. The clean jacket and jeans threw me, but he could have stolen those from this house. Bret's otherwise unkempt appearance fits with Bree's impression, and his boots definitely looked old enough. Stealing new shoes is harder than clothes.

But I didn't see any signs that Bret might be high; his eyes were clear, and he wasn't jittery or anxious like he would be if he were going through withdrawals. And if he is homeless, then what's he doing up in Big Bear?

"He's probably just a lonely old bachelor," I decide. "It's hard to be homeless up here. Too cold for that. He'd be down in the valley where it's warmer. Anyway, we shouldn't make any assumptions yet."

"I guess," Bree concedes with a sigh.

"I need to get some sleep," I say.

"You'd better eat something first," Bree says. "And I should check your bandages."

I turn and reach for the bag with our food in it, but Bree catches my arm to stop me. "Go lie down. I'll handle the food."

"Thanks," I reply as I angle for the empty bed.

I kick off my boots, take off my jacket and gloves and drop them at the foot of the bed, then crawl under the covers. My stomach grumbles at the thought of food, and I watch hungrily as Bree pulls crackers and cans of tuna from the bag.

My eyes feel like lead, and they're closing by themselves. I fight to keep them open, but I'm losing that fight fast. Each time I open my eyes, Bree has jumped to a different part of the room.

Now she's standing between the beds passing out paper plates with crackers and tuna on them to my mom and kids.

Blink—

She's reaching into the duffel bag.

Blink—

Handing out bottles of water...

I feel movement on my bed. An arm drapes over me. I turn my head sleepily, expecting to see Bree.

But it's my daughter, Gaby. She's crawled into bed beside me, peeking over my injured ribs. She squeezes me hard in a one-armed hug, and my wounded side aches.

"Careful," I groan.

"Sorry."

Her head drops to the pillow beside mine. Her blue eyes drill into me, and she says, "I love you, Daddy."

I smile weakly and mumble back, "I love you, too, kiddo."

Bree comes over with a plate of crackers and tuna and a bottle of water that she sets on a night table between the two beds. I sit up, and Gaby curls up against me in a semi-fetal position—her knees drawn up, her head tucked under my arm, nestling against my wounded side.

"What about your bandages? Maybe we should change them first," Bree says.

I shake my head and lie through a mouthful of crackers, "It's not that bad."

"Are they going to find us here?" Gaby asks while I eat.

Bree goes to sit on the other side of the bed,

squeezing our daughter between us.

"They're not looking for us," I say.

"How do you know?" Gaby presses.

I swallow a dry mouthful of tuna and crackers, and wash it down with a swig of water from the bottle that Bree left beside me. "Because the Union surrendered, and we're not out there causing trouble for the invaders. There's no reason for them to come after us."

"Then why did we have to leave the other house?"

I smile wryly at that. She has me there. "We left because we didn't want to risk staying in a place that they'd attacked earlier, and all of the broken windows would have made it hard to stay warm. They had plenty of time to come and get us, and they didn't, so that means they're not looking for us."

"Who are they looking for?" Gaby asks.

"No one, sweetheart," Bree says. "The fighting is already over."

"But what if it's not over?"

Bree and I trade knowing looks over Gaby's head. These questions could go on for a while. "We're safe here. Daddy will keep us safe."

"But what if they get him?"

"I'm not that easy to get."

"But—"

"Shhh. Daddy needs to rest now, darling."

"If he's asleep, who is going to keep us safe?"

"You saw those robots in the black suits?"

Bree asks.

Gaby nods, her head brushing against my side.

"They're watching the house for us. They'll let us know the minute that they see anything, and they have sensors that can see much better than our eyes, even at night."

"But what if one of them comes here?"

"Then I'll shoot it dead," I say.

"But what if they just want to say hi?" Gaby asks. "Maybe they're not bad. Maybe they're friendly."

"Even better. Then we don't have anything to worry about."

I lean over to place my empty plate and the water bottle on the night table. Zachary is watching us from the other bed. Our explanations served equally for him, but the fact that he hasn't asked any questions of his own tells me that he knows better than his little sister: he's old enough to know that his parents don't have all the answers.

Just as I'm lying back down and pulling the covers up to my chin, Bree comes over with a first aid kit that I didn't realize we'd packed. "Not yet," she says, opening the kit on the bed. "Let's get a look at your side."

I pull up my black hoodie sweater to reveal a bloody smear that has leaked all the way down to the waistband of my pajama bottoms. Blood has seeped through the sheet tied around my ribs, turning it dark red.

Bree grimaces as she works to untie the sheet.

"Does it hurt?" Gaby asks, crowding in to get a look.

I shake my head. "No, sweetheart."

Bree pulls away the sheet, but it's too dark to see much. "Let's get some light on it," she says, reaching for the lamp on the nightstand beside me.

"We should keep the lights off," I object.

"Turning it on for a minute won't hurt," Bree insists.

The lamp blazes to life, dazzling my eyes.

Bree sucks in a sharp breath, and I tuck my chin to my chest to get a look at what she's seen.

There are three parallel gashes in my side. They're each about four inches long, but mostly superficial. The wounds have congealed, but they're still open, and I don't see how they can close on their own. "I'm going to need stitches. Any chance there's a needle and thread in that first aid kit?"

Bree bites her lower lip and shakes her head as she searches briefly through the plastic box.

"Maybe we can find one somewhere in this house," I suggest. "We just need a sewing needle and some fishing line. Looks like this place belonged to an outdoorsman. I bet we can find the fishing line out in the garage."

"Fishing line," Bree says while fixing me with

a skeptical look.

"What? It'll work, and it'll be stronger than plain old thread," I insist.

"We should take you to a clinic in town. Even if there's no one there, they'll have the supplies we need. Including something for the pain. Pills at least."

"And risk running into something along the way?" I counter. "Not worth it."

"I'll go get Niles to take a look in the garage," my mom suggests. She gets up from the other bed and heads for the door.

I watch her go. Bree's eyes drill into mine. "Even if she finds what we need, sewing you up is going to hurt. A lot. You need at least a dozen stitches."

That sounds about right. "There's alcohol by the bar. After a few shots, it won't hurt that bad. Find me something to bite on, and I'll be good."

"Like what?"

"Some socks, or a glove... Niles was wearing leather gloves. Get me one of those."

Bree snorts and flashes a crooked smile at me. "Who do you think you are? Clegg Hannigan?"

I wink at her and raise an index finger to my mouth and blow as if it's the smoking barrel of an old-fashioned revolver.

"You're a crazy bastard."

"Crazy for you."

"I'll be back," she says, patting my hand as she leaves.

The door opens, then clicks shut behind her.

Gaby sits staring at my injured side. It's not bleeding at the moment, but it looks pretty ugly. She's transfixed by all the dried blood.

"I bet the aliens aren't really mean," Gaby says, as if the gashes in my side might have happened by accident. "They just came here because they wanted to make some new friends."

"That's *so* stupid," Zachary mutters.

I'm tempted to agree with him, but Gaby's six, so her innocence just makes me smile.

"Is not," Gaby insists.

"Is too..."

"Is *not!* You're stupid!"

I'm too tired to play referee. My eyes are sinking shut again. It could be a while before Bree and my mother get back with the things they need to stitch me up.

"Daaad, she called me stupid."

And that's the last thing I hear before falling into a deep, dreamless sleep.

CHAPTER 15

Someone is shaking me.

"Chris, wake up," Bree's voice coaxes gently beside my ear.

I crack an eye open to see her smiling at me. She holds up a sewing needle. Her other hand holds a spool of fine fishing line. "Looks like you were right about finding fishing line in the garage."

My mother sets a bottle of vodka on the night table and pours a full glass.

"How did you get into the garage?"

Niles crowds in beside my wife, holding out one of his leather gloves.

"We found the door opener. Seems like the generator is powering the garage, too."

I nod, too tired and sore for a verbal response.

Bree is busy threading the needle, then cleaning it in a second glass of vodka. I glance between her and my mother, watching as they hesitate and regard one another. They're trying to decide who should stitch me up.

"Bree, you can do it," I say, knowing that my

mother has the weaker stomach and that Bree has steadier hands.

"I have more practice with a needle and thread," my mother objects.

True enough, but I don't want her passing out and adding to our problems. "You can watch and give advice," I suggest.

Bree lets out a shaky breath. "Well, we need to clean the wound first." She lifts the bottle of vodka in one hand and casts about, as if looking for something.

"I'll get a clean towel," my mother suggests. "I think I saw a linen closet between the bedrooms." She heads for the door and strides out quickly. We wait a few seconds, and then she's back with a stack of clean white hand towels.

"Perfect," I say.

My wife proceeds to douse the first towel in vodka. "Lie on your side," she says.

I'm already lying on my side, but she probably means for me to turn the wounded side closer to her. I do that and raise my arm, pinning it behind my head.

Another shaky breath from Bree.

My mother grabs Niles' leather glove and holds it in front of my mouth. I clamp down on it.

"Here goes..." Bree says.

And then she's rubbing away the crusted blood with a vodka-soaked towel. My side lights up in blinding agony. Flashes of light flicker before my eyes, and my head swims with the pain. Grabbing a fistful of the pillow behind my head, I bite down hard on the glove and release an agonized roar that's muffled by the glove in my mouth. It feels like someone is scraping my bones with sandpaper.

Then, a moment later, it's over, and Bree drops a blood-soaked towel on the floor. My side is bleeding freely again, and the blood is coursing hotly down my side.

Gaby scuttles away, fleeing to the armchair by the fireplace and the bay window. Zach looks on with a horrified expression. My mother looks paler than I've ever seen her in my life. She sits down on the other bed. Niles looks on with a grimace.

And Bree is hesitating again. I spit out the glove. "I'm going to bleed out if you don't stitch me up soon."

"Get me another towel, quick!" Bree says, snapping out of it. Niles grabs one from the stack.

My mother moans and sways dizzily.

Bree presses the towel firmly to my side. "Hold it there," she tells Niles. "Keep the pressure on."

He reaches past her, and she casts about again. Grabbing the needle and line from the glass of vodka, she holds the needle up to the light, checking the knot that holds the line.

"This better work," she says. Then she douses her hands in vodka and bends to the task of stitching the first cut.

This time the sounds that tear past my lips aren't muffled by the glove, but Niles promptly stuffs it in my mouth again.

It feels like the pain goes on forever. One endless moment of blinding agony that comes in waves, with peaks and valleys. Each prick of the hook is a peak. The valleys are when Bree is pulling the line through my ragged flesh.

At first I'm focusing on those sharp pricks, trying to count the stitches since I can't see past Niles. But soon my head is too light, and I'm too weak to make sense of anything anymore. I'm getting close to passing out, either from blood loss or the pain. But I no longer care. At least I won't be able to feel anything if I'm unconscious.

Bree leans back from me, wiping tear-stained cheeks with the backs of bloody hands.

"Keep the pressure on," she says to Niles.

To my ears it sounds like she's underwater. Or maybe I am. But the pain is down from a twelve to a six.

"You did good," I manage to croak out.

And then my eyes are sliding shut again.

I hear people arguing about whether or not I should be allowed to sleep.

"I'm just tired," I say.

"Let him rest," my mother insists.

I feel people cleaning my side, wiping away all the blood with spare towels and whatever's left of the vodka. I realize that they forgot to give me that drink.

Oh well. Too late now.

* * *

"Chris. Chris!"

This time the whisper that wakes me is a sharp one.

My eyes spring open to see Bree leaning over me. The room is much darker than it was before. The lights are off. I sit up quickly—and immediately regret it as the stitches in my side pull and blood leaks out hotly.

"Careful," Bree hisses.

"How long was I out?"

"It's four AM," Bree says, as if that answers my question.

It's then that I notice my mother is by the windows, peeking through the curtains. My kids are sitting up on the other bed, wide awake and alert.

"What's wrong?" I whisper.

"We heard something outside," Bree explains.

"What did you hear?" I ask, staring at my mom.

"Car doors opening and shutting. Voices," my mother answers. "I think someone stopped at the top of the driveway."

"They must have seen our vehicles."

I gingerly climb out of bed to check the window, wondering why the CDUs haven't alerted us. Or maybe they have and Niles is busy giving them orders.

My mother steps aside to let me look, but I can't see anything past the pine trees at the back of the house.

"It could be the owners of this place," I say.

A soft knock sounds at the door. I start in that direction to answer it, but Bree beats me there.

"Hello?" she whispers through the door.

"It's me," Niles says.

She opens the door. "Paul and Jeremy have detected two humans and two bots outside."

My theory about it being the owners is sounding even more likely now.

But what Niles says next shoots it down: "It's an Army unit."

"How do you know?" I ask.

"Their bots made comms contact with mine. I gave them permission to approach. They'll be here any second. I thought maybe we should greet them together, go find out what they know. Maybe there have been new developments?"

I rub the sleep from my eyes. "Yeah, okay, that's a good idea. Better warn Bret so he doesn't overreact when he sees them."

"I already did. He heard me, but he doesn't want to come out of his room."

I go find my boots and try to put them on, bending carefully. In the end, I need help from Bree to get them fully on. Then my jacket. I'm able to shrug into it, but have to move carefully to avoid tearing the stitches. Bree hands me one of our two shotguns.

"Thanks," I say.

"You think it's a good idea to greet them with weapons?" My mother asks.

I shrug while pulling back the pump action to check the ejection port and make sure the gun is loaded. I can see a shell in there, the brass gleaming in the dark.

"It's better than going out empty-handed. We don't know what their intentions are yet."

"They're soldiers, not criminals," my mother argues.

My father was a career soldier—a captain in the Army, so she has plenty of respect for servicemen. Having been in the service myself, so do I, but something about this encounter feels wrong. What's a team of two soldiers and two bots doing up here in the middle of the night? I wonder if these guys ran away from whatever peace-keeping role the military has taken in the wake of the Union's surrender. If so, technically that *does* make them criminals.

But rather than tell my mother any of that, I walk out the door with Niles, and tell Bree to shut and lock it behind us.

"Don't open for anyone that isn't me," I add.

She nods quickly, but before she shuts the door, she passes the other shotgun out to Niles.

"Is it loaded?" I ask.

Bree nods. "I loaded it while you were asleep. I thought we should be ready in case something found us here."

I smile crookedly at her. "Smart woman."

"Be careful," she adds, not rising to the bait to banter with me. She hates when I refer to her generically like that.

"You know how to handle it?" I ask Niles as we turn to leave.

I hear the door click shut and springs twanging as she turns the knob to lock it.

Niles nods slowly, but he's holding the shotgun like an umbrella, with the barrel pointed at the ceiling. A second later he drops it across his chest, and the barrel swings into line with my head.

"Woah..." I duck out of the way. "Always aim away from people that you don't mean to shoot." I show him, cradling my gun in one arm with the barrel pointing down my hand holding the action and the stock leaning against my shoulder.

"You mean aim it at my feet?" he echoes incredulously.

"Next to your feet. And it's a lot better than aiming at my head. Anyway, Mossbergs have a safety. Right here." I turn my gun to show him the slider on top of the weapon between the stock and the barrel.

He flicks his safety off to test it, but I reach over to flick it back on.

"Let's keep that on for now. Just in case. Come

on. Those soldiers must be standing right out-side by now."

I lead the way past the pool table, wondering if showing Niles the safety was a bad idea. The last thing I need is for Bree to wind up using an-other sewing needle to fish around for shot in my ass.

CHAPTER 16

Niles and I leave the games room, walking past the CDU that he stationed here. I think about telling Niles to have it follow us for added security, but if these soldiers want to cause trouble, having an extra civilian defense unit around won't stop them.

Besides, I doubt they're a threat to us, even if they really did go AWOL.

We reach the front door to find it shut with a heavy wooden wardrobe in front of the door with the broken window. Niles must have had the CDUs drag it there at some point. We both set our guns down to push the furniture aside. Niles does most of the work, but I help as best as I can while minding my injuries.

The other CDU is standing right outside the doors with its back to us and a stun gun drawn.

We both pick up our shotguns and I open the broken door to step outside. I hear boots crunching steadily through the snow, along with the soft whirring of the MAUs—Mechanized Assault Units.

The bots approach us first, without their human counterparts. Both bots have their rifles ready, but not aimed. Their faces are less anthropomorphized than the CDUs, with only a vague resemblance to human features. The adaptive camouflage built into their armor has changed colors to match their surroundings—dark white and gray that helps them blend with the snow. I wait for them to come within spitting distance of us before saying anything, but the MAUs speak first.

"I'm Corporal Lawrence, and this is Private Duran," one of the bots says, jerking a thumb to the other. They're using human names and voices, not robotized ones, so I know I'm talking to the human soldiers.

"Chris Randall," I reply. "Formerly UNA Corporal Randall," I reply. "And this is Niles Pearson," I add, nodding sideways to indicate him. "Where's your sergeant, Corporal?" I ask the bot who's speaking.

"She's dead, sir."

"You came up from the valley?"

"Yes, sir."

"What's the situation down there? I heard we surrendered."

"Officially, yes, but there are still pockets of resistance. Both military and civilian." The bot speaking to me heaves its shoulders in a shrug. "Doesn't matter much. We have the numbers, and they have the tech. One of them is enough to kill ten of us, and the flying ones have these four-legged bastards the size of bears out there doing most of the fighting for them."

I remember Niles' description of creatures like that emerging from a lander and tearing his neighbors apart.

"Do they have guns?" I ask, wondering if those four-legged ones are more like attack dogs than sentient aliens.

"Yes, sir. Lasers and plasma. And some kind of shields to protect them. Don't know if you heard, but LA is gone. Nothing but smoking craters and fires raging out of control. San Bernardino is in better shape, but it was also hit pretty hard, and we saw plenty of hostiles on the ground, harassing civilians and attacking army units."

"But we surrendered."

"Yeah, tell that to them. Seems like their idea of surrender is we let them do whatever they want with us."

"Maybe they're waiting for us to lay down our weapons," Niles suggests. "Maybe they're only attacking people that are armed?"

"Maybe," Corporal Lawrence admits. "But our comms are being jammed, so that makes it hard to figure out what provokes them and what doesn't. We lost contact with our unit and got cut off by enemy forces. That's when we decided to come up here and regroup rather than add to the casualties."

I wonder if that's true or if it's just a story they're telling to avoid admitting that they ran away from the fighting.

"Were you followed?" I ask.

"Enemy drones tailed us for the first twenty miles or so, but we lost them in the mountains."

"Same here," Niles says.

"Did you see any sign of the enemy up here?" I ask.

"Negative. The town looks like it took a few hits, but it seemed clear. We didn't take the time to conduct a thorough sweep."

"Understood." I'm relieved by that news, but I know better than to let my guard down because of it.

"You should come inside," Niles says. "You're sitting ducks out there."

I hesitate before echoing that sentiment, wondering if sheltering a military unit makes us a target.

The corporal clears his throat and says, "Thank you for the offer, sir, but as you say, we may have been followed. We noticed a guest house on the property, right above the garage. Would you mind if we holed up there for a while?"

"Go ahead," I say, grateful for a safer alternative.

"Thank you. Comms seem to be clear around here. We'll let your CDUs know if we see anything."

"Likewise," I say. "Stay frosty, Corporal."

"Hooah."

I watch both units turn and march back up the driveway to the guest house.

"Why didn't they come introduce themselves in person?" Niles asks as they leave. "Kind of suspicious, don't you think?"

I shrug. "Not really. That's what the MAUs are for. They always get sent in first. Saves lives."

"I guess." Niles sighs. "We should have asked them more questions."

"Like what?"

"I don't know... I just hoped they would have more news for us."

"Or *better* news," I mutter. "Come on. Let's get back inside."

CHAPTER 17

We return to the games room and gather our families to discuss the arrival of the soldiers. I add my thoughts, and so does Niles. In the end, we're pretty much evenly divided on it.

"You had no right to let them stay here," Jessica Pearson says. She glowers darkly at me from where she stands behind the bar, working a corkscrew into a bottle of wine. Her lips are pressed into a thin, disapproving line.

"Technically, it was your husband who invited them to stay. And we're all squatters anyway," I say from where I sit casually on the edge of the pool table, facing her and the others. The kids and my family are on the couches and chairs along the windows and sliding doors to the deck outside. The only light coming in is from those windows, but the stars and the full moon make the lake shine like a mirror and fill the games room with a pale silver light.

I go on smugly, "Niles suggested they come in here, but they wanted to stay in the guest house instead."

"Well, you're both fools, then," Jessica declares as she gulps down a glass of the Riesling that she just uncorked.

"Excuse me?" Niles says with his eyebrows raised. He's sitting on the back of the couch where his kids are curled up on either side of their robotic nanny, Emily.

But Jessica doesn't retract her judgment. "They could have been followed here," she explains.

"Then why aren't we already under attack?" I counter. "Having them here is a good thing. Unlike your bodyguards, military bots *can* use lethal force, and they're deadly as hell. Not to mention the soldiers themselves. We need that firepower. It might be the only thing that keeps us alive if we do run into trouble up here."

"And yet, they ran away with their tails between their legs. Their firepower obviously wasn't enough, and you said it yourself, they've probably gone AWOL, so what makes you think they'll stick around to defend us?"

"They're not really AWOL if we're in a state of anarchy right now," I point out.

My wife stands up from the sitting area and walks over to join me. "She might be right, Chris." Bree softens the blow of siding with the woman who fired me by taking my hand and wrapping it around her waist.

"We should vote on it," Jessica says. "All in favor of telling the soldiers to leave?" Her hand shoots up while she sips her second glass of wine. Followed by Bree's. Then my mother adds hers.

"That settles it," Jessica says. "Niles, would you please go tell our guests to find somewhere else to stay?"

"Hang on," I say. "That's only three against. What about Bret?"

"Even if he sides with you, that makes it a tie," Jessica says, looking far too reasonable as she sips her wine. "How do you propose we break it?"

I can feel a vein throbbing on the right side of my head. My thoughts spin restlessly. "We let the kids vote."

Jessica snorts derisively at that.

Before we can argue any further, a rattle of gunfire shatters the night, followed by another, and then—a man shouting a phrase that I recognize all too well: "Frag out!"

There comes a muffled *boom*, and then a momentary silence.

"It's too late! They've found us!" Bree whispers sharply. Gaby whimpers, and Zach jumps to his feet with his fists balled. But the look on his face is pure terror.

"Shhh," I say, silencing them all as I stand up and snatch my shotgun off the pool table. The touch of cold aluminum clears my head. I look in the direction of the guest house, my ears straining through the silence for any sound that might indicate an ongoing threat. I'm hoping that frag grenade put an end to whatever it was.

But then a pair of heavy *thuds* echo around us, and Haley Pearson lets out a muffled scream. I spin around to see their nanny bot, Emily, lying on the floor at Haley's feet. Not only that, but Paul, the CDU assigned to guard the entrance of the games room, has collapsed in the open doorway between us and the great room.

"What the hell?" Niles demands in a strained whisper.

"She just fell over..." Haley's brother, Sean, says.

"Another EMP," I say, but this time there's no explosion to explain it, and I'm left wondering if the EMP in the valley might have actually been caused by something other than a nuke. Maybe it's a strategic weapon being used by the invaders.

There comes another shout from the direction of the guest house, followed by a scream, and then more rattling roars of gunfire.

"What do we do?" my mother asks in a barely-contained shriek.

"Well?" Jessica hisses at me. She's irate, her eyes flashing darkly in the moonlight, but I don't have time to appease her. I'm already snapping into motion. "Get everyone into that bathroom and lock the door," I say, pointing to a shared bathroom between the two bedrooms on this side of the house. "Niles, get your shotgun and follow me."

Rather than do as I asked, Bree runs to the bedroom where we left our things. My heart beats erratically in my chest, and I take two steps to follow her before I realize that she's retrieving guns and ammo. She races back to my side with both Glocks and a box of shotgun shells.

"Here," she hands me the box of shells and one of the Glocks, while keeping the other for herself. "Don't do anything stupid."

I nod quickly as I empty the box of shells into one of my jacket's outer pockets and snap the holstered Glock into my belt. "Keep the kids quiet," I say.

And then Niles and I are striding out and stepping over Paul on our way to the back entrance of the house.

The gunfire from the soldiers has gone ominously quiet. Gripping my shotgun tighter, I wonder what chance Niles and I will stand if the soldiers and their automatic weapons have already been neutralized.

CHAPTER 18

Niles grabs my shoulder before we've made it more than two steps toward the main entrance of the house. "Wait. What about Bret?" he whispers. "We could use his help."

"Go get him and meet me by the doors," I reply.

Niles hesitates, maybe wondering at the wisdom of us splitting up. But I'm not planning to engage hostile forces on my own. Niles races toward the hallway that separates the great room from the master suite. I hurry past the kitchen, then the formal dining room, and cross the den at the main entrance of the house. I peel back the curtains and peek out the windows.

The full moon and stars reflect off the snow outside, making it easy enough to see. No sign of the soldiers or whatever attacked them, but from here I can only see one side of the guest house.

It's the side with the stairs that provide access to the living area above the garage. If something goes up there or if the soldiers come out, I should be able to see it from here.

No movement yet.

As I study the possible entry points of the guest house, I find myself wondering why we didn't take it for ourselves. It's closer to the road, but there's only the one entrance at the top of those stairs to worry about. All of the windows are on the second floor.

Then again, who knows if that matters. That alien I fought could fly, and for all we know the four-legged two-armed ones that Niles saw are good climbers.

A flicker of movement at the top of the stairs catches my eye, and I watch as one of the two human soldiers comes limping out and creeping down the stairs. When no one else follows, I'm left wondering what happened to the other one.

The man reaches the bottom of the stairs, pauses, and peeks around the corner with his rifle.

An otherworldly hooting sound fills the silence, and the soldier opens fire on something that I can't see. The roar from his rifle only lasts for a second, and then he turns and starts limp-running straight toward me.

Odd, hooting snarls accompany the frenzied crunching of heavy footfalls through ice-crusted snow. It sounds like a stampede.

A jolt of adrenaline courses through me. Whatever creatures are making those sounds, this soldier is leading them straight to the house.

I glance over my shoulder, checking for

backup, but Niles isn't here yet. Maybe he chickened out. Either way, I have to do something. That soldier is still alive, but he won't be for long if I don't help.

Running to the back doors, I body-check the wardrobe to push it aside, wincing at the dull ache in my injured leg and the sharp stabs from the stitches in my side. I only have to move the wardrobe a few inches to gain access to the door that Bret didn't break on his way in. Unlocking it, I crack the door open—

Immediately on the other side of it I see the Pearsons' other bodyguard bot crumpled in a useless heap on the doorstep.

"Over here!" I call to the soldier in an urgent whisper. He hears me and pours on a burst of speed, but he's not fast enough.

Three giant, four-legged creatures appear, each of them the size and color of a rhino. They're hairless with wrinkly gray skin and rippling muscles showing between thick black plates of armor. Two thick arms protrude from the front of their chests. Short snouts hang open revealing sharp white teeth. Two dark, gleaming red eyes sit above the snout, and a bony crown of horns atop the head. Between the bony horns are four flexible stalks with cone-shaped tips. These creatures aren't wearing helmets like the one I faced, but I can see what look like weapons holstered between their arms, and something that might be a sword on their backs.

Snow sprays out in all directions from the creatures' churning legs as they gain on the soldier running toward me. Oddly enough, none of the three have drawn their weapons.

The soldier sees them closing in and lets out a terrified scream.

My shotgun snaps up to my shoulder, my thumb flicks off the safety, and I take aim on the nearest monster.

CHAPTER 19

I aim for the side of the nearest beast's head and pull the trigger. The shotgun goes off with a *boom.* Horns splinter and the creature wails in a throaty roar. Its stride falters, but it keeps coming. One of the two behind it pulls even with the first. I pump the action to chamber another shell and pull the trigger again.

Boom.

A second shell to the side of the head takes the monster down, and it goes skidding through the snow on its chin, carried by its momentum.

The next creature in line snags the limping soldier with one of its massive arms. I catch a glimpse of long black claws flashing through flesh. The soldier cries out and falls face-first into the snow, just ten feet away from me. The monster's jaws yawn wide and gleaming teeth crunch around the soldier's thigh. He cries out with the sound of his femur snapping and twists around to take awkward aim with his rifle. I'm pumping my shotgun and shooting his attacker in the side of the head just as he empties his magazine into the other side of the monster's head. A rattling roar of bullets joins the intermittent booming of my shotgun. The monster shudders and roars under the combined assault, then releases the soldier's leg. Bright red blood spurts all over the snow as the monster collapses on top of him.

He screams as the weight of it adds to his injuries.

The third one arrives, moving fast and spraying snow. Just as I'm adjusting my aim and reloading, it skids past him and takes a running bite. Jaws close around the soldier's head, and there comes a sickening crunch. I'm pumping the action and pulling the trigger as fast as I can. Three more shots take the final monster down, but then I'm out of ammo and reaching for the extra shells in my jacket pocket.

Seeing that the soldier is beyond my help, with his head separated from his body and halfway down an alien monster's throat, I retreat to shut the door and lock it while I slot shells into the loading port in front of the trigger.

"Are they all gone?" a small, shaky voice asks through the ringing in my ears.

I glance back to see Niles standing frozen in the hallway from the den to the dining room. He's nothing but a blank cutout made of reflected moonlight and shadows, but I can imagine the glazed look of shock in his eyes. I've seen it often enough on the faces of soldiers after their first time in combat.

"Where the hell were you?" I hiss back at him.

"I went to get Bret..."

And that conveniently took just long enough for him to miss all of the action? Or was he standing there in the hallway this whole time, frozen with terror?

I scowl at Niles and look away, back to the doors. The wardrobe is still blocking the one with the broken window, and both are locked by the deadbolt between them. I can't see anything through the frosted glass, so I step over to the windows in the den and peer outside. The dead soldier and the three dead rhino-like creatures all lie just outside the porte-cochère that extends from the entryway.

A huge swath of the trampled snow around the soldier is stained red with his blood. The aliens seem to have died far cleaner deaths. Rather than red, the snow around them looks dark and muddy.

Niles joins me by the window and sucks in a shallow breath at the sight of the carnage. I glance at him. His breath is steaming the glass as he leans closer to it.

"Is that what you saw kill your neighbors?"

He nods slowly.

I wait a couple of beats, and then look back outside, studying the aliens once more. Four legs and two arms just like Niles described. Massive jaws and sharp triangular teeth that protrude slightly from their faces and interlock when closed. Two eyes. Four flexible stalks on top of their heads, nestled between at least a dozen horns.

"Bret decided to hide in his room?" I ask.

"He didn't reply when I knocked on the door."

"I guess he's a deep sleeper." It seems like I won't be able to count on either Niles or Bret to have my back. "We should take a closer look at those things," I say, nodding out the windows.

"What? Why?" Niles half-whispers, half-shrieks at me.

"Know your enemy," I say, heading for the doors.

"What if there's more of them out there?"

I pump the action of my shotgun to chamber the first shell. "Two blasts at point-blank to the side of the head seems to do it. They're no harder to take down than a bear." Well, maybe a little harder, because one shot at point blank would do it with the average bear.

I move to the door and turn the deadbolt to unlock it. "Ready?" I ask.

Niles looks terrified at the prospect, but he licks his lips and draws his shotgun up a little higher across his chest.

"Don't forget the safety at the back," I tell him. Niles hefts the weapon higher for a better look, peering at it in the dim light and through his glasses. I reach over and slide the safety off with my index finger.

"Remember to keep your finger outside the

trigger guard and the barrel aimed at the ground until you've got a target lined up."

Niles nods woodenly and drops his aim to the floor.

I turn and pull the door open. The frigid night air steals my breath away and makes my nostrils stick together as I stride across the back steps to reach the dead soldier and the three massive gray heaps of alien corpses piled around him.

My eyes flick up to the driveway and then to the wooden staircase along the side of the detached garage. The other soldier must have died in there, but these monsters didn't come from there. Did they have a shootout through the windows before the other guy made a run for it? Soaring snow-dusted shadows of pine and cedar trees line the property on both sides. No sign of hostiles.

Bringing my eyes back down, I cross over to the nearest bear-like creature—the one that snapped the soldier's femur in its jaws. Stopping just a foot away from it, I flick on the tac-light beneath the barrel of my shotgun to get a better look.

Niles gasps as the headless soldier appears in garish white light.

"I think I'm going to be sick," he says, and promptly proves himself right, spilling whatever he ate for dinner into the snow.

I ignore the carnage and my increasingly useless battle buddy to instead focus on the aliens. Hairless gray skin covers thick knots of muscle all over their bodies. They have dark, viscous black blood like crude oil. The jaws are broad and high with the jutting, interlocking white teeth that I saw before. They occupy fully half of the creature's skull.

A soft, whistling sound catches my ear, and I notice little puffs of white steam issuing between the teeth. The neck is slowly inflating and deflating like a frog's with each breath.

"It's alive!" Niles hisses at me.

Aiming for the side of its head with my shotgun, I carefully toe the creature's foot with my boot. It twitches and whistles a bit louder between its teeth, but otherwise doesn't move.

"Barely," I say. Rather than put it out of its misery, I take a minute to study the beast. The feet are fat and round with three thick black claws at the front, but no real toes to speak of. The arms, however, end in giant hands with three fat fingers, two of which look like thumbs.

"They look like Rhinos," Niles says, noting the same resemblance that I did earlier.

But it's a vague resemblance at this point— both have four legs; they share the same size and coloring, but everything else about these monsters is alien. For some reason, *Behemoth* is the name that comes to my mind.

Another whistling sound draws my attention to the one in front of me, and I'm tempted to put it out of its misery, but there's a clear reason not to.

My eyes flick up and scan our surroundings once more.

"What are you looking for?"

"Their master," I say quietly. "These are the grunts, or the slaves."

"How can you be sure? On the radio I heard someone say that we're now a part of the Kyron Federation. That implies multiple different species in an alliance, working together."

I shrug. "Maybe, but then why aren't the different species in that federation all running into combat together? Why three of these Behemoths and none of the flying ones? You saw something similar when you were up on the roof of your house, right? Just these four-legged ones ran out after your neighbors?"

"Well... I didn't stick around for long, but what does it matter which species is in charge?"

"It matters because we need to know who's sending out these strike teams, and what they want. It could help us to defend ourselves, or at least to avoid becoming their next targets."

There's no sign of the winged alien that I suspect sent these Behemoths after the two soldiers. "I need to take a look inside the guest house."

"Wha-what for?" Niles stammers.

"Stay here and guard the entrance," I tell him. "Lock the door. I'll be right back."

And then I'm running past the dead soldier

and his alien killers. I don't bother to take the assault rifle from the dead man. The military switched to smart-locked weapons years ago, so their rifles won't be of any use to me.

Racing up the driveway, I stop at the bottom of the wooden stairs and wait for my breathing to quiet and slow. I can see from here that the door at the top of the stairs is open, and I remember seeing that soldier come limping down as fast as his feet could carry him. What was he running from? Not the Behemoths, because they came from the street.

As soon as I'm able, I sneak soundlessly up the stairs and stop on the last step to peek around the door jamb.

What I see on the other side sends an electric jolt of terror sparking through me, and I quickly duck back from the opening to avoid being seen.

My back is to the wall, my eyes on the open door beside me. Shotgun held across my chest, my frozen palms suddenly slick on the cold metal frame of the weapon.

The split-second image of what I saw on the other side is burned into my mind's eye. My heart is fluttering in my chest. My mouth's dry.

I was right. The Behemoths aren't the ones we need to worry about. The sound of bones crunching and of wet chewing noises coming from inside the guest house makes my stomach churn. I cringe and hold my breath, hoping to God that *thing* didn't see me. Or hear me.

But it must have heard my shotgun and the soldier's rifle going off—the shrieks of the Behemoths dying.

It has to know we're out there even if it doesn't know that I'm standing here on the stairs, listening to it feed.

My breath shudders out. I can't hold it any longer. I ease back down the stairs, moving as fast as I dare.

And then my Glock slips out from my belt. It clatters down the last three steps with the slide rattling noisily.

I freeze on the second to last step and my gaze snaps to the open door at the top of the stairs. My breath is frozen in my chest once more, my ears straining for any sound other than the steady drumbeat of my own pulse.

Nothing. No sound, or sight of the winged creature I saw inside gnawing on a severed human leg as if it were a chicken drumstick.

Maybe it didn't hear me drop the gun. Or maybe it's known the whole time that I'm out here, and it simply doesn't care because it knows that I'm not a threat?

Like the one I faced in the Pearsons' home, this one is wearing a suit of black armor, but unlike that one, it had its helmet off, revealing a bald head with translucent white skin, bony, and whorled with snaking black veins in fishscale patterns. I also glimpsed four of those antennae-like stalks on top of its head. It wasn't facing me, but I remember clearly the demonic, red-eyed countenance of the one that was somehow speaking *through* the president.

Jumping down the remaining steps, I sprint for the house, running faster than I have ever run before in my life. My legs feel numb, like they don't even belong to me.

A prickle of dread raises the hairs on the back of my neck, and I glance over my shoulder to see if the demon is following me—

It's standing at the top of the stairs, watching with keen red eyes. The lower half of its face is covered in blood, but I can't see its mouth past the black grille of the mask that it's wearing.

This creature is identical to the one I saw on the TV. It's maybe only five feet tall with two skinny legs, bent slightly at the knee. Two slender arms are folded against its chest.

As I watch, its legs snap straight and it springs into the air, flying high over the railing of the staircase. Before it can begin to fall, it spreads a pair of translucent wings and swoops down toward me.

I twist around while running and bring my shotgun into line, hastily lining up a shot. *BOOM.*

Bright specks of white light flare all over the creature's armor and in front of its face. The same thing I saw the first time I fought one of these things. It has some kind of energy shield.

My gaze lingers too long. I stumble and trip, going down hard in the snow. The creature swoops by overhead, and I both hear and feel its wings *wooshing* as it climbs steadily higher into the night, flying off in the direction of the town. Scrambling back to my feet, I track the creature with my shotgun, and pull the trigger with another BOOM.

But it's too far away, and this time I see only one or two pinpricks of light as the shot is absorbed by the creature's shield.

My body feels cold and numb as I stand staring up at the vanishing black shadow soaring above the trees. I have that surreal, stuck-in-molasses feeling from my worst nightmares. That flying alien was *eating* the remains of the other soldier.

Primal dread overcomes me. It's fear, so potent that I can taste the metallic tang of it like pennies on the back of my tongue.

I've never been this scared, not even in the Army, in the middle of a firefight with Chinese guerrillas in the Qin Mountains.

This is the fear of a six-year-old child, who upon waking from a nightmare is told by his parents that monsters aren't real.

Now I'm an adult, and I must have said the same thing to my kids at least a hundred times.

But I've just realized that those reassurances are lies.

Monsters *are* real, and they've taken over Earth.

CHAPTER 20

Niles comes running over to me, out of breath, his eyes wide and gleaming with moonlight behind his glasses.

"What the hell was that?" he breathes, his gaze darting frantically between the treetops to check if it might be coming back.

I can still feel adrenaline sparking along my nerves. A nonsensical croak escapes my lips. I try again. "Let's go inside." Then I'm taking the first wobbly steps in that direction, walking backward to keep us covered. We stumble through the open door of the house, and Niles slams it shut and locks it behind us. It takes a few seconds for my eyes to adjust to the dim light inside. The tac-light of my shotgun is still on and shining brightly at the floor, but I don't want to go waving it around carelessly and lighting up the windows. Who knows if more of those flying demons are out there.

"This is bad." Niles breathes a shaky sigh and goes to the windows to check if something is creeping up on us. I join him there. No signs of anything.

"There are definitely two different species," Niles says slowly. "The bear-things and the flying ones."

"Behemoths and Demons," I suggest.

Turning to Niles, I see him studying me curiously, as if waiting for an explanation. "It fled after you shot it," he says, prompting me.

"Yeah. They have some kind of energy shield." It sounds like something out of a holovid. That tech is science fiction, not real. And yet, recent experience proves otherwise. "Its shield is probably only strong enough to absorb one shot."

"It didn't even try to shoot you?" Niles asks.

"No," I confirm, shaking my head.

"Maybe that means they're not after us? Just the military."

"How would they know the difference? Besides, they promised reprisals against anyone who doesn't lay down their arms. I shot it. And I killed three of those Behemoths. For all we know, it left to get reinforcements. Or to order an air strike on this house. We need to get our families and leave."

"And Bret?" he asks.

I shake my head as I move away from the windows. "He's been useless so far. He can stay."

Niles nods quickly and rushes ahead, leading the way down the entry hall. My tac-light illuminates our path as we hurry past the den, then the dining room and the kitchen. Angling to the left, I check the windows facing the lake and the deck outside for signs of any Demons lurking there. Nothing that I can see.

We enter the games room, stepping over the disabled CDU, and run to the bathroom where I told everyone to hide.

Knocking lightly on the door with my knuckles, I whisper, "Bree?"

No answer.

Then I try the door. It pops open with a soft wooden creak. It's not even properly shut, let alone locked.

My guts heave in a sickening lurch. I push the door all the way open. My tac-light is pointed at the floor, but it radiates far enough through the five-piece bathroom to reveal tangled human shadows lying on the floor.

"Bree!" I cry, lurching into the room, suddenly terrified that my family is dead.

Niles pushes past me to check on Jessica and his kids.

* * *

"They're not waking up!" I'm shaking Bree, then my mother, then Zach. There's no sign of Gaby anywhere. My head is spinning. My heart in my throat.

"Jess!" Niles cries, no longer being careful to keep his voice down. "Shit. Sean! Haley!"

I take a second to calm down and think. It's then that I have the presence of mind to check for a pulse. Pressing two fingers to my wife's throat, I wait—

And feel her carotid artery skipping steadily under my fingertips. Reaching by her, I check Zach, then my mother. Same result.

"They're alive," I say. "Turn on the lights!"

Niles doesn't hesitate. The bathroom lights snap on, and I squint against the sudden swell of illumination. Then I'm checking everyone for signs of injury. There's no blood. No scorch marks to indicate lasers. "They're stunned," I realize.

"How?" Niles asks. "The only stun guns we have are the ones the CDUs were using, and those are smart-locked."

I'm shaking my head as I look around again, checking for the one who's missing. "Gaby!" I whisper fiercely. No reply.

Pushing off the floor beside my wife, I do a more thorough check of the bathroom. She's not around the corner by the toilet. Nowhere else on the floor, and not in the tub or the shower. She really is missing. I can only hope it's because she had the presence of mind to hide while everyone else was being stunned. I step over the rest of my family to reach the window above the bathtub. It's big enough that Gaby could have crawled out.

But it's latched and shut.

"Bret," Niles says slowly.

"What?" I whirl to face him.

"Who else could have stunned them? He was the only one inside."

Rather than mention the darker possibility that aliens were sneaking in from the deck while we were fending them off at the back entrance, I seize on that possibility and storm out of the bathroom. "Wait here," I say.

But this time Niles doesn't listen. He follows me out of the bathroom.

"I said wait! Whoever stunned them could come back."

"And stun them again?" Niles counters. "Your daughter is missing. Whoever did this was after *her.* If he'd wanted to kill any of the others, he would have done so."

I realize Niles is right as I'm stepping over the broken-down CDU. And a child abduction speaks to darker, more twisted motivations than any I would ascribe to our alien invaders—their demonic appearance and grisly diet notwithstanding. Why abduct a child and stun everyone else?

It had to be Bret.

I fly across the great room, forgetting for a moment to check for hostiles that could be waiting for me or skulking outside on the deck.

But no bright green lasers lance through the windows to cut me down. Reaching the hallway to the master suite, I cross it in three strides and then hammer on the door with my fist. "Bret! Open up!"

No reply. I'm seeing red. My heart is slamming in my chest. I never should have argued to stay here with an unknown quantity like him. I can't believe it, but Jessica was right. We should have left.

"Stand back," I say to Niles. Taking a step back myself, I raise my good leg to the door and give it a sharp kick. The door shudders violently, but holds.

"Get ready," I say.

I try again, this time body-checking the door. My shoulder sparks with pain, but the door gives way, and I stumble through. My shotgun is up and sweeping, the tac-light bouncing around the master suite. The bed is unmade, sheets rumpled. No one in it. A sitting area in front of a fireplace by the windows along the deck is also empty.

Turning back the other way, I see the hallway to the en-suite bathroom. Storming in that direction, I stop as another doorway appears to my left. Opening the door and shining my shotgun in, I get a glimpse of two blood-covered bodies propped up against a wall of boots and tennis shoes. It's an elderly couple. It takes less than a second for me to recognize them from the photos in the hall.

"Chris..." Niles trails off. "There's blood on the floor."

Shining my tac-light along the floor in the closet, I see a trail of it here, too.

"He killed them," Niles says with a sharp intake of breath. Suddenly he's standing right beside me, leaning past my shoulder to get a better look at the bodies.

I place a finger to my lips and nod to the bathroom. He could be in here.

An image jumps to mind: Bret's dirty hand wrapped around Gaby's mouth. A hunting knife pressed to her throat.

Forcing the image away, I lead the way to the bathroom, my tac-light flashing off the wooden walls and floor.

I can see the open door, a double vanity. My own reflection dimmed by the bright eye of the tac-light reflecting off the mirrors. And something else. Crimson scribbles on the mirrors. Writing?

Stopping at the threshold, I peek around the door jamb, being careful to keep my body behind cover.

The light reflecting off the mirrors illuminates just enough of the bathroom for me to see that it's clear.

My heart sinks and a wash of cold dread floods my system. Stepping into the bathroom, I hurriedly check every inch of it just to be sure: behind the door, in the tub—even though I can already see that it's empty.

"He left," Niles says.

With my daughter! Every fiber of my being is screaming: terrified and enraged at the same time. And yet I feel weak, like I need to sit down.

My gaze finds the writing on the mirrors. It looks like blood, but I quickly realize that it's just red lipstick.

I silently read the words even as Niles reads them aloud.

"I am not a killer. I am not a killer. I am not—"

Bret ran out of room for more words. The lipstick is lying discarded in the sink.

"He's a total psycho," Niles says, as if that wasn't already obvious. But the conflicted nature that this denial suggests isn't that of a cold-blooded killer. Rather that of a mental patient with aggressive tendencies. That could make him even more dangerous. It means he's unpredictable and that his actual motives might not be what we would suspect.

But maybe that *is* better. Maybe it means he's not trying to hurt my daughter. Maybe he thought he was saving her. I can only hope.

My brain switches gears. How the hell did Bret stun both of our families and abduct Gaby without either me or Niles hearing so much as a stifled cry?

He must have stunned Gaby, too, otherwise she would have screamed, and that means he carried her out. But to where?

I remember the footprints we saw leading here. Maybe he went back to wherever he came from. And if he's carrying Gaby, he'll be slower than us.

"Come on," I say, already running back the way we came. I hope he doesn't have much of a lead on us. There might still be time to stop him.

CHAPTER 21

Back in the games room I run to the sliding glass doors to check if they were unlocked from the inside. The door pulls open without the least bit of resistance.

This is where Bret went out. Two sets of footprints are visible in the dusting of snow on the deck. Flashing my tac-light over them, it takes me a moment to read the prints. There's a smaller set leading right up to the sliding doors where we stand. I can see indentations from three splayed toes, or... claws. A small heel. Narrow foot. It's bird-like. No question about what could have made these prints. The fact that there aren't any others leading to them gives another clue. One of the Demons flew down and landed here. But there are more prints leading away from them to a set of stairs that go down to the lake. It flew down, then walked away.

"I don't get it," Niles says, frowning at the footprints as I flash my tac-light back and forth over them.

The other set of prints is definitely human

and coming from the opposite end of the deck —down by the master suite. The human prints seem to be following the alien ones, but there's no sign of a struggle.

My impression of Bret does a brief one-eighty. Maybe he didn't take Gaby. Maybe he's innocent.

But he did kill that elderly couple, didn't he?

I didn't check their injuries to see what killed them. Maybe it was one of the aliens.

Regardless, a possible scenario gels in my mind. While I was fighting the invaders out back and Niles was guarding the doors, another one flew down here, broke in, and quietly stunned our families. Then it carried my daughter out. Remembering the Demons' diminutive size, I wonder if it chose her because she was the only one small enough for it to carry.

The why is a mystery, but everything else seems to fit.

The lingering question is where does Bret fit in? Did he hear or see something and go investigate?

"We need to follow those prints," I say.

Not waiting for Niles to reply, I rush out onto the deck and down the stairs to a big, flat, snow-covered area before the lake and the pebbled beach.

The prints stop abruptly here, and they're smeared around in what looks like some kind of a struggle. No, not a struggle, I realize.

Bret fell down suddenly. Then he was dragged away. The drag marks end where the footprints do. Suddenly vanishing without any explanation.

Walking over to the spot, I shine my tac-light around, checking for bodies. But Bret and Gaby are nowhere to be seen.

This is the end of the trail.

"I don't get it," Niles says.

But I do. Walking quickly around the flat snow-covered area, I find four more prints. These ones were made by landing struts.

"There was some kind of vehicle landed here. A transport."

"The invaders?"

"Who else?"

I can't believe they managed to fly in and fly out without us hearing or seeing a thing, but I guess our attention was elsewhere at the time.

"So it wasn't Bret who took Gaby," Niles says.

"No."

"What would they want with a six-year-old girl?"

A dozen half-formed theories flash through my mind in an instant. Medical experiments. A slave. Curiosity. A pet. A snack...

I wince at the last one, remembering how the Demon I saw was eating the remains of that soldier. But it seems like a lot of trouble to go to for food. And sneaking in and incapacitating everyone seems harder than simply killing us and then feeding on our corpses.

No, this is about something far less primitive than the biological imperative to eat. And what's even more curious is that Bret followed the one who took my daughter, only to wind up abducted himself.

"Chris?" a trembling voice calls out from above. It's Bree.

"They're awake," Niles whispers, his breath steaming the air.

"I'm down here!"

No point in being quiet anymore. The enemy already knows exactly where we are.

CHAPTER 22

"She's gone!" As soon as I reach the top of the stairs, Bree grabs my arms in a taloned grip, her nails digging in.

"Careful," I say, noting that her hand is dangerously close to the trigger of the shotgun I'm holding. Bree releases me. "What did you see? *Who* took her?" I ask, even though I'm fairly certain I already know the answer.

"We didn't see anything. Someone knocked on the door. We thought it was you or Niles. As soon as I opened it, something pushed in, but I couldn't see anything. Then there was this flash of light that came out of nowhere and hit me in the chest. I collapsed after that."

"They shot me right after her," Jessica says, speaking from the open door to the games room. She has an arm wrapped protectively around each of her kids.

"And nobody screamed?" I ask.

Bree bites her lip. "I don't know. It all happened so fast."

"Where's Zach?" I ask, moving quickly to

cross the deck and get back inside.

"With your mother," Bree says just as Jessica steps aside to let me in. Zachary and my mother are sitting on one of the couches just inside the entrance.

"Dad!" he cries when he sees me. He comes running and wraps his arms around my waist in a fierce hug.

Bree comes in. "What are we going to do? We have to find her!"

Niles slides the door shut behind us.

"It looks like they flew away in a ship," I say. "Did you see or hear it land?"

Everyone shakes their heads.

"We heard the shooting outside," my mother explains. "But that was all."

"Okay..." My mind is racing. That doesn't give me anything to work with. This is bad. We have no idea where they went. For all we know they took Gaby to that floating aircraft carrier that I saw heading for LA the night that they arrived.

"Maybe there's a lander up here," Niles suggests. "I saw those four-legged things, the Behemoths, come out of a ship on our street in San Bernardino. The ones we faced here were coming from the direction of the street. Maybe they walked here from the town? We could check for prints. Follow them to the source."

"Good idea," I say. "The Behemoths might have been following the soldiers. Or even Bret's prints. The other Demon flew off in that direction, too. We should hurry. They could leave at any time."

"We?" Jessica echoes. "Who's we?"

I look to Niles. He nods.

Jessica lets out an incredulous snort. "Surely you're joking. We need you here, Niles, to protect *us*. You'll just get yourself killed if you go after them."

I can see indecision warring on Niles' face. Jessica might be right, but I don't like my chances doing this on my own.

"What if it were Haley?" he asks.

"It's not."

"But if. You would be arguing for Chris to go after them and get her back."

Jessica says nothing to that.

"It's the right thing to do."

"Fine, go be a martyr, then!"

"Staying or leaving?" I ask Niles. "I can't afford to wait any longer."

"Leaving," Niles confirms. "We'll find her."

I nod to him, grateful for the support.

"What about us? We can't stay here," Jessica says. "What if they come back and abduct more of us?"

"Go to one of the neighboring houses," I suggest. "Break in if it's empty and hide there. Wait for us to return." I'm looking at Bree as I say that. She nods quickly. "Go," she breathes.

Leaning in for a quick kiss, I whisper, "I love you."

"I love you, too," she says.

Turning to Zach, I can see his cheeks are streaked with tears. He's tall for his age, already encroaching on my chest at four-foot-eleven.

"Don't go," he mumbles tearfully.

"I have to find your sister."

"They could come back," Zach argues.

"You won't be here, and they won't know where you went."

"But they could find us."

"Maybe. But your mother has the rest of our guns, and she knows how to use them. She'll protect you."

Zachary shakes his head vigorously. "No."

"I need you to be brave. We can't just let them have Gaby. You understand?"

A nod.

"Good." I lean down and kiss him on the top of his head. "It's going to be okay. I'll be back soon." Bree is watching me with big eyes. Looking at her, I add, "I promise."

My mother comes over, and I pull her into a quick hug.

"Be careful. I love you," she whispers beside my ear.

I return the sentiment, and then nod to Niles, and we go running back through the house to the rear entrance. I feel sick to my stomach, tired, cold, terrified—

But there's an icy fist of resolve clutching my heart that keeps me focused. I *will* find Gaby.

I have to.

CHAPTER 23

Outside, Niles and I check what we can recover from the dead soldier. His guns are all smart-locked, so they're useless to us, but the frag grenades are the old-fashioned kind. Maybe old military surplus. Who knows. Whatever the case, I'm grateful for it. It takes some wrangling to get the soldier's vest off his shredded body and put it on over my jacket. The pockets are stuffed with grenades. Three frag, one smoke to signal for an air extraction.

Not that anyone will be coming to get us, but maybe it will come in handy at some point.

"What about me?" Niles asks.

Rather than point out that having him handling frag grenades could get us both blown to hell, I say, "There's another soldier in the guest house."

But before we leave, I also want to see what the big four-legged aliens were carrying. I saw guns holstered to their chests, and some kind of sword on their backs.

Setting my shotgun down in the snow, I

check the chest holster of the nearest Behemoth. It holds a hefty black gun with a short, fat barrel and a thick grip, which makes it awkward to hold.

Taking aim for the top of the driveway, I try the trigger. It's a hard pull, and refuses to give. Thinking there might be a safety, I play around with one of the buttons on the side of the barrel. The weapon thrums to life, vibrating subtly in my hands, and a glowing display appears in the air above the back of the weapon, but the readout is filled with alien symbols, so I don't know what to make of it.

Trying the trigger again, this time with both hands, I manage to squeeze it, and a blinding pulse of orange light snaps out and explodes in the snow ten feet away. The snow hisses into steam, and the asphalt under it rains pebbles over us.

"Impressive," Niles says.

"Yeah..." I play with another button. It's a big rocker switch. Maybe that's the safety?

Trying the trigger again, this time a solid beam of white-hot fire jets out, roaring and hissing as it evaporates the snow on contact. It only extends about nine feet from the barrel, and I can feel the heat radiating back at me. It's some kind of flamethrower. A plasma gun?

I test it on the hindquarters of the dead Behemoth that I took the weapon from. It cuts through flesh, bone, and plates of armor with a hissing roar and a sickening stench of burning flesh and composites. The leg drops off into the snow, glowing a fiery orange at the shoulder where I severed it.

"Wow," Niles says.

"Yeah. Let's get another one for you."

We grab another of the plasma guns from one of the other Behemoths. Having seen them at work, I wonder why they didn't draw these weapons and use them on the fleeing soldier. Maybe this species is not very bright. If so, then the weapons they're carrying might not be theirs, at least, not designed by them. These thoughts fuel my grunt / slave theory about the four-legged aliens. The flying Demons seem much smarter.

We struggle to find a way to holster the plasma weapons, but eventually have to detach the harness-style holsters that the Behemoths were wearing. We tie them awkwardly around our torsos. The guns are heavy, but shorter than our shotguns.

Now I'm feeling much more confident about our chances once we find the enemy. The swords strapped to the Behemoth's backs look interesting, but why bring a knife to a gunfight?

"Let's go." We've delayed here for at least five minutes, and I'm anxious to get on the road and figure out where these things came from.

Setting off at a run, I lead the way up the driveway. My hands are numb on the cold aluminum frame of my shotgun. I'm using the tac-light to illuminate the way, but with the full moon it's not really necessary. Spare shotgun shells jangle together in a zippered pocket of my jacket as I run.

At the top of the driveway we find the metal gate has been forced open. I can't imagine it hold-ing against one of the Behemoths. They prob-ably just charged straight through. Their giant circular footprints trail away on the other side of the gate, leading away all down the center of the street, highly visible and easy to track in the moonlight.

I start sprinting down the street, following the tracks—

Then stop suddenly.

We don't know how far they came. It's freez-ing out here, and we're not entirely dressed for the weather. It would be better to take one of the cars. Not to mention faster.

Turning back the other way, my gaze skips over the Tesla SUV, the Suburban, and the Sol-diers' hulking electric JLTV.

"Let's take the Jilvee," I suggest.

"The what?" Niles asks.

I explain the nickname, frustrated by his ig-norance but understanding it at the same time. He has lived a life of luxury and comfort, and probably had no contact with the military until now.

"Where are the keys?" Niles asks.

"They don't use keys."

"Then...?" Niles trails off questioningly.

I run back down the driveway, cursing myself for not thinking of this while I was stealing the soldier's vest and grenades. I'm just in time to see my family and Niles' disappearing through the line of Cedar trees between this house and the neighboring one. Good. At least they're away now.

Upon reaching the dead, headless soldier and the alien monsters that killed him, I lay my shotgun down and pull a knife off the soldier's belt. Grabbing his right hand and pulling the guy's glove off, I start cutting out a square of skin.

"You're taking his implant? Will that work?" Niles asks. "I thought they're automatically deactivated after you die."

"They are, but with our infrastructure and satellites disrupted, the system that deactivates them is probably offline."

Peeling away the skin I find the tiny silver wafer that is this soldier's ID. Taking it out carefully, I put it in my pajama pants pocket and then grab the soldier's rifle.

Aiming for the sky above the trees, I pull the trigger. A single shot cracks the night, and a grim smile curves my lips. The spare magazines are already in the vest that I'm wearing, so there's no need to search for them. I'm tempted to head up to the guest house to get the other rifle and ID implant for Niles, but we've wasted enough time as it is. "Take my shotgun," I tell Niles.

He grabs it while I steal the dead soldier's gloves and pull them on.

"Let's go," I say, straightening and sprinting up the driveway.

Niles runs beside me, carrying both shotguns by the forestock, barrels aimed at the sky. Between those, the alien plasma guns, grenades, and the E9 automatic rifle I took off that soldier, we're packing a hell of a lot of firepower.

I just hope it will be enough.

CHAPTER 24

With a military ID chip in my pocket to authorize me, starting the Jilvee is as simple as pushing a button.

I start executing a three-point turn to get the bulky armored vehicle facing back the other way. Sitting beside me in the front, Niles has both shotguns on the floor, pinned between his legs with the barrels pointing up.

"Make sure those safeties are on," I say, worried he could accidentally shoot the roof and ricochet shot all over us. The pellets would go through a regular car roof, but won't get past the Jilvee's armor.

Niles busies himself checking the safeties on the Mossbergs while I complete my three-point turn. I have the E9 army rifle balanced in my lap, barrel aimed at the door. Awkward, but I'd rather that to being unarmed.

The giant footprints of the Behemoths swing into view under the Jilvee's headlights. The whole street is trampled. I hit the accelerator and the armored vehicle kicks forward with surprising agility.

I keep to a modest twenty miles per hour, following the tracks as quickly as I dare. As I drive, I'm keeping one eye on the digital screen hanging where an old-fashioned rearview mirror would be. That screen is connected to cameras on all sides of the vehicle with night vision and thermal overlays. I dim the headlights to avoid blinding the forward camera. I don't know if these aliens are warm-blooded, but the fact that they were up here in the snow gives me a clue. Cold-blooded creatures wouldn't be able to stand winter. Not without substantial protection. Jury's out on the flying Demons with their full-body armor, but the Behemoths had to be warm-blooded. Their armor was perfunctory at best. It didn't stop my shotgun, that's for sure.

"Looks like they came the whole way on foot," Niles says after about five minutes of driving. "We're getting close to town already."

"Yeah," is all I can bring myself to say. My mind is elsewhere. I'm hoping that we're not dealing with two different groups. If we are, then Gaby might have been taken in a completely different direction, and these tracks could be taking us farther away from her, not closer.

No cars are on the street besides ours. None in the air, either. The night is utterly dark and silent. None of the neighbors on Eagle Drive have their lights on, which means homes with generators are rare. Not even the flickering orange glow of firelight illuminates their windows.

We pass a 7-Eleven on the left, a McDonald's on the right. Coming to a T with Big Bear Boulevard, I hit the brakes and check our surroundings with my eyes and the thermal view from the cameras. No sign of enemy contacts. Dead ahead is some kind of motel or maybe a resort. A wall of trees soars behind it. The windows are all dark, and only a couple of cars are parked in the lot.

The Behemoths' tracks lead across the boulevard to that parking lot.

"What's through there?" I ask Niles, pointing to the parking lot.

"That's the Silver Pines Resort," Niles says. "They have pretty extensive grounds. A tennis court. Several clusters of buildings."

"Looks like that's where the Behemoths came from," I say, and then kill the dimmed headlights with a stab of my finger. "You ready for this?" I whisper.

Niles nods and pushes his glasses higher up on his nose. "What's the plan?"

I give the matter some thought. We could drive around to recon the area, but we'd be spotted for sure. Even with an electric motor, this vehicle is too big to be quiet.

"This is our stop," I decide. "We'll have to go the rest of the way on foot. I'll lead. You watch our backs. Keep it quiet. We don't want them to see us coming."

Niles sucks in a shaky breath. Reaching for

one of the shotguns he flexes his leather gloves on the stock and barrel. "Ready when you are."

A stab of my finger kills the engine, and the screens all go dark. Popping open my door, I step down, landing in the snow with the E9 up. I notice the rifle's scope has a thermal overlay. I activate it and scan our surroundings. Staying close to the Jilvee, I focus on the resort across the street, looking for heat signatures. Still nothing.

I wave quietly over my shoulder for Niles to follow as I move across the main boulevard. Five lanes of trampled and tire-tracked snow. The Behemoth tracks lead straight across to the resort. On the other side of the street, the alien tracks become more chaotic in the resort parking lot. Several human bodies lie face down beside the open doors of an SUV. The snow around them is dark with blood. We're not using our tac-lights, so thankfully I'm spared the grisly details.

Niles comes alongside me as I stop behind a pine tree to scan for targets. He's staring wide-eyed at the dead bodies in the parking lot. One of the windows to the main office of the resort appears to have been broken. Rather than speak to Niles, I catch his eye and point to where the alien tracks lead around the side of the main building.

Leading the way, I dart across the parking lot to the side of the main office, sticking to the eaves and the shadows. Sweeping my rifle around with one eye on the scope and the thermal view, I can see there aren't any hostiles lurking behind the main office, but there are more buildings back here—two-story structures for the guests. The tracks lead straight by those buildings, through the trees at the end of the parking area, to a snow-covered clearing.

Moving quickly, I race to the end of the parking lot, sweeping left to right with my rifle and the scope.

Still nothing. Reaching the edge of the clearing, I can see where the tracks end. Right in the middle of a snow-covered field. My heart sinks and my blood runs cold.

"They already left," I whisper to Niles.

It's the same thing we saw at the house. A vehicle might have been landed here at some point, but it's gone now.

Walking on in a daze, I follow the tracks to their origin. A broad, flattened area that might have contained a boarding ramp. The snow around it is pressed in six circular patches. I'm reminded of Niles' description of the lander he saw. Six cylindrical engines arrayed around a central hull. The lander was big, at least twice the size of the tennis court to my right.

Niles looks to me, his expression grim. "I'm sorry, Chris," he says.

I have no words for a reply. This was the only hope we had to find Gaby. There's no way to know where they took her now.

I walk aimlessly around the field, trying to find some other sign or clue. Something. I don't even know what I'm looking for. Human foot-prints, maybe. Gaby's footprints.

But the only ones I see are the claw-shaped prints of the Demons and the big circular hooves of the Behemoths.

"Maybe the ones that took her went some-where else," Niles suggests.

But that isn't any better. I walk to the nearest circular depression in the snow. There's no sign of it melting, so the invader's engines don't pro-duce any heat. Or at least their landing thrusters don't.

I go down on my haunches for a better look—

And my forehead slams into something solid, knocking me over. I land on my ass and sit in the snow, stunned and blinking up at whatever I just hit.

But the space is empty.

"What the hell?" I mutter.

Springing off the ground, I spare a hand from my rifle, reaching out like a blind man—

My hand encounters something hard and smooth.

Something invisible that follows the curva-ture of the indentation in the snow.

Hope ignites in my chest, and I step back quickly, my rifle up and tracking.

"What's wrong?" Niles asks, looking around suddenly.

"Shhh." My gaze darts around for threats, but there's no sign of anything. Nothing visible, anyway. "They're still here," I explain, walking quickly past Niles to the point where the alien tracks began.

Going down on my haunches, I find another invisible surface angling up from the ground.

A landing ramp.

CHAPTER 25

"What are you doing?" Niles asks, watching as I feel my way along invisible surfaces like a mime trying to get out of a box.

Rather than reply, I wave him over. He crouches down beside me, and I grab one of his hands and place it against the landing ramp.

His eyes widen and he flinches away from the ramp.

"Wha-what is that?" he stutters.

"Their lander," I whisper back. Standing up, I fix my gaze on the point where I imagine the top of the ramp to be. "It's some kind of cloaking shield."

Nothing is coming out, at least nothing that I can *see.* But I have to find a way inside. Gaby could be in there.

"Now what?" Niles whispers, looking up at the invisible lander with me. "Do you think they know we're here?"

"If they do, they don't consider us a threat," I reply, flexing my hands restlessly on my rifle. Maybe that's because there's no way that we could possibly get inside the lander. But I have an ace in the hole. Maybe the Demons haven't noticed it yet, or maybe no one is actually watching us. Either way, I need to act fast.

Putting a foot to the landing ramp, I feel the angle of it, then take another step. There's some kind of grip on the ramp, making it easier to walk up it than I was expecting. Holding out a hand in front of me like a blind man, I continue up the ramp as quickly as I dare.

"What are you doing?" Niles hisses at me. "We can't just... we need a plan."

But I have a plan. After just a few more steps my outstretched hand hits a solid surface.

Wrangling the alien holster and plasma gun to one side I expose a mounting clip on the vest that I stole, and hang the E9 there. Drawing the plasma gun, I hold it in an awkward two-handed grip and aim it at what I can only imagine is a door.

I take a step back in case there's some kind of weapon splash effect, and then pull the trigger. A blazing, white hot beam shoots out. It extends four feet from the barrel before ending in a molten spray of unknown alloys. Big glittering silver beads dribble out, hissing as they hit the invisible landing ramp and roll down past our feet. Tracking the beam up, a molten orange furrow appears in the air. The beam of plasma is so bright that I'm nearly blinded by it.

I quickly trace out a rough oval—a door. It

takes me about ten seconds to finish the cut. Releasing the trigger, I blink rapidly to clear the after images from my eyes. The seam is cooling. As my vision clears, I notice that the center of the cut is now opaque and clearly visible. The hull of the ship is a dark, non-reflective black, and the cut I've made is illuminated from within the ship.

"Now what...?" Niles asks.

I'm actually surprised that none of those Demons or Behemoths came out while I was busy cutting a hole in the side of their lander. Maybe nobody's home?

Rather than waste my breath with a verbal reply, I step closer to the cut and deliver a sharp kick to the center of the severed section. It shudders and elicits a hollow *bang,* but doesn't give way.

Aiming the plasma gun once more, I pull the trigger and cut straight across the bottom. As soon as I've finished, the severed section of hull drops a couple inches lower with molten slag oozing out. It begins leaning out, toward me and Niles. Seeing that it could crush us, I shout, "Get clear!" And then turn and leap off the landing ramp into the field below. I land hard in the snow just as the severed hull hits the ramp with a *boom.* Spinning around with the plasma gun, I find myself staring at a ragged opening into a dimly-lit interior. The light fixtures are a dark, alien blue that looks fuzzy to my eyes.

Niles picks himself off the ground beside me, aiming his shotgun into the opening. It looks like some kind of antechamber with another door on the other side. Probably an airlock. At least the interior is visible.

"Come on. There's another door to cut through."

"What if they're waiting for us on the other side?" Niles asks as I go vaulting back up the landing ramp. We can see where we're stepping thanks to the severed hull section that's lying on top of the invisible ramp.

Inside the dimly-lit airlock, I stop in front of the inner doors. There's a control panel beside them, glowing with alien symbols.

Rather than try my luck opening the doors, I take aim with the plasma gun again.

Before I can pull the trigger, the door springs open, parting in the middle.

"Shit!" Niles cries, and I hear his hurried footfalls as he retreats.

I dart sideways into cover behind the door frame. Peeking around the edge of the open doors, I can see that the interior is empty. There's no sign of either species of aliens. But *someone* had to have opened the door for us.

It feels like a trap.

As I peer around the edge of the doors, my skin prickles with sweat under my layers. The space on the other side of the airlock could be a cargo area, or some kind of troop bay. There are six extra-wide doors, three to either side of a hexagonal floor. No, not hexagonal. Octagonal. Three doors in each of the sides, one where I stand, and a pair of curving, illuminated tubes at the back. The floor is covered in metal grates with what looks like machinery and crawl spaces below.

Dim blue light strips frame the edges of the floor and the ceiling, which is at least twelve feet high. I can't help thinking that this area has been designed to accommodate the Behemoths. Those six doors probably lead to sleeping quarters, or maybe to cryo pods like the ones UNSF uses for interstellar missions. Regardless, we only encountered three Behemoths, so where are the other three?

"Chris," Niles whispers beside my ear.

I flinch at the sound and glance over my shoulder to see him crouching there. He quietly crawled back into the airlock after fleeing a moment ago. "I don't see Gaby anywhere," he says. "We should go."

"Maybe they haven't come back yet. The vehicle that landed at the house had to be much smaller than this one."

"So who opened the doors?" Niles asks.

"They must have left someone at the controls." My gaze snaps up to the ceiling. "For all we know there's a dozen decks above this one. Gaby could be on any of those."

"You said they might not be back yet."

"Might. We don't know anything. The only way to find out is to go inside."

"That's what they want us to do. They opened the door to lure us in," Niles says.

"Or to stop me from cutting it open. Look, I can't leave until I've found my girl."

"They could be invisible, just like this ship," Niles argues. "They could kill you before you even know that they're there."

He makes a good point, but I don't know what other choice we have. My mind races for a way to safely enter this part of the ship. Remembering the thermal scope on my rifle, I holster the alien weapon and unclip the E9. Peeking around the door frame with my right eye pressed to the scope, I see nothing but cold blue surfaces. But that doesn't mean anything. What would be the use of a cloaking shield that only works for the visible spectrum of light?

"See anything?"

"No."

I briefly consider spraying the interior with bullets, but I could miss. Or hit a shielded Demon and not even realize it.

I grind my teeth as I work the problem.

Just then I remember something: the smoke grenade.

Opening a few of the pouches in the vest, I feel around for the cylindrical shape of it as opposed to the roughly spherical bulb of a frag. The second pouch contains the smoke. Pulling it out, I set my rifle down and then pull the pin. I toss the grenade into the center of the octagonal deck. It hits with a tinny *clunk* and crimson smoke that looks purple in the blue light hisses out noisily. Peering around the edge of the doors, I watch the shape of the emerging smoke cloud for disruptions that might indicate a solid but invisible body interrupting the flow.

For the first few seconds, nothing happens.

But then a small, almost child-like silhouette appears: two short, skinny legs lead up to a torso and a sharply-angled head. No arms that I can see, but I remember the way they extended straight from the aliens' chests.

The silhouette stands there, frozen, waiting. Maybe it hopes that I still haven't seen it.

Drawing the plasma gun, I flick the rocker switch to set it back to the other fire mode, take aim—

And pull the trigger.

A bright flash of light erupts from the barrel as a ball of super-heated plasma shoots toward my target.

But it's no longer standing there.

"Where did it go?" Niles whispers sharply.

A flash of green laser fire strobes back at us, narrowly missing my head with a scalding burst of heat. I duck back into cover, cursing and patting my hair in case it's on fire.

"Does that answer your question?" I ask. This is bad. We're pinned down by an invisible adversary, and I still don't know if Gaby is even here. A second beam of emerald light flashes out of the smoke, from a new angle this time. I'm covered, but Niles isn't. He cries out as it burns straight through his arm. A tongue of flame erupts from his jacket, filling the air with a sickening stench.

"Get down!" I cry, giving him a shove just before a second laser can pierce his torso. He squeezes into cover beside me, patting his arm frantically to put out the fire.

My pulse is thundering in my ears. Invisible aliens could come creeping in here at any second to finish the job. We can't shoot what we can't see, so they've already won.

Unless.

I reach into one of the other pouches for a frag grenade. Pulling the pin and releasing the "spoon," to activate the fuse, I toss it through the open door, aiming for the center of the chamber on the other side. The kill radius of the grenade is five meters. Big enough to blanket the entire deck with shrapnel.

Shrinking even further into cover, I hold my breath in anticipation—

The grenade goes off with an echoing *boom* and a subsequent roar of shrapnel plinking off the bulkheads.

Silence rings loud in the wake of that explosion. I'm already reaching for another frag to finish the job in case that wasn't enough.

But Niles catches my arm to stop me. "Look,"

he whispers through teeth that are gritted from the pain of his laser-burned arm.

There's a dark shadow lying on the floor just outside the open doors of the airlock.

It's the size and shape of one of the Demons, and it's not moving.

CHAPTER 26

"Let's go!" I shout to Niles before launching myself out of cover and spraying the deck left to right with a burst of suppressive fire. Then I run past the alien corpse into the middle of the deck. The smoke from the first grenade is dissipating. It's not meant to be harmful, but in the enclosed space it still irritates my eyes and lungs. I take shallow breaths to inhale as little of it as possible. Running to the back of the chamber where I saw those illuminated tubes, I scan the physical control panel glowing between them. Hitting alien symbols randomly, I wait for some kind of response. The tubes look roughly analogous to elevators and extend all the way up to the ceiling. My random, haphazard attempts to operate them don't yield any result.

"Over here!"

I turn to see that Niles has found something else—a broad ramp with guide rails and hand holds along the ceiling that curves around behind the elevators. An alternative access to the other decks? This one looks like it was built for the Behemoths to use.

I take point up the ramp, clipping my E9 rifle to my vest and drawing the alien plasma gun as I go. The first "landing" is huge, and the doors are equally oversized. Definitely built to the Behemoths' dimensions. Flicking the plasma gun back to beam mode, I cut a hole through the doors and kick them in. They fall in with a *bang* to reveal a gleaming room that looks like a laboratory of some kind. It's brighter in here, and the light is white rather than blue. I can see three separate cubicles arrayed around the space, each of them transparent with a big gleaming metal bed inside. Two of the three beds are occupied, and I recognize both occupants—one of them is a familiar little girl with dark hair.

Niles sucks in a sharp breath, and a strangled noise escapes my lips as I run to the cubicle with my daughter inside. One of my palms lands on the glass. "Gaby!" I cry, heedless of who or what might hear me.

But she doesn't respond. Her jacket is off, and her shirt ripped open. Three fat tubes are snaking out of her bare chest, one red with blood, another black, the third one clear. There's also a glossy black helmet on her head, with wires snaking from it to a wall of equipment behind the bed. Blinking lights and rhythmic chiming sounds make me think they're monitoring her vitals.

"I'm going to fucking kill them!" I grind out.

"Quiet," Niles whispers. "Unless you want them to kill you first."

"Watch the door!" I snap at him. If there are any other aliens crewing this ship, they already know we're here.

"Hurry up," Niles adds.

Not bothering to look for a door, I use the plasma gun to cut another hole. Pushing through with a *bang* as the severed section hits the deck, I hurry to Gaby's side. Her eyes are shut, but roving rapidly behind her lids, as if she's in REM sleep. At least I know she's alive.

I reach for the tubes in her chest, then hesitate. What if she bleeds out? These tubes are as thick as my thumb, and at least one of them is red with her blood. My best guess is that they lead straight to her heart.

Holstering the plasma gun, I look for a way to disconnect my daughter without killing her. The helmet looks like the easiest to remove, so I try that first. It slides off with only minimal resistance, revealing spongy pads inside that might be adjustable for different head sizes.

Now that the helmet is off, I can see that Gaby's ears are bleeding. My heart gives a painful stab in my chest. Her eyes have stopped roving, but she's not waking up. Fearing for what that might mean, I pull off a glove and check her pulse. Slow, but steady. She's okay. I heave a sigh.

The bundle of tubes in her chest is next.

"Hurry up, Chris!" Niles says.

I glance back at him, checking for signs of enemy contact. But we're clear—

As far as my eyes can tell.

Niles is right. We can't afford to delay. If another one of those Demons slips in here with a cloaking shield engaged, we'll never know until it opens fire.

Grabbing the three tubes in my bare hand, I can feel liquid pulsing through them in time to each beat of Gaby's heart. It's just as I suspected. I can't remove them, but what if I can tie them off somehow? Better be a hell of a good seal.

I have to do something.

"Chris!"

"Just hang on a minute!" I grab the tubes and bend them to put a kink in the lines. An alarm immediately starts screaming from whatever machine the tubes are coming from. I grimace, and awkwardly grab the plasma gun in my other hand.

Aiming at the bundle of tubes where they lie on the floor, I try to pull the trigger to sever them. Maybe the heat of the plasma will seal them off, too. I can only hope.

It takes every ounce of my strength to pull the trigger one-handed. A white-hot beam snaps out and severs the lines. Red, black and clear fluids dribbles out, but the pressure is low, and the molten end is quickly cooling into a mangled-looking seal. Fluids stop leaking, and I slowly release the kink in the lines to test it.

Nothing leaks from Gaby's end. Pressing fingers to her throat once more, I hold my breath—

And let out a shuddery sigh. Her pulse is still skipping lightly beneath my fingertips.

I pick up the severed end of the tubes. They're about three feet long, but there's no time to figure out how to shorten them. Wrapping them around her waist like a belt, I scoop up my daughter and run from the cubicle.

Niles is standing guard by the hole that I burned through the metal doors at the top of the access ramp. "What about Bret?" he asks.

I glance back at the other occupied cubicle to see him lying on another metal bed with wires and tubes trailing from him.

"There's no time," I say. "Besides, he killed those people, remember?"

"He's still human."

"Barely," I reply, jerking my chin to the ramp that we came up. "You need to lead the way. I can't carry her and handle a gun at the same time."

"Right," Niles replies. His eyes are wide and staring at the bundle of tubes protruding from Gaby's chest, but rather than waste time with questions, he flicks the safety off on his shotgun and runs out.

I follow him down the ramp, with Gaby clutched protectively to my chest. Even under all of my layers and weapons I can feel that she's still warm and *alive*, but I'm whispering frantic, repetitive prayers to any god that'll listen for her to please, *please* stay that way.

It was a miracle just to find her here. Another miracle if we escape. Is it too much to ask for a third? She can't die.

CHAPTER 27

Niles and I fly back down the landing ramp and stomp our way across the snowy clearing to the resort parking lot. Trees and buildings flash by in a blur. Gaby is still not waking up.

The tubes in her chest are a serious concern. Somehow we need to remove them without doing even more harm.

I snap a glance over my shoulder. No sign of pursuit.

But the bird-like Demon we met inside the lander was invisible, and those things fly anyway, so who knows if we're being followed or not. I turn back to the fore, straining my ears to listen for an extra set of footfalls—or wings *wooshing* as one of them chases us from the air.

We reach the resort's main office with the broken window. I spare a glance at the bodies in the parking lot.

Dead ahead I can see the boulevard. Our Jilvee is just on the other side of that, all sharp angles gleaming in the moonlight.

We race across the snowy street, me half-stumbling as I cradle Gaby and swivel my head side to side, looking for incoming threats. Niles pulls even with me and I see him scanning frantically for targets. The town is deserted. Anyone with any sense is hiding indoors.

My lungs burn from the cold. Realizing that Gaby is no longer wearing a jacket, and her pajama shirt has been ripped open to make room for the tubes in her chest, I cradle her closer to me. I'm not sure how much warmth I can convey to her through all my gear and layers. I have two different weapons strapped to my chest. If anything, the metal will scald her bare skin. Shifting my grip, I place my bare hand to her cheek.

Ice cold.

Shit.

Next, I'm feeling her neck for a pulse...

Thready, but it's still there.

We reach the other side of the street. I yank open the driver's side door, then think better of it and wave Niles over. "You drive."

"Me? I don't know—"

"It's the same as your SUV!" I snap at him, while yanking open one of the rear doors. "I need to sit with Gaby in the back." I wonder if Niles will be able to start the vehicle without the ID chip in my pocket, but I think I'll still be sitting close enough.

Niles nods woodenly and climbs in just as I slide in the back.

Laying Gaby across the back seats, I remove

the alien holster and plasma gun, then unclip the E9 rifle.

Niles gets the truck started. It comes whirring and clicking to life.

"Where are the headlights?" he asks.

"Forget them. You want to draw more of those monsters to us? The moon is bright enough."

And it is. Reflecting off the snow, we can see clearly for hundreds of feet in all directions.

Shrugging out of my army vest, and then unzipping my jacket underneath, I work quickly to wrap it around Gaby.

Niles is putting the truck through a lurching set of maneuvers to get us turned back the other way. I find myself staring at the tubes in Gaby's chest while rubbing her icy hands between mine to warm them up.

"Stop!" I tell Niles.

He hits the brakes suddenly, and my shoulder slams into the front seat. Gaby almost falls to the floor of the truck.

"What's wrong?" he asks, his head twisting every which way to see.

"Easy!" I say. "You almost cracked my skull."

"Then don't startle me!"

I take a breath and let it out slowly. "Gaby needs a doctor. Are there any hospitals that might be open?"

"Ordinarily? The Community Hospital would be. But right now it's probably abandoned just like everything else."

"It has an ER?"

"Yes."

I grind my teeth briefly. Even if all of the medical staff have evacuated, there will be supplies there that we can use. I have some basic medical skills from my time in the Army, so I'm pretty confident that I can stitch Gaby up if that's all that's required.

Big if.

But maybe one or more of the doctors or nurses stayed at the hospital when the shit hit the fan.

"Take us there," I say.

"Are you sure? What if—"

"Just do it, Niles! We don't have time to argue."

"Right. Hold on—"

The truck lurches around again. I brace myself, sitting sideways and pushing against the front seat with my leg and arm while holding Gaby with the other.

I'm tempted to tell Niles to stop being a fucking lead foot, but he's jackrabbiting around because he's scared shitless and in a rush.

And right now, I'd rather that than have him driving like my mother.

So I bite my tongue.

And start praying again.

I've never been much of a believer in higher powers. But show me a parent who doesn't secretly whisper a prayer when their kids are in trouble, and I'll show you a liar.

* * *

I was half-expecting that the hospital would have the lights on, but all of the windows are dark. The sign that reads, *Big Bear Community Hospital* is dark. So is the one that reads *Emergency Room* above the glass doors.

Gaby hasn't woken up yet, and I'm starting to lose my shit. Did they put her into a coma? Is it my fault for disconnecting her without knowing what that helmet and the tubes in her chest were for?

The Jilvee grinds to a halt in front of a covered loading zone for ambulances. I pop open my door and carry Gaby out. It's freezing outside without my jacket on, but at least Gaby feels warmer now.

Running with Niles to the glass doors of the ER, I curse under my breath when they don't open automatically for us.

Either the hospital's generators aren't on, or someone disabled the doors. Either way, we're going to have to break in.

I can't see any signs of life or activity inside. Stepping back from the doors, I nod to Niles and say, "Shoot them."

He hesitates, looking at the shotgun in his hands, then back up at me. "Won't the noise be a problem? What if something hears?"

He makes a good point. "Then find something else. A rock, or—"

Niles grabs the shotgun like a club and swings it into the doors. They shatter in a pebbly rain of safety glass.

"Or that," I say.

I'm the first one through.

The reception and waiting area are deserted. Looks like we're on our own. Scanning the interior, I realize it's too dark to safely navigate, and I don't want to trip over something with Gaby in my arms.

"Turn on the tac-light," I say.

"The what?"

"Under the barrel." I make an awkward gimme gesture to Niles while holding Gaby.

He comes over, I point to the flashlight clipped to the barrel of the shotgun. He finds the button on the back and turns it on.

"Where are we going?" he asks.

"Those doors over there," I reply, nodding to a pair of swinging doors that lead deeper into the hospital.

Niles takes point and pushes through to a room full of curtained cubicles, some open, others shut. Hospital beds and equipment line both sides of the space.

One of the curtains is parted—an eye peeking out. The curtain parts another foot. The beam of the tac-light bounces off the pale, wide-eyed face of a young, pretty woman with long, dark hair and a white doctor's coat. She looks like a deer caught in headlights.

My heart skips a beat. "We need help!"

"What's wrong with her?" The doctor blinks and then squints at us, belatedly throwing up a hand against the glare of the tac-light.

"Sorry," Niles mumbles as he sweeps the shotgun away from her. That's probably why she was so scared. Not used to having a gun pointed in her face. What did she think we were going to do? Raid the hospital for drugs?

Niles starts bringing the barrel of the shotgun into line with Gaby so he can shine the light on her, but then he appears to remember what I said about not aiming a gun at things he shouldn't shoot.

The doctor pulls out a smaller pen light instead. She aims it at Gaby, sees the tubes in her chest, and sucks in a sharp breath. That wide-eyed look of shock is back.

"How did..." she trails off.

"The invaders abducted her," I say. "Her vitals seem stable, but she's not waking up."

Snapping out of it again, the doctor says, "We need to get her to a bed. This way."

She turns and Niles and I follow her to one of the curtained cubicles. The tac-light illuminates a bright green circle of the curtains before the doctor throws them aside to reveal a bed.

"Lay her down."

I do so, and then watch, wringing my hands as she plucks Gaby's eyelids open and shines the light into them one at a time.

"Pupillary reflexes are normal."

"What does that mean?" I ask.

"It means she's not brain dead."

I nod quickly, feeling suddenly numb, but not from the cold. Brain dead. I didn't even consider that as a possibility, but I'm glad that it's been ruled out.

The doctor puts a stethoscope in her ears and listens to Gaby's chest.

"Heartbeat is slow and erratic. Breathing shallow."

"Shit."

She checks the severed end of the tubes protruding from Gaby's chest. "It's not leaking. Did she lose any blood?"

"Some, not much," I say, but then hesitate. "But we don't know what they did to her."

"I'll have to run some tests."

"Can't you just wake her up? Give her a shot of adrenaline or something?"

"Not until I know why she's unconscious. Sometimes comas are the brain's way of protecting itself. It could also be from hypoxia, or swelling in her brain. Did she suffer a head injury?"

"Fuck, I don't know!"

"Okay, okay." The doctor sucks in a deep breath, appearing to take a moment to steady herself. Going to a nearby piece of equipment, I see her pull out a line and turn the machine on. It starts beeping. She clips something to Gaby's index finger and I hear the familiar beep, beep, beeping of a vital signs monitor. The screen at the top of the device is showing various numbers in different colors.

"Well?"

"Pulse is forty-five. O2 saturation ninety-four percent... blood pressure is sixty-one over forty-three."

Those numbers all sound way too low to me. "What do we do about it?"

"With these symptoms it could be..." She trails off into silence, biting her lip in the muted glow of the life signs monitor.

My heart is hammering with anticipation. I'm starting to feel like this woman is an impostor. Maybe she's a nurse, not an actual doctor. Or worse, maybe she's neither.

Before she can come up with an answer, Gaby's left hand twitches. Then her arm. And then her entire body starts skipping and jumping on the bed, flopping around like a fish. The life signs monitor starts to scream with an alarm.

"She's seizing!" the doctor cries. "Help me turn her on her side!"

I run over to help just as Gaby starts foaming at the mouth. We get her turned on her side, and chunky vomit comes spilling out of her mouth. It smells like rotten tuna from the meal we ate earlier.

My daughter's eyes are rolling and her lids are fluttering.

"Come on, Gaby! Wake up!"

Her mouth starts opening and closing like a fish, as if she can't breathe.

"Her airway's blocked!" the doctor cries. "Hold her!"

She darts away, comes back with a scalpel and a breathing tube. I know what she's going to do even before she cuts a vertical slit in Gaby's throat.

Emergency tracheotomy.

She puts the tube in, and air starts whistling in and out.

Gaby's seizure abruptly stops, and her eyes fly wide. She sits bolt upright, then doubles over, gagging and coughing up the remains of her midnight snack.

I hold her by her shoulders, careful to mind the tube in her throat and the ones in her chest. She's awake. And alive.

After a minute of coughing, Gaby finally subsides, slumping against me. Then she appears to notice the tubes in her chest and her throat, and she screams hoarsely.

"It's okay! Gaby! Calm down! We're going to get them out."

She's sobbing inconsolably, air whistling through the tube in her throat. Between the doctor and I, we manage to keep her hands away from the tubes. She starts to calm down. Her mouth is moving, but only muffled sounds escape her mouth.

"Don't try to talk," the doctor says. "You won't be able to talk right now."

Gaby nods slowly, swallows and winces in pain as she does so.

"It's okay," I whisper, and kiss her on the top of her head. "You're going to be okay."

But the truth is, I'm still scared as hell. We still don't know what they did to her. Or why. And my mind is busy filling those blanks with all of the most terrifying possibilities imaginable.

CHAPTER 28

I watch from Gaby's side, holding her hand for support. With my free hand, I'm shining the doctor's penlight for her as she checks that Gaby's airways are clear, then removes the breathing tube and dresses the opening.

"What's your name?" I ask.

"Willow Turner," she says.

"Nice to meet you, Willow. I'm Chris. That's Niles, and the little trooper you're patching up is Gabrielle."

"Hi, Gabrielle."

She starts to move her mouth, but Dr. Turner stops her with another warning. "Not yet. You can talk when I'm done, but it would be better if you didn't say anything until you're better."

Gaby makes a sad face, but nods and swallows wincingly once more.

"My little soldier," I say. "You're being so brave."

"What can I do?" Niles asks.

I glance at him. He's standing at the foot of the bed, biting his nails, fidgeting, shifting from foot to foot. He looks like he's on the verge of a total nervous breakdown.

"Go get the others and bring them here," I suggest.

"What, by myself?"

"Yes."

"The others?" Doctor Turner asks, looking up from her work patching Gaby's throat.

"Her mother and grandmother, my son. Niles' kids and wife."

"Oh. Yes, bring them." The doctor glances at Niles, her gaze lingering on the shotgun. "You have any other weapons with you?"

"A few. Some are in our truck. The rest are with our families."

"Good, then you can help guard this place. Especially since you broke the door."

"Has anything tried to come in?" Niles asks.

"Not yet. But I've seen them..."

"Which ones?"

"The big gray, four-legged ones."

"Behemoths," I suggest.

"That's their name?"

"Good as any," I reply.

"They were walking around in the parking lot, sniffing at the doors. That's when I turned out all of the lights. The generator is still running, but I thought it would be best if I didn't draw attention to myself."

"Smart. Are there any other patients?"

"No."

"Staff?"

Dr. Turner shakes her head. "It was a quiet night when the invaders came. The patients were all ambulatory, and they fled with the staff as soon as we heard the first explosions going off. I guess they thought they'd be safer outside."

"You've been here by yourself all that time?"

Doctor Turner nods.

I make it sound like it's been a week or more, but the invaders only arrived last night. This is the middle of night two. Just over twenty-four hours now.

The conversation lulls. I look back to Niles. He's still standing there biting his nails.

"Let's go," I say.

He flinches to life, eyes focusing belatedly on mine. "You're coming?"

"Just to the truck. I left my weapons in the back."

"Oh," Niles sounds crestfallen.

"Relax. You'll be fine."

"Maybe you should go? I could stay and watch Gaby."

I give Gaby's hand a squeeze, then leave her side to join Niles. "That's not happening. I'm not letting Gaby out of my sight. You'll be fine."

Glancing back at the doctor, I nod to her and say. "I'll be right back."

I hand her the penlight and then follow Niles through darkness to the waiting room, now icy and cold from the door we broke to get inside. I shiver at the sudden change of temperature.

Outside it's even colder. Our breath turns to steam, and I'm wishing I hadn't left one of my gloves in the alien lander when I pulled it off to check Gaby's pulse.

Reaching into the back of the Jilvee, I pull out the utility vest, the E9 rifle, and the alien plasma gun with its holster.

Niles climbs in behind the wheel and lays the shotgun across the passenger's seat.

I reach into the right pocket of my pajama pants and hand him the tiny silver wafer that is the dead soldier's ID chip.

"You'll need this to drive the truck. Keep it somewhere safe."

He pockets the chip with a grimace. Looking at the Army E9, I realize that I won't be able to use it anymore without the ID chip.

"Let's switch," I say, nodding to the shotgun.

He passes it back over and I hand him the rifle.

"Safety's here," I say, showing him where to flick it off. "The rest is easy. Point and shoot. Scope's set to thermal. It'll show you heat signatures."

Niles nods quickly, but he has a glazed look in his eyes that makes me wonder if he's really listening.

"Don't shoot unless you have to, and don't delay. The faster you can get back here the safer you'll be."

"Yeah…" he breathes a cloud of steam in my face.

"Good luck. I'm counting on you."

He nods again and then pulls the door shut. The Jilvee whirrs to life and spits snow from its tires as Niles hits the accelerator too hard and jack-rabbits away.

I watch him go. The shotgun like ice against my bare hand. The tac-light is still on, blazing bright against the snow.

I wait a few more seconds, watching to see that Niles doesn't run into anything as he rejoins the street and flies down it to the boulevard once more.

Seeing nothing, I turn and run back inside, illuminating the way with the tac-light. As I approach the doors to the patient treatment area I see that they're limned with light. Pushing through, I find Dr. Turner inside with one of the overhead lights on. She's using the light and a handheld scanner to examine the area around the bundle of tubes protruding from Gaby's chest. A holographic screen is projected beside the bed, which shows the colored imagery from the wand-like scanner. I see spidery blue and red veins, fat red and blue arteries, Gaby's heart… and at least a hundred silver hairs snaking to and from the arteries, invading everything in sight.

Setting my vest, shotgun, and the alien weapon down at the foot of Gaby's bed, I hurry over to study the results of the scan.

"What are those?" I ask, pointing to the silver hairs.

"The other end of the catheter in her chest."

"Can you remove it?" I ask.

Doctor Turner glances at me, her hazel eyes sharpening on mine. Gaby's gaze finds me next. I flinch at the sight of how bloodshot her eyes are. Is that normal? Or another symptom of whatever was done to her? She still has dried blood around her ears from where it was leaking out when I found her.

Gaby looks terrified. Her mouth starts to move, but then she appears to think better of it. I reach for one of her hands with my gloveless one and give it a squeeze.

"There's no direct involvement with the heart. It looks like the tubes break into hundreds of much thinner strands and invade all of the major arteries leading to and from the heart. But they're incredibly thin... I don't think we need to worry about what will happen when we pull them out. Her normal clotting response will handle any bleeding."

"Okay. Do it."

Doctor Turner sets her scanner aside and starts looking for a way to detach the trunk of tubes. She tugs at it, then looks to Gaby. "Does that hurt?"

Gaby shakes her head.

Another tug.

"Looks like it's stuck to her with some kind

of... glue maybe?"

As she pulls, I can see hundreds of sticky strands appearing beneath a sucker-like pad, but no welling of blood to worry about.

"It's coming out..." I can tell Doctor Turner is having to exert herself now.

Gaby makes a stifled sound that could be a sign of pain.

"Doc..." I say warningly.

"Almost there..."

And then the bundle of tubes comes away in the doctor's hands and she stumbles back a step.

She stands to one side blinking at it. We both look at Gaby to check that she's not bleeding. She isn't, but it left a mark where it was attached: a clearly defined circle of dark red pinpricks. At least a hundred of them.

We look back to the device, and see that the strands of adhesive were actually the hairline filaments that Dr. Turner identified on the scanner. They're about five inches long and sagging under their own weight, looking vaguely like a horse's tail.

"That was easy," Doctor Turner says.

"Yeah," I agree, my eyes back on Gaby now.

A weak, trembling smile graces her lips, and she tries to talk again. This time a recognizable croak comes out. "Cold," she says. And then I see her teeth start to chatter.

Placing my bare hand to her forehead, she feels like fire to my ice, but that could just be because I haven't been wearing a glove since we left the lander.

The doctor nods and says, "She's running a light fever."

"Since when?" I ask.

"Since she got here. I thought you knew. Thirty-seven point three. It's really not very high. Nothing to worry about, anyway."

How do you know? I want to scream at her. But biting the hand that heals isn't a good idea.

"I'll give her something for it," Doctor Turner says, heading for a cabinet outside the curtained area where Gaby is. "Antibiotics in case of infection. Tylenol to bring it down. She'll be fine," the doctor insists.

I nod along with that, hoping she's right. But then something else occurs to me. I give Gaby's hand another squeeze and then push through the curtains to find Doctor Turner. She's using syringes to suck out samples of the three fluids that were in the tubes in Gaby's chest. One red, one black, one clear.

"What are you doing?" I ask, even though the answer is pretty obvious.

She glances at me, and I can see the wheels turning behind those hazel eyes, as if she's debating whether or not to let me in on a secret.

"Taking samples," she says slowly.

"Yeah, but why?" I want to know if her suspicion is the same as the one that just occurred to me.

"A precaution."

"You want to know if the fever is from an *alien* infection," I suggest, speaking in the barest whisper.

Doctor Turner grimaces, and I know that I've just read her mind. She holds up the severed tubes by way of explanation. "The clear one could be for hydration, or to deliver medication, right? It looks like saline, and maybe it is. The red one is obviously Gaby's own blood. But what is the black one?"

I swallow thickly. This conversation is digging dangerously close to the source of my lingering fears. I still can't fathom a motive for any of this. What possible purpose could there be to experimenting on a six-year-old? And what about Bret? What do the two of them have in common? Maybe nothing. Maybe they were randomly selected.

"How do we find out?" I ask.

"I'll know more once I get a look at these samples under a microscope. Stay here. Keep Gabrielle company. If you need me, I'll be right through those doors, at the end of the corridor, on the right." Doctor Turner points to another set of swinging doors at the far end of the patient treatment area.

"Okay," I say, and watch as she hurries off. She didn't hook Gaby up with those meds that she was promising, but she probably wants to know what she's dealing with first.

Heading back to Gaby's side, I find her sitting up, looking pale and frightened. I wince, wondering if she overheard us talking about her.

"It's okay, Gabs," I start to say.

"Did you hear that?" she asks hoarsely.

"Hear what?" I ask, glancing around quickly. Not waiting for her to reply, I grab my shotgun off the floor at the foot of the bed.

"There..." Gaby whispers.

I frown, my ears straining for a hint of whatever she's hearing, but the room is perfectly silent.

"It's talking," she says.

"Talking?"

"Not talking. Making sounds," she says.

"What kind of sounds?"

She shakes her head, and winces as she swallows.

I still can't hear anything. My eyes focus on the dried blood around her ear lobes, and wonder if it has anything to do with that.

"Lie down sweetheart," I suggest.

Switching to a one-handed grip on the shotgun, I pull the blankets at the bottom of the bed up over her, tucking her in. Her teeth are chattering again. I stroke her hair, watching as her eyelids grow heavy, slowly sinking shut.

"Can you still hear it?" I ask in a whisper.

She rocks her head from side to side on the pillow. "No."

"Good." Add hallucinations to Gaby's symptoms.

I glance back at the doors where Doctor Turner disappeared, silently willing her to hurry up with examining those samples.

CHAPTER 29

Gaby is resting, so I stand sentinel in the darkened waiting room of the ER, watching the broken doors with my shotgun, waiting for Niles to return with the rest of my family and his. I have my jacket back, since Gaby was getting hot under her blankets, and I managed to scrounge some gloves from the lost and found behind the reception desk. My legs feel like ice again, but at least I'm not freezing to death.

My mind wanders to the invisible lander where we found Gaby. If it weren't for all the snow, we never would have found it. The footprints leading to the ramp were the only sign it was there. That and the flattened patches underneath. I wonder how many other invisible landers are out there, quietly abducting people for alien experiments.

So much for peaceful coexistence. The Demons have a reason for being here that they're not talking about. At least, not that I've heard. We only saw that one broadcast. Maybe we should try turning on another holoscreen to see if there have been any new ones. Maybe we'll find out the invaders have abducted others like Gaby, and what happened to them.

A sigh escapes my lips in a puff of steam.

Niles where the hell are you?

How long has it been? Twenty minutes? Thirty?

At least that. I hope he didn't run into any trouble along the way. Maybe I should have gone with him.

Shit.

My eyes drift out of focus on the snowy moonlit world outside. How long would it take me to get back to the end of Eagle Drive on foot? I feel like it can't be more than two or three kilometers. So about ten or twenty minutes at a brisk jogging pace.

Just as I'm about to go find Doctor Turner and tell her I'm leaving, I see a dark blur go racing down the street and skidding through a turn into the parking lot.

It's Niles' Suburban, not the UNEA Jilvee.

Running out the broken entrance of the ER, I reach the side of the vehicle just as it stops in front of the hospital. The doors fly open, and the Pearsons' kids come boiling out, followed by mine, and then Bree and my mother.

"What took you so long?" I demand of Bree in a strained whisper.

She shakes her head. "There are more of the four-legged ones on the main street. We had to go around before they could spot us."

Zach nods along with that, his eyes huge.

"We'd better get our things inside," Niles says, heading for the back of the Suburban. Jessica glares at me as she strides past with Sean and Haley.

Maybe she blames me for running into the invaders on the way here. But she could have stayed. Niles too. My family could have come here on their own. The fact that Jessica is here means that she realizes we'll stand a better chance by sticking together. I shouldn't be surprised by this. After all, my replacements are just hulks of scrap metal now.

We hurry to unload the vehicle, carrying our bags inside as quickly and quietly as we can.

By the time we're done, everyone is breathing hard from the exertion. Bree asks me through gasping breaths, "How is she?"

"She's okay. She's resting." I decide not to mention Gaby's fever, or the way we found her with those tubes in her chest. I'm not sure how much of that Niles already said, but I don't want to worry my wife yet. Hopefully we'll soon have more concrete info from Doctor Turner.

I'm on my haunches beside the gun bag, taking stock of what's left. I lost my Glock on the stairs of the guest house while running from that Demon, but Bree put hers back in the bag. We still have both shotguns, one of which is in the bag, the two alien plasma guns with their holsters, the Army vest, the E9 rifle that I gave to Niles, which he's still holding; three flashlights, five road flares, and a scoped hunting rifle chambered for .30-06. It's a bolt action, but the caliber alone makes up for the awkwardness and gives it better accuracy. Pulling out the flashlights, I pass them around. One for Bree, another for Niles, the last one for myself. Then I zip up the bag, thinking we can pass out guns later. For now, it's good enough Niles and I are armed.

"Where is she?" Bree asks as I straighten up with the gun bag in my left hand, my shotgun resting on top of it, and a flashlight in my right hand.

"Through there," I say, nodding at the swinging doors to the patient treatment area. I'm already leading the way.

As soon as I push through the doors, I see that Doctor Turner has pulled Gaby's curtain completely aside, and she's wearing a canary yellow hazmat suit.

That fact alone tells me more than I wanted to know about what the invaders did to Gaby.

Bree streaks by me, cursing steadily under her breath.

"Wait!" I call to her, but self-preservation doesn't stand a chance against a mother's love, nor a grandmother's. I watch my mother follow in Bree's wake, but she comes to her senses halfway there.

Doctor Turner sees Bree coming and holds

out both palms to stop her.

Bree slows, but doesn't stop. Zach and I stand off at a distance of ten feet, while the Pearsons stay right inside the doors, keeping as far from Gaby as possible without leaving the room entirely.

"What's wrong with her?" my wife demands of the doctor. "Why is she so pale?"

"Mom..." Gaby croaks. Her eyes and cheeks are wet with tears, her face scrunched up in misery. "It hurts..."

My heart aches sharply with those words. All I want is to run to Gaby's side and cradle her in my arms.

But I have another kid to think about, and I need to know why Doctor Turner is wearing that suit.

Bree tries to get by, but the doctor steps sideways to block her.

"You can't get too close. She could be infectious," Doctor Turner explains.

"Infectious?" Bree echoes incredulously. She glances back at me, then again to the doctor. "Let me by, right now!"

Turner looks to me, her expression pleading behind the bulky mask.

"What did you find?" I ask.

"A virus... at least, I think that's what it is. I've never seen anything like it before. It was in the tube with the black blood. And that's what's in Gaby's system right now. It's multiplying at an alarming rate."

"What is she talking about?" Bree asks.

"Mommy," Gaby moans, her back arching off the gurney.

My mother takes a halting step toward her. "She's in pain!"

Bree makes another determined attempt to dart past the doctor, and this time Turner grabs her by the shoulders and physically pushes her back. "Chris, you need to keep your wife back! Help me!" she says through gritted teeth.

I set the gun back down and rush in to do just that. Fear for the rest of my family has overtaken my fears for Gaby.

I pull Bree back several steps with her kicking my shins and punching my arms, struggling and cursing and vowing to *fucking leave me* if I don't let her go.

"Bree! That's enough! Stop it!"

She subsides somewhat and breaks down sobbing. "Just let me go," she mumbles tearfully.

"We can't help her by getting sick, too," I whisper in Bree's ear.

"Your husband's right," Doctor Turner adds.

My wife glares death at her.

"This is an unknown pathogen, and until we know how it spreads, you need to isolate from your daughter."

"What do you mean isolate?" Bree asks, as if those simple words have lost their meaning.

"I mean, you can't get close to her unless

you're wearing one of these suits."

"You have more?" I ask.

The doctor nods. "Just one."

"Give it to her."

Doctor Turner says, "Follow me."

I catch Niles' eye where he's standing with his family by the swinging doors between the waiting area and the patient cubicles.

Leaving Bree's side, I hurry back to the gun bag, grab my shotgun and the heavy duffel with the rest of the guns.

Striding over to Niles, I pass him the bag, and he sags beneath the weight. "Go watch the entrance. Stay out of here until we know more."

He nods stiffly, and stumbles back through the doors into the waiting area with his wife and kids.

"Is she going to be okay?" a small voice asks. I turn to see Zachary standing in front of my mother, halfway to the doors at the far end of the treatment room which Bree and Doctor Turner are steadily approaching.

"We're going to do everything we can for her," I say as soon as I reach my son's side. Turning him away from Gaby by his shoulders, I add, "Follow your mother."

"You're not coming?" my mother asks. At forty-three, it's easy to forget that in her eyes I'm still her kid. I shake my head. "Someone should stay and watch Gaby."

Another cry comes from her direction. I

glance back in time to see her subside, but she's obviously suffering.

And for a moment, I don't care that she could infect me. All I care about is that my little girl is in pain.

"Go," I croak at my mother.

My mother gives a stifled sob and flees the room with Zach. I watch from a distance as Gaby's back arches with another wave of pain. It takes every ounce of my will not to run to her side. But there's nothing I can do for her.

Helplessness leaves me grinding my teeth. "It's okay, Gaby!" I call to her. "You're going to be fine. We're going to help you!"

But she doesn't appear to hear me, and somehow that makes watching her suffer just that much worse. She's only six years old. It isn't fair. Why didn't those fuckers take me instead? Why my little girl?

Impotence builds to rage, and rage to hate. I find myself fantasizing about all the ways that I'm going to make those Demons suffer if I ever encounter one of them again.

CHAPTER 30

I'm jealous watching Bree and Gaby interact from where I stand two cubicles over with Zach and my mother.

After a while of tending to Gaby, Doctor Turner leaves Bree and comes over to speak with us.

"I see you're all keeping your distance," she says. "That's a good idea."

"How is she?" I ask, my eyes fixed on Gaby's face.

"Better. The meds are starting to take effect."

"But?" I can hear the hesitancy in the doctor's voice. There's something she doesn't want to say.

She glances at Zach, then back to me, as if asking my permission to say whatever it is in front of him.

I nod for the doctor to go on. Better that he knows what his sister has so that he treats it with the right amount of respect.

Doctor Turner says, "This is a completely novel virus. Worse, it's an *alien* virus, and it doesn't even look like any of the viruses we have on Earth. I call it a virus because of how it behaves, but it's really a much more complicated organism than we're used to seeing."

I shake my head. "What does that mean?"

"What is it doing to her?" my mother adds.

"It's inserting new DNA into her cells, and hijacking them to reproduce itself, just like any other virus would."

"I thought you said it doesn't look like viruses from Earth," I object.

"That's the curious part... ordinary viruses corrupt infected cells, forcing your immune system to attack and destroy those cells, but your daughter's immune system isn't reacting."

"Then why is she getting sick?"

"Because her cells are changing. The virus is invading them and rewiring her body completely. New cells are growing that weren't there before. Old ones are dying off. She's getting symptoms because the virus is systematically changing her on a molecular level. We can see some of those changes already. For example, her blood is getting darker and her skin is getting lighter. Even her eyes are changing color. They were blue, but they're getting redder by the minute."

"My poor baby," my mother says through tears, wiping her eyes. "Why would they do this to her? Why *her?*"

"Redder?" I ask. That detail clicks in my brain, and leaves me reeling with horror. The Demons have red eyes. So did the Behemoths. They were also as pasty and pale as the moon itself.

Doctor Turner nods.

"Why change her into something else?" I ask.

Doctor Turner appears to consider the question for a moment. Her brow furrows deeply inside her suit. "That depends. Our bodies are uniquely suited to life on Earth, but there are certainly ways in which we could be improved, or simply changed so that we're better adapted to different conditions. Given that this was done to your daughter purposefully, and by a vastly superior species from an entirely different planet..." The doctor trails off, letting me fill in the blanks for myself.

"You think they're changing her in ways that are more useful to *them*."

"That, or else they believe that a virus is the easiest way to wipe us out, and it's actually more like our earth-borne viruses than I think."

"But we surrendered. We're not a threat to them."

"Did we?" Doctor Turner asks. "That's what those Union drones said. It's what we heard the president say on the news, but that doesn't make it true. She was obviously coerced, and our drones could have been hacked. Or maybe we *did* surrender, but there are still pockets of resistance everywhere. They might have lost patience with us."

My mother looks as horrified as I feel. "But

Gaby's six! She's not a threat!"

Bree sends us a sharp look from where she stands by Gaby's side. I wince and hold a finger to my mouth. "Shhh. Keep it down," I tell my mother. "We don't want to scare her."

"Sorry."

"Gaby is small and easy to abduct," Doctor Turner says. "She was probably a target of opportunity. Maybe one of many."

"We've all already been in contact with her," I point out. "It might be too late for us to avoid catching this."

"It might," Doctor Turner admits. "But I did see something while examining the samples to make me cautiously optimistic."

Desperate for some kind of good news, I seize on that. "What did you see?"

"The virus appears to be neutralized as soon as it leaves the host. It's extremely vulnerable to drying, a lot like STDs. So the mode of transmission is probably the same, via an exchange of infected fluids. Possibly also through food or water."

My mind flashes back to the tubes that the invaders put in my daughter's chest, and I realize that they were probably infecting her like that. With those fluids. We didn't get to her in time.

"So it's not airborne," I say, looking for the silver lining.

"No."

I let out a shuddery breath. "Well, at least

there's some good news."

"But surely you can do something for her," my mother says. "Please. You have to help her."

"I'm doing everything I can. But her immune system simply isn't responding, so everything I've given her isn't working. The only thing I can think of that might work is to inject a nano virus that's programmed to specifically hunt and kill the invading organism."

"So do that!" I snap.

"I don't have the expertise. You'd need a nanobiologist, and even if we could find one to help us, we would only stop the virus from making more changes, it wouldn't undo the ones that have already been made. Gaby would end up in some kind of limbo between her original physiology and the emergent one. If that didn't kill her, she would likely have pain and debilitating chronic symptoms for the rest of her life."

Dread solidifies in my gut, and suddenly my whole body feels heavy and weak. I watch as Bree strokes Gaby's head, brushing sweat-matted hair away from her face. "So basically, you're saying there's nothing you can do."

"All we can do now is wait," Doctor Turner confirms.

Silence rings loud in my ears, pressing hard against my eardrums. My pulse is hammering against them from the other side.

"She thought they were here to make friends," Zach says, breaking the silence in a quiet voice.

I look at him. Somehow that makes this so much worse. They took the most innocent person they could find as a subject for their experiments. Now they're corrupting her and turning her into something else. It's either that, or they're killing her, and I'm not sure what would be worse.

CHAPTER 31

Nine Hours Later...

I wake up to the sound of an alarm screaming, and a strange hissing, snapping sound. Followed by a human scream. Sitting up quickly, I'm blinking my eyes to clear away the sleep. Two beds over from me, my daughter is wrestling with someone. Niles. His hand is bleeding, and she looks sicker than ever. Her eyes are bright red and feral. Teeth snapping and smeared with Niles' blood.

Swinging my legs over the side of the bed, I race over to help him subdue her. Grabbing Gaby by her shoulders, I try to pull her away from Niles. She lets out a snarl and turns those snapping jaws on me, not a hint of recognition in her eyes.

"Gaby! It's me! Dad!"

"She's delirious," Niles grits out. "She fucking bit me!"

Muscles and thick black veins stand out on Gaby's skinny arms like cords. She's a lot stronger than I remember. It takes both Niles and I to avoid her snapping teeth and wrestle her back into bed, but she's bucking and kicking. One foot catches Niles under the chin and his teeth clack together loudly. I see a flash of long black nails that look more like claws than toenails.

"Fucking hell!" Niles cries, spitting blood. He obviously bit his tongue.

"Doctor Turner!" I yell.

"Where is she?" Niles roars. He steps back from Gaby, and I struggle to hold her down by myself. Her arms and face are chalk white, and I can see bald patches of her scalp where her dark hair is falling out in clumps. Thin trickles of black blood are dried on her cheeks, having leaked from her eyes like tears. Bree comes running in with my mother and Zach with Doctor Turner right behind them in her hazmat suit.

Gaby's snapping teeth angle for my arm, narrowly missing my wrist. Bree crowds in, helping me hold Gaby's head. "Watch her teeth!" I warn her as Gaby struggles to reach her mother.

Then Doctor Turner arrives. Not wasting any time, she goes straight to a nearby cabinet, fills a syringe and plunges it into Gaby's arm. My daughter subsides a few moments later, those feral red eyes rolling up in her head.

"Shit," I mutter through a shuddery breath.

"What happened?" Bree asks, her eyes flicking from me to Niles and back.

"She woke up in a fit, screaming and snarling," Niles explains. "I thought it was a seizure so I tried to restrain her, and then she bit me!"

He's holding his bleeding hand out as evidence, his blood splattering on the floor.

I look to Doctor Turner for an explanation. She's shaking her head. "Let's get you cleaned up."

Niles follows her to the adjacent cubicle.

"It's like she didn't even recognize us," Bree whispers to me.

"She didn't," I confirm.

Bree's face is etched with horror. "What does that mean?"

"I don't know."

"What if she never remembers us?" Bree asks, her voice pitching up to a panicky register, her eyes wincing. My mother approaches her, wrapping Bree in a hug.

"Let's not jump to conclusions yet," I say. Heading over to Doctor Turner and Niles, I'm just in time to see her spraying his hand with disinfectant. The bite is a clearly defined horseshoe. Each of Gaby's teeth have made a bloody indentation. Raising two kids, I've seen the occasional bite mark, but nothing like this. This could have been made by an animal.

"What if she infected me?" Niles asks.

Doctor Turner looks up from bandaging his hand. Her expression isn't encouraging. "Unfortunately, that is a very real possibility."

Niles jumps off the bed, looking frantic. "So

what, then, I'm going to turn into that?" He gestures offhandedly at my daughter.

"We don't know anything yet."

"But that's what the virus does, right? You said so! It changes the hosts cells into something else. That's why she looks like that."

"Yes," Doctor Turner confirms. "I'm sorry. I explained the danger of getting too close to the girl. You had to know the risk you were taking when you ran to help her."

"You said it's transferred by fluids. I didn't think she was going to bite me!"

"I'm sorry, Mr. Pearson, I don't know what else to tell you."

I swallow thickly, feeling guilty that I didn't wake up faster. We took turns through the night, alternately watching the entrance. He just happened to be on his watch when Gaby went into distress. Niles came running in, the good Samaritan, and now he's in the same situation as my daughter.

"Where is Jessica?" I ask.

Niles looks around quickly, as if suddenly remembering that he has a family. His gaze fixes on the swinging doors to the ER waiting room. I notice there is light spilling in around those doors now. It's past sunrise. If Jessica Pearson and his kids were waiting there they would have heard the commotion and come running. He must have left them somewhere else for the night. Somewhere warmer, where the icy air wouldn't be gushing in through that broken door.

"It should be okay for you to see your family," Doctor Turner says. "But you need to be careful with direct contact. And we don't know for sure that you're infected. Try to be positive."

"How soon will we know?" I ask.

"Your daughter was infected last night, correct?"

"Yes," I confirm.

"So, it's taken less than twelve hours for her to get to this point. That's an extremely fast incubation period. Assuming the same holds true for Niles, we should know by tonight whether or not he has been infected."

Niles blows out a frustrated breath and goes storming off, heading for the doors to the waiting room.

"Where are you going?" I call after him.

"To say goodbye to my family!" he calls back.

Bree catches my eye as I look away from Niles, then both of us turn to stare at Gaby's unconscious form. Niles has just breathed our fears to life. Gaby isn't dead, but she's fast becoming unrecognizable to us. What if we already missed our chance to say goodbye?

* * *

Night has fallen again. I've spent the entire day watching Gaby alternate between fighting her restraints and vomiting into a bucket. Bree has been standing by with that bucket ever since the stomach symptoms began. That was around 5:00 PM. Gaby has been throwing up at least twice every hour since then. I see her subside, my wife stroking her head. She's past the violent, delirious stage, and now she recognizes us again, but if anything, she seems sicker than ever.

I'm forced to watch from a distance, helpless and afraid. I thought I knew fear when I was facing one of the Demons, but this is *real* fear: one of my kids is in trouble, and I can't do a thing to help.

Gaby is still in there somewhere, fighting, holding on to her identity if not her humanity. My little soldier.

She looks more alien than human now. Her eyes are completely red. Her skin as pale as the Demons', her blood as black as tar.

Her hair has almost completely fallen out, and her scalp has four lumps on it that look almost like vestigial horns. That reminds me of the four snake-like stalks rising from the tops of the Demons' heads. Is that what's happening to her? Are they turning Gaby into one of them? I wonder if she's going to sprout a pair of wings.

It's a ridiculous thought, but I'm not smiling. Gaby convulses and sits up as far as her improvised restraints will allow. She rolls to one side and retches into the bucket that my wife is holding.

I hear a gasp and a groan from across the

room. Niles is sitting up. Like Gaby, we've taken the precaution of restraining him. When we did that, I took the military ID off him along with the rifle, and used surgical tape to affix the ID chip to the grip of the rifle before storing it in our gun bag. We might need that weapon later. Niles is awake now, but he's been drifting in and out of consciousness all day.

"That's what I have to look forward to," he croaks, his eyes on Gaby.

Swinging my legs over the side of the bed, I cross the room to him. He's pale as death and running a fever, eyes bloodshot and getting redder by the hour. His hair has started falling out. This is what Gaby looked like last night. So far his transformation is tracking hers pretty evenly. Doctor Turner is in the lab, running more tests. Not that it will make any difference. Her clumsy attempt to program a nanovirus to target the alien one raging through Niles' system didn't work. The alien virus reconfigured itself to evade the detection algorithms, and now it's too late to try again. He's too far along to risk aborting the transformation.

"You're still lucid," I point out. "That's a good sign."

"Is it? I'd rather not be fully aware of what's happening to me."

I don't mention that he can't be far from the violent, delirious stage that resulted in Gaby biting him and passing on the infection.

On the bright side, Doctor Turner no longer thinks the virus will kill its host. And neither do I.

If this virus were some random pathogen, it wouldn't be making such organized changes, and it wouldn't be smart enough to change its own form when attacked. The invaders are clearly using this infection to transform us. The question is, why?

What will they do with us once they've turned us into human-alien hybrids?

DAY THREE

CHAPTER 32

"**H**ow are you feeling?" I hear Doctor Turner ask.

"Much better," Gaby says in a deeper, huskier voice than I'm used to hearing from my six-year-old.

"Thank God for that," Bree breathes in a voice that's still strangled with fear and horror.

I know just how she feels.

Gaby is fully lucid now. Her hair is almost entirely gone, and she's no longer throwing up. It's just after three in the morning. Everyone else is asleep on the other side of the hospital, safe and warm in the maternity wing, except for my mother who is keeping watch with one of our shotguns in the ER waiting room. She knows how to use a gun, so I'm not worried. But I hope she doesn't fall asleep.

Bree looks to me with a strained smile, then back at our daughter. I'm keeping a wary distance of about four feet. The snarling and shrieking sounds Niles is making as he fights his restraints on the other side of the room are a helpful reminder of why I should keep my distance. I know what will happen if I get infected.

Doctor Turner is checking Gaby with that handheld scanner, and glancing from time to time at the vital signs monitor next to her.

"She's still running a high fever..."

"How high?" Bree asks, her voice pitching up in alarm. The suit should muffle her words, but external speakers in the hazmat convey the sound clearly.

"Forty-one degrees Celsius," Doctor Turner says.

"She should be dead," I say.

"And yet..."

"She feels fine," Bree finishes. "You're not feeling cold or hot, are you, sweetheart?"

Gaby shakes her head. Stringy, sweat-matted strands of dark hair fly across her pillow. She has about as much hair as a hundred-year-old man. I grimace at the sight of her bloodshot red eyes as they fix on mine.

"What's wrong, Daddy?" she asks. Her voice sounds alien to my ears.

I try to smile and shake my head. "Nothing. Nothing's wrong."

"You look worried."

"Shhh. You shouldn't talk. Remember your throat is still healing," I say, and then immediately feel guilty for trying to shut her up. That voice is unnerving me even more than her appearance. Somehow, I expected the changes to all be superficial—the pale, almost translucent skin. Baldness. Red eyes. The strange lumps growing under her scalp.

But hearing an entirely different voice coming from Gaby's now-black lips, makes me wonder if she is only pretending to remember us. For all we know, Gaby has changed just as much on the inside as the out.

"Actually," Doctor Turner says, reaching for Gaby's bandage. "Incredible..."

"What?" I try to lean in for a closer look.

"It's completely healed," the doctor says, removing the bandage and pointing at a clean, chalk-white patch of skin.

"That's amazing," Bree says.

"So why does her voice sound like that?" I ask.

"The acid from her stomach may have injured her throat," Doctor Turner suggests. "She's been vomiting constantly for hours."

"Yeah." I peer deep into Gaby's eyes, trying to figure out what is lurking behind that blood-red stare.

"I'm hungry," she says.

"That's a good sign," Doctor Turner says.

"What would you like?" Bree asks.

"Ummm, maybe some... some chicken? Or a hamburger. Or steak."

"She's craving protein," Doctor Turner says. "I think we have some diced beef in the cafeteria. I can go heat some up for you, would you like that?"

Gaby nods. "Is it..." She grimaces, and I catch a flash of black gums. "Cooked?"

"Of course, it's cooked," Bree says.

"But I want it raw."

A sick weight settles in my gut. Bree looks to me, her gaze full of concern. Apparently, Gaby isn't just craving meat. She's craving raw meat.

An image flashes through my mind's eye: the memory of that Demon in the guest house, gnawing on the dead soldier's leg as if it were chicken.

"I'll go get you some food," Doctor Turner says, interrupting my thoughts.

Another shrieking snarl from Niles brings my head around to see him pulling hard against the cable ties that we used to secure his hands to the sides of the bed. We did the same with Gaby, and wrapped the ties with gauze to pad them so they wouldn't injure themselves when they struggle.

I wonder how Gaby is going to eat with those ties around her wrists. Looking back to her, my eyes narrow on her gaunt, bony white face. Her chin and cheek bones are more prominent than I remember. Did she lose weight, or did those bones grow in the last twenty-four hours?

Gaby gazes unblinkingly back at me, her alien eyes boring into mine. The soft, innocent expression that I'm used to seeing is long gone. They say eyes are the window to the soul. I can't help wondering whose soul I'm seeing now.

This could be a trick. Act normal and get us to cut her free so that she can eat.

Then what?

Maybe she takes a bite out of one of us.

CHAPTER 33

I wonder what time it is and go check the swinging doors to the waiting room. My mother is there, guarding the broken entrance. It's still dark outside. Hearing footsteps, I turn to see Doctor Turner coming back with food from the cafeteria. I return to Gaby's bedside and watch as the doctor adjusts the incline of Gaby's bed until she's sitting up. But rather than cut her free, she hands the food to Bree to feed her. Doctor Turner might secretly be worried about the same things as I am, about whether Gaby is as alien on the inside as she now looks on the outside.

I watch my daughter eat her diced beef in big, greedy bites. Greasy meat, fat, and sauce dribble down her bony chin.

When the tray is almost empty, she pauses and cocks her head suddenly to one side, listening.

"Who said that?" she asks in mid-chew, her eyes darting around.

"Said what, honey?" Bree asks.

No one has said a word. The only sounds

were of Gaby's chewing and Niles' snarling and struggling.

Gaby's expression twists up in a mixture of confusion and... fear? At least, I think that's what I'm seeing.

"Who has to die?" she asks.

Now I'm the one who's confused.

"Die? What are you talking about?" Bree asks.

"She's hearing voices again," I say.

"Again?" Bree asks.

We both look to Doctor Turner.

"When was she hearing voices?" the doctor asks me.

"Last night. Before everyone else got here. When you went to examine the samples, she told me she was hearing something."

"Not like that," Gaby says. "This time it's different."

"Different how, honey?" Bree asks.

"Now, it's words. Last night it was sounds. Now he's talking."

"Sounds?" Bree asks, looking from me to Gaby and back again.

"How do you know it's a *he?*" Doctor Turner asks.

Gaby shrugs. "Because it sounds like a he."

We all look around once more, just to be sure that no one else is actually in here with us. It's possible that someone is hiding behind the curtains in one of the other cubicles, but if someone was actually talking, we would have heard them, too.

"What else is he saying?" Doctor Turner asks.

Gaby turns her head, as if listening to an actual voice. "Now he's saying that he hates hospitals. And doctors."

"Is he in here, with us?" the doctor asks in a sharp whisper.

Gaby shakes her head. "No. He's outside in the snow. He's looking for a way in."

Adrenaline spurts through my system like ice. Cold, electrifying. Clarity seeps in, and suddenly I'm striding two cubicles over to the bed where I've spent most of the past day. Grabbing my shotgun from the floor beside it, I hurry back to Gaby's side.

"You think she's actually hearing someone?" Bree asks, looking and sounding skeptical behind the bulky helmet of her hazmat suit.

"I don't know, but it wouldn't hurt to take a look around."

Doctor Turner nods, then says, "It's possible that she has better hearing now, but we're too far from the doors and windows. Not even a dog would be able to hear someone outside the hospital from in here."

"All the same," I say. "It's something to do."

Bree nods to me. "Go. I'll stay here and watch Gaby."

"Yeah." I lean in and drop my voice to a whisper. "There is one thing you should know. The invaders have some kind of technology that can make them invisible."

"Invisible?" Doctor Turner asks. "You mean camouflage?"

"No, I mean invisible. There could be someone in the room with us and we wouldn't even know it."

Both Bree and Doctor Turner look terrified by the possibility.

"So, what do we do?" Bree asks in a sharp whisper.

I turn and nod to the gun bag where it sits on the floor by the head of my bed. "Keep a weapon close," I suggest. "I'll be back soon."

* * *

"I haven't seen anyone trying to get in," my mother says.

Rather than worry her with the possibility of invisible enemies, I say, "I'm going out to take a look."

"I'll come with you," my mother says.

"No. You need to stay here and guard the doors."

"Be careful!"

I pass through the broken door, my shotgun up to my shoulder, the tac-light on and shining. Snow is falling in big, fat white flakes.

The beam of the light illuminates bright cones of dancing flurries. Shadows scurry away, taking refuge in the trees. But the movement is all light and shadow, nothing of substance. No signs of life outside the entrance of the ER. None of the hulking gray Behemoths. No humans.

Remembering that the Demons can fly, I jerk the shotgun up to scan the dark sky. Unlike the previous nights, there's no moon. Nothing to light the way besides the beam of my flashlight.

Taking a few crunching steps through the icy snow, I check the roof of the one-story hospital building. No Demons up there, either.

Not visible ones, anyway.

But if Gaby really did hear someone, I don't think it was an alien. Aliens wouldn't use words that we can understand.

Bringing my shotgun back down, I start walking the perimeter of the building. The air is frigid, searing my face and ears. My legs are already feeling cold through my pajama bottoms, and my hands are fast turning to ice on the grip and stock of the shotgun. I'm feeling like an idiot for marching out here in the snow to chase a kid's hallucination.

I decide to walk once around the building, just to say I did it. Following the square, straight edges of the walls, and wading through snow drifts and snow-covered bushes, I notice that there's no light leaking out from any of the windows. For all anyone would know, the hospital is abandoned. At least Doctor Turner has been careful. The ER treatment area doesn't have any windows, so the lights we turned on in there aren't drawing any unwanted attention to us.

I check each of the windows and the emergency exits as I walk by. There's no sign of break-ins. The doors are all sealed and locked.

I reach the far back corner of the hospital, slow down, and peek around the edge. There's no sign of life around here, either.

Definitely hallucinations. Even if there was something out here, there's no way that Gaby heard it from all the way inside. Walking faster now, I'm motivated by the thought of getting back inside where it's warm. I'm halfway down the back of the hospital when I hear the *boom* of a shotgun going off, followed by a scream.

That was my mother.

I try to break into a sprint, but the deep snow around the back of the hospital sucks my boots in deep and doesn't want to let go. Each lunging step takes precious seconds to extract. I'm wading through the snow like it's deep water.

Another *boom* shatters the night, and I hear a distant hooting sound, echoing through the trees. Alien monsters calling to each other. It's the Behemoths. They heard the gunfire and now they're letting each other know.

Fuck.

Another shotgun shell explodes.

I pull away from the eaves to get out of the snow drifts and run down the other side of the hospital. It takes me just a few seconds to arrive. I see my mother standing out front, her shotgun up and aimed at the trees on the other side of the parking lot, a cone of falling snow illuminated by the tac-light under the barrel.

I reach her side, coughing from the cold and seeing spots from the sudden exertion. But that's all I'm seeing. There's no sign of whatever my mother was shooting at.

"What's going on?" I hear Bree call to us from the waiting room.

Glancing over my shoulder, I can see her and Jessica Pearson both standing in the shadows, peering out at us.

Rather than answer, I'm scanning the trees with my mother for signs of whatever she was shooting at.

"What happened?" I manage to whisper between gasps for air.

"I saw something moving," she whispers back in a shaky voice. "Over there."

She points with the barrel of her gun to the trees. Keeping my shotgun aimed in the same direction, I cross the parking lot to see if anything is hiding in those shadows.

Gray and brown tree trunks. Green, snow-laden branches. But no sign of—

A glimmer of something catches my eye. A scrap of reflective black material that doesn't look at all like tree bark.

And then it steps into view, and I come face to face with a red-eyed creature wearing a shiny black ski jacket. It's holding a sleek, long-barreled black pistol, aimed straight at my chest.

I dive to one side just as emerald fire erupts from the barrel. Then I scramble into cover behind the nearest tree.

"Chris!" my mother calls to me.

"Don't shoot!" I call back, thinking that she'll hit me if she does.

Peeking around the trunk of the tree, I catch a glimpse of whatever-it-was dashing through a hedge between me and the street. I take aim with my own shotgun, but can't get a clear shot through the trees and bushes. The creature vanishes in a matching hedge on the other side of the street, and I relax my aim.

My brain takes a second to catch up. That wasn't one of the short, crouching winged aliens. It was a fully erect humanoid wearing blue jeans and a black ski jacket. The jacket was open, the white shirt underneath torn and blood-stained. Chalk-white skin, red eyes, four short snake-like appendages terminating in cone-shaped openings above its bald, bony head. The attacker was thoroughly alien, but given what it was wearing, there's no question about who it actually was.

Turning around, I sprint across the parking lot to my mother. Bree and Jessica are both there, standing behind her.

"What was it?" Bree asks.

"Bret," I say. "Or it used to be, anyway."

CHAPTER 34

Back inside, I hurry through the swinging doors to the treatment area. Gaby watches me with bright alien eyes as I stride in.

"What happened?" she asks. "I heard you shooting."

"Nothing, sweetheart." A glance at my daughter sends an electric jolt through my system. She looks exactly like Bret, with the exception of those four flexible stalks rising above her head. She has four lumps instead. I wonder how long before they emerge.

Doctor Turner steps out from where she was hiding with my son behind the curtains in one of the other cubicles.

Footsteps echo after mine, I glance back to see both Bree and Jessica following me.

Niles shrieks and strains against his cable ties, tendons standing out on his neck as he fights senselessly against his restraints. He's drooling all over himself. His bloodshot eyes track me across the room, as if he's slavering at the thought of sinking his teeth into warm flesh. *My* flesh. He's reached the delirious, violent stage. If his symptoms keep following Gaby's, in a few more hours he'll be vomiting, and then lucid.

But changed. Just like my daughter. And Bret.

Reaching my bed, two over from Gaby's and across the room from Niles, I bend down to rummage through the gun bag. It's time to get everyone armed. Pulling out the alien plasma weapon and its holster, I set that on the floor beside me. The Army vest is here, along with the E9 rifle and the ID chip that I taped to the rifle's grip when Niles got bitten.

I hesitate, waffling between the awkward anatomy of the plasma gun and the more familiar rifle.

Bree stops right behind me, and Zach comes running over, but Bree stops him with an upraised hand. "My suit could be contaminated," she explains. He nods and runs to my mother instead.

Jessica and my mother are both standing two steps back from Bree. My mother has her shotgun half-raised and aimed at the doors to the waiting room. I wonder if Jessica's kids are still hiding in the maternity wing on the other side of the hospital, and why everyone thought it was a good idea to leave the broken entrance of the ER unguarded.

"What if he comes back?" Bree asks me.

"It's not *him* that I'm worried about," I say.

"Then who?"

Rather than tell her about the alien hooting noises I heard after my mother fired her shotgun, I reach into the bag for the Glock, eject the magazine to check that it's full, then pass it to my wife. She hesitates. I gesture for her to accept it, then I get it. She won't be able to handle a gun very easily in the hazmat suit. Not to mention those suits cut peripheral vision down to almost nothing.

I pass the sidearm to Jessica instead.

"You know how to use it?" I ask before letting go.

"Point and shoot, right?"

I grimace at the simplification. "The only safety is the trigger itself, so don't touch it unless you mean to shoot whatever you're pointing at."

Jessica nods woodenly as she takes the weapon from me and holds it in an awkward two-handed grip with the muzzle aimed straight up at the ceiling, like she's some kind of spy. At least she's not waving it around carelessly. But I still correct her.

"Muzzle down, toward the floor. If you do fire it by mistake, you'd rather lose a toe than your head. Or someone else's."

She gives me a dark look, but complies, lowering the weapon.

Doctor Turner joins us, looking shaken inside her bulky yellow suit. "What did you see out there?"

"Another experiment." I nod to Gaby. "He

looked just like her, but farther along in his transformation."

Doctor Turner nods back.

"We were staying in a house with him up on Eagle Drive," I add. "The Demons took him when they took Gaby."

"Demons?" Doctor Turner asks.

"The flying ones."

She nods again.

"Anyway, he was using one of *their* weapons."

Bree blinks at me. "You think he took it when he escaped?"

"Maybe." I spend a few seconds studying her through a frown. "Or maybe he was released and they gave him that gun for a reason. Either way, we all need to be armed, so you should get out of that suit."

"Let me help you," Doctor Turner says, and Bree turns so that she can start undoing magnetic clasps and Velcro seals.

Taking the moment while they're busy, I put the Army vest on over my jacket, then clip the rifle to it. Between that and the shotgun, I should be good, but the plasma weapon is harder to use, so I can't give that to Bree. She should take the shotgun while I use the alien weapon. Strapping the alien holster awkwardly over my vest, I tie the thick padded gray straps around my torso in two different places.

As soon as Bree is out of her hazmat suit, I hand her the shotgun. Reaching into my jacket pocket, I divide the spare shells between her and my mother.

Now all of us are armed. All except for Doctor Turner. I look at her, and she shakes her head.

"I've repaired enough gunshot wounds to never want to be the one pulling the trigger."

"Not even if your life depends on it?"

"Not even then."

She's one of those people—hates guns on principle. On a good day, I can respect that, but an honest-to-God alien invasion ought to be enough to bend those rules.

Rather than try to argue with her, I say, "You can take a flashlight." Dropping back down to the bag, I grab one of the two flashlights and toss it to her. I keep the other for myself. Bree and my mother have the tac-lights, and I'll need to see what I'm shooting at somehow. Realizing that I can't handle both the flashlight and the plasma weapon at the same time, I find another roll of surgical tape and use that to tie the flashlight on below the barrel of the alien weapon. A bit awkward, but it will do.

"All of this for one escaped patient?" Doctor Turner asks, glancing around at each of us.

Now is probably time to warn them about what we're really up against. "It's not for him. You remember the four-legged ones?"

Doctor Turner nods, her brown eyes wide behind her helmet. My wife grows pale, and my mother glances back at us. "Is that what that sound was?" she asks.

I nod. "They heard you shooting, and they started calling to each other. They could be here any second."

CHAPTER 35

"**A**re there any other entrances besides the ER?" I ask Doctor Turner.

"Only the emergency exits," she says.

"Good. Okay..." My thoughts are racing as I try to figure out how best to secure this building from an unknown number of those rhino-sized Behemoths. Two shotgun blasts at point-blank to take one down. But they had guns. What if this time they decide to use them? We don't even know how many could be coming. "Jessica, your kids are safe?"

She flinches and glances behind her, as if only now remembering that she left them alone.

"I'm sure they're fine," I add, striding past her with the plasma gun. I'm heading for the doors to the waiting room. "We would have heard them otherwise." I don't add that Niles and I heard nothing when they took Gaby.

Pushing partway through one of the two doors, I use it to cover me as I peek into the waiting room, sweeping the shadows with the flashlight taped to my weapon. Cold air swirls into the treatment area. No sign of anything in the darkened waiting room. I push the rest of the way through. "Bree, Mom, watch the entrance. One on either side," I add, sparing a hand from my weapon to point at the broken doors. "Stay behind cover as much as possible."

"What about Zach?" Bree asks.

"I'll take him to the Pearson kids. They'll be easier to protect if they're all in the same place."

"Okay," Bree says, and then the two most important women in my life go running to the entrance. Turning to my son and Jessica next, I notice that Doctor Turner has also followed us. She's flicking her flashlight around, the beam jittering as her hands shake. "Doctor, you lead the way."

"Where?"

"Maternity."

"Of course."

She nods and starts across the waiting room to a matching set of swinging doors on the other side. I keep pace with her.

Zach and Jessica follow us. I shine my light into the shadowy alcoves to the bathrooms and the empty space behind the reception desk. No sign of anything or anyone skulking in here. So far so good. There's a small chance that while we were busy arming ourselves, Bret might have realized we left the front entrance unguarded and snuck in through the broken door.

If he did, there's only a few places he could

hide. Inside the bathrooms. And through here, on the other side of the hospital. We're in front of the maternity wing doors and Doctor Turner has a hand up, ready to open them.

I take a quick step to get in front of her and shake my head. "Wait here," I say. I need to clear those bathrooms before we go anywhere.

Pushing through the door to the men's room first, I aim straight down to the end. The restroom is arranged in a typical hallway configuration: sinks to my left by the door. Four stalls further down, urinals opposite them on the right, and a small window at the end.

Clear so far. I move past the sinks, kicking open the stalls one at a time. First one—clear. Second one—clear.

Third one—

A guttural roar is my only warning before the stall at the end bursts open, and a pale-faced monster rushes out. I bring the plasma gun around just in time for it to be ripped out of my hands. The light goes with it, and I go stumbling backward through near perfect darkness, wrestling with a red-eyed monster that looks just like an adult version of Gaby.

Spittle gleams on Bret's black lips. He bares his teeth, hissing at me. I can feel sharp nails digging through my coat. He has both of my arms clutched in his, making it impossible to reach for the rifle clipped to my vest. He backs me up against the door to the men's room just as it starts swinging open.

"Chris!"

Bree's voice.

"I found him!" I grit out, while struggling to free even one of my arms. Bret is wickedly strong. I can bench three hundred pounds, but somehow this guy, who's probably never seen a gym in his life, is actually stronger than me.

The door behind me bumps against my back as Bree tries to force it open. Bret slams me against it, and the back of my head makes a re-sounding *boom* against the hollow metal door. Dazed, I try again to free my arms, but the opposite happens. He's forcing them up beside my head, and snapping teeth are inching closer to my throat. Is he still in the violent delirious stage? Wasn't he firing a gun at me earlier?

He grins at me, and I could swear that his teeth are sharper than a human's should be. "I am the future," he says. "Take a good look."

"Fuck the future," I say. And then I bring one of my knees up into his gut as hard as I can. The air leaves his lungs in a rancid whoosh that makes me wonder if he's already been dining on raw meat.

He eases up, just enough that I'm able to wrench one of my hands free. Rather than reach for the rifle, I deliver a ham-fisted right hook to Bret's jaw. His teeth clap together loudly, and he stumbles back a step, releasing my other wrist. Now I go for the rifle. He dives for the floor, and reaches to a holster on his hip.

Too slow. I pull the trigger and a deafening crack sounds. The muzzle flash dazzles my eyes in the darkness. Bret cries out and struggles to bring his alien sidearm into line with my chest. I take a quick step forward and kick it out of his hand. The weapon goes skittering across the floor.

The door bursts open behind me, and my wife rushes in with the shotgun aimed at Bret's chest. The tac-light illuminates him fully, and she sucks in a quick breath.

Bret grins up at us, his teeth smeared black with the blood of an alien hybrid.

There's a small pool of it below his lower abdomen where I shot him. He's lying on his side, clutching the wound.

"You fools," he says. "You can't fight us. They'll kill you all for resisting the occupation."

Bree and I trade glances with each other. I notice Jessica standing with Doctor Turner in the open door to the men's room.

"Is everything okay?" my mother calls from the doors to the ER.

"Just fine," I call back.

"What do you mean, *us*?" Bree asks. "Who is us?"

"The Chimeras," he says. "Others like me and your daughter."

"There are more of you?"

"Of course. Soon there will be millions of us."

"Millions?" Bree asks in a trembling voice.

"So this is why they came?" I ask him. "To turn us into hybrids? What for?"

Bret pushed himself up to a sitting position, and I'm shocked to see that his gunshot wound has already stopped bleeding. He's in remarkably good shape to have been shot by an E9 rifle at point-blank range. Add enhanced healing to inhuman strength. The invaders are definitely making a few improvements to our natural physiology.

"I didn't understand either," Bret says. "I was like you, ignorant and stupid. Until they explained to me my purpose."

"And what exactly is that purpose?" Jessica asks.

"To keep the peace while the Kyra rebuild our cities. And to help them recruit new conscripts for the Kyron Guard."

I shake my head. "The guard?"

"Their military," Bret says. "The Kyra are at war. They need more soldiers. That is why they came."

I take a few seconds to process these revelations, but something still doesn't fit with what Bret is saying. "They took my daughter. She's six. What good is a six-year-old in a fight?"

"She has another purpose."

I take a quick step toward Bret, hefting my rifle higher and aiming it at his head. Enhanced healing be damned. Let's see him survive a bullet

between the eyes. "What purpose?"
"To breed more soldiers."

CHAPTER 36

I almost pull the trigger right then and there. "To *breed?* She's *six,*" I grit out.

Bret grins and lets out a hissing laugh. "Not *now* you stupid *Dakka.* When she comes of age. If it works, she will be among the first of a new caste of Chimeras. A ruling caste of K'sari. The others are all sterile because of the virus, but some of the Kyra believe that turning your species before you reach maturity is the key to retaining your fertility. Time will tell."

"What is your name?" I ask. Maybe I can settle the question of whether or not a person's personality and memories remain intact after the virus changes them.

"My name is Bret Anderson Wallace," he says.

At least he remembers that much. But the agenda he's espousing is not his own, so to some extent he was definitely brainwashed.

"We need to tie him up," Bree whispers.

"We have more zip ties in the treatment room," Doctor Turner says from the door.

"Go get them," I say.

"I'll go with you," Bree adds, and both their flashlights vanish.

Shadows come racing back in, but the light pooling beneath the plasma weapon that Bret tore out of my hands is enough to see the dark outline of his body, and the gleam of his eyes and teeth. I keep my aim and my gaze fixed on the smugly grinning alien hybrid in front of me. He was a psycho killer even before the invaders changed his appearance to match.

"I'm going to check on my kids," Jessica says.

"Take Zach with you," I add, thinking that we've neutralized the immediate threat.

"Okay," Jessica confirms.

If those Behemoths come charging in, I don't want my son standing around in the waiting room, right in the line of fire.

"How do you know all of this?" I ask Bret. "The Demons told you?"

"Not in so many words. The Kyra put a brain scanner on my head. They used it to teach me their language and to learn ours. They know everything that I do now. It's how they're learning about us."

"So they know that you killed the people in that house? They know that you're a murderer?" Even as I ask that, I wonder if it will matter to them.

Bret cocks his head curiously at me. "You thought that was me? I'm not a killer."

That provokes a derisive snort from me.

"Yeah, I read the note you left for us on the mirror."

"And you didn't believe it? Oh, I see, you thought I was crazy."

"If the shoe fits. Why write that on the mirror if it wasn't you? Who were you trying to convince? Yourself?"

Bret's grin vanishes. "I found them like that," he says, dodging my question. "With their throats slit from ear to ear. The Kyra have no use for old people. They can't breed, and they're not worth the time and training it takes to make them into soldiers. The Kyra consider them a waste of resources."

I wonder what that will mean for my mother. Are the invaders actively exterminating anyone who's past their childbearing years?

Hurried footfalls interrupt our conversation. I start to turn toward the sound, then catch myself. Too late. Bret is lunging for the plasma rifle by the urinals.

I don't even hesitate before pulling the trigger, and this time the bullet goes straight through his heart. Bret collapses and jerks a few times before lying still.

A wash of regret courses through me, mostly because he was giving me good intel, and now he can't.

The door behind me bursts open, and I turn to see Bree standing there with Doctor Turner. My mother is standing right behind them, looking terrified.

"Chris!" Bree says in a sharp whisper. "They took her. Gaby is missing, and so is Niles."

CHAPTER 37

"**T**hey didn't go out the front. I was watching the doors the whole time," my mother says as I recover the plasma weapon and clip the rifle to my vest once more.

Doctor Turner is staring at Bret's dead body, her eyes wide. "You killed him," she says in a flat voice.

I don't have time to explain myself. I stop in front of her. "What about the emergency exits? How many are there?"

"Three."

"That's probably where they're headed. Come on!" I do a quick check of the waiting room as I run through it, but there's no sign of anyone in here other than us.

My gaze stops on the doors to the maternity wing, and I freeze in my tracks, remembering that Zach and the Pearson kids are hiding somewhere through there. "We should split up. We'll be able to search faster like that. Mom, go with Bree, check the maternity wing and the exits on that side. Doc, you're with me."

"Be careful," Bree says.

"You, too," I reply.

And then we each run for our respective doors, our flashlights and tac-lights bobbing in the dark.

I wish our ARCs and comms were still working so we could use them to keep in touch while we're split up like this.

Reaching the doors to the treatment area, I push through one of them and aim my plasma gun around the edge as I do so, using the door for cover.

"Clear," I whisper for Doctor Turner's benefit.

It's just like she said. Niles and Gaby are both missing.

Seeing no sign of any potential threats, I run through the room, glancing at the gun bag near Gaby's bed as I go. I remember the bolt action rifle that should still be in there. Maybe Niles is already past the delirious stage of the infection, and like Bret, he's working for the Kyra now.

Would he have taken a gun?

I detour to confirm the rifle is still in the bag, then move through the room as quickly as I dare, clearing each curtained cubicle along the way.

"We already checked everywhere in here," Doctor Turner says after I throw the curtains aside in two of the cubicles.

Something could have come in here to hide while we were distracted with Bret. We need to hurry if we're going to find Gaby before the

Kyra can take her back to one of those invisible landers.

I reach the doors at the far end of the room and repeat the process of shielding myself with the door as I push through. The darkened corridor on the other side is empty.

I run through with Doctor Turner. A glowing red EXIT sign lights the far end of the corridor. I sprint down the corridor to the end, heedless that there could be any number of hostiles hiding behind the doors flashing by on either side of me.

I hear Doctor Turner's footsteps echoing after mine. Reaching the exit, I slam into the push bar—

And only manage to open the door about two feet. There's a snow drift on the other side. Scanning the snow with the tac-light, I check for footprints that could belong to Gaby, Niles, or one of the Kyra with their skinny, taloned feet.

But the only footprints I see are mine from earlier when I was running around the perimeter.

Pulling the door shut, I look to Doctor Turner. "Where's the next exit?"

She nods to another crimson EXIT sign blazing at the end of the hallway to my left. Bobbing flashlights arrive just before two familiar-looking shadows push that door open.

"Anything?" I call to them. "Look for footprints!"

"I can see…" Bree trails off. "One set of boot prints!"

"Those are mine. Anything else?"

"No!"

Bree and my mother come running to join us on our side of the hospital.

"You checked the other exit?" Doctor Turner asks them.

"Yes," Bree says between gasps for air. "No sign that anything went out there, either."

"What does that mean?" my mother asks.

My gaze is locked on the swinging doors to the treatment area where we came from. "Either they're still in here or they went out the front."

"But we came from there," Bree says. "Wouldn't we have seen them trying to sneak by us?"

"Hopefully," I agree. I don't add that if they did get by us, they're probably boarding one of those invisible landers now, and we're never going to find Gaby after that.

CHAPTER 38

Doctor Turner says, "Your daughter was lucid, so she would have put up a struggle if someone tried to take her, and Niles was completely out of it. He would have attacked anyone who came near. The only way to get them both out of the room without us hearing would be to somehow incapacitate them and then drag them out."

"Last time they stunned everyone in order to take Gaby."

"How far would one of those little winged ones get dragging or carrying two people?" Doctor Turner asks. "That's a lot of dead weight."

She makes a good point.

"We need to check all the rooms in this corridor," I say in a whisper. "Is Zach safe?"

Bree nods. "He's locked in a recovery room with the Pearsons."

"Good." A locked door probably isn't much of a deterrent, but it's better than nothing. "Bree, Mom, you take the rooms on the right. We'll take the ones on the left."

"Wait," Doctor Turner says.

I stop with my hand on the knob of the first door. "Someone needs to stay in the corridor to make sure nothing sneaks out of the other rooms while we're searching."

"Sounds like a good job for you," I say. "Shout if you see anything."

"But you said they could be invisible. How will I know if I see something?"

"It or *they* came for Gaby and Niles, right? It's not going to leave without them, so unless they're invisible, too..." I let her fill in the rest for herself.

Doctor Turner's chin dips in a shallow nod. She doesn't look reassured. Probably because she's figured out that an invisible adversary could also pick us all off at its leisure and then take Gaby and Niles out once there's no one left to stop it.

I open my door. It groans on old hinges in need of oil. My tac-light flickers over stainless steel counters arranged in two rows. There's lab equipment on those counter tops—microscopes, glass beakers and vials. Cabinets line the walls, but none are big enough to hide a person, let alone two and one or more aliens.

Shadows shift and swirl through the room, fleeing under the counter tops and scurrying into corners. There's nowhere that anything could hide in here. Not without the advantage of invisibility, anyway.

I shut the door to this room and move to the next one. Bree and my mother are busy doing the same on the other side of the corridor.

This time I read the sign on the door.

Radiology.

Turning the handle, I pop the door open to see a big X-ray machine, a bed, several holo-screens and projectors. Lead vests hang along one wall.

There's more room to hide in here, with all of these big machines, but I should at least be able to spot a foot or an arm sticking out. I'm assuming that Gaby and Niles are both unconscious and have been dragged into a corner somewhere. Just to be sure, I actually go into this room and walk a quick circle around the equipment in the center of the space. Nothing.

My mind wanders: how long does it take to recover from a stun bolt? Our stun guns are all electrical, and recovery is usually measured in seconds, but the alien version seems to last at least a few minutes. My best guess is maybe ten or fifteen, based on how long it took before Bree stumbled out of that lake house to ask where Gaby was.

I shake my head and get back on task. The radiology room is clear, so I head for the open door to the corridor.

I reach it just in time to hear a startled scream, followed by a *thud.*

My heart slams in my chest. I check the corridor in both directions, with the plasma gun braced against my shoulder. I have both fingers wrapped around the alien trigger, ready to unleash hell.

But I'm too late. There's nothing here, and Doctor Turner is on the ground. Her flashlight rolls to a stop by her feet.

Bree and my mother emerge from a door six feet down and across from mine.

"What happened?!" Bree asks as she runs over and drops to her haunches beside the doctor. I'm back to scanning both sides of the corridor, my eyes wide and burning with the need to blink, but I force them to stay open. I can't afford to miss any movement.

"Doctor!" Bree says, shaking her.

My mother stands guard with me, also scanning for targets.

"It has to be invisible," I whisper.

"Is she dead?" my mother asks.

"I can't see... there's no sign of an entry wound."

"It stunned her?" I ask.

"I think so," Bree replies.

"It doesn't want to kill us," my mother says, as if that means it might be friendly.

"Let's not make any assumptions," I say.

"It could pick the rest of us off right now if it wanted to," my mother goes on. "So why doesn't it just keep shooting?"

"Maybe because we'll see where the shots

come from and shoot back. It's just being cautious."

Bree looks up from examining the doctor. "We need to get her someplace safe."

I shake my head. "If they'd wanted her dead, she would be. We need to finish searching the other rooms."

"There are three doors left," my mother says.

A loud hooting sound draws our attention to the treatment room.

"What was that?" Bree whispers.

"Reinforcements. We'd better hurry. Stick together and watch each other's backs. On me." With that, I hurry to the next door in line and rip it open.

CHAPTER 39

Bree and I quickly clear the next room together, leaving my mother by the door to watch our backs. I make sure to keep her in sight, but she has the sense to close the door and watch the corridor through the square window at the top.

It only takes a second for me to recognize where we are. This is a pharmacy. There are three aisles of medications behind the counter. A few fridges sit around with soda and bottled water in them. Aisles stacked with junk food, diapers, wipes, and vitamins. A cash register.

Finding a low door beside the cash register, I step over it and hurry down the first aisle. It's clear. Peeking around the back of it, I see Niles unconscious and propped up against the racks of medicine. One aisle over, Gaby is lying on her side, curled into a fetal position.

"Bree!" I call as loudly as I dare. "I found them!"

Stepping over Niles I rush to Gaby's side and begin slapping her cheek lightly to wake her. "Gaby!" I say.

She stirs and moans, mumbling something between her black lips.

Bree arrives and falls on her knees next to us. "Is she okay?"

I nod quickly, even though I have no clue.

Setting my weapon down, I scoop Gaby into my arms. Her eyelids flicker with that movement. Then bright crimson eyes flare wide, and she sits up suddenly. "Where am I?" She glances around quickly, alarm registering on her alien features.

"It's okay," Bree says, rubbing Gaby's arms. "You're safe."

I see tears sparkling in my daughter's eyes, and they course swiftly down her cheeks as she tucks her head against my chest. She lets out a stifled sob.

This is still my little girl. No matter how she looks and sounds. It's still her. Maybe the Kyra didn't have time to warp her mind and reprogram her to pursue their agenda like they did with Bret.

Another hooting call catches my ear, and this time I hear heavy, plodding footsteps to accompany it. I stand up quickly, and grab my plasma weapon again, leaving Gaby to stand on her own two feet.

"What was that?" she asks in a quavering voice that is still a full octave lower than it should be.

Rather than risk a reply, I hurry down the

aisle and step over the door and around the counter to join my mother by the door. She has her back planted to it, her eyes wide and terrified. She's sunk down to a crouch to keep out of sight of the window at the top.

I can hear those heavy, plodding footsteps more clearly now. At least two Behemoths are outside, walking down the corridor.

Shit. Doctor Turner is out there. Bree was right. We should have at least dragged her into one of these rooms.

And then the thudding footfalls stop, right outside the door. My mother's eyes fly wide and she looks like she's just about to jump up and start shooting.

I give my head a shake and hold a finger to my lips. Maybe they know we're in here, maybe they don't.

I hear another alien hoot, but this time there's more nuance to it. The sound modulates up and down, interrupted by guttural growls and snarls. Then it pauses, and a similar voice replies with more hooting. It's an alien language. If bears and geese could talk, this is what it would sound like.

Then comes a third voice, but this one is completely different: deep and husky, it's a chattering mixture of shrieks, hisses, and growls. Despite those discordant sounds, it has an almost musical, sing-song quality to it. Like a broken flute.

My mother is visibly shaking now, and the pump action of her shotgun is rattling.

My hand snaps out to silence it.

A strident shriek issues just outside the door, as if someone heard us and said: "I found them!"

But I'm positive that they already knew we're in here.

I gesture hurriedly for my mother to come away from the door. She crawls over to me, then stands up with her shotgun raised and aimed from the shoulder. We're both ready and waiting to ambush anything that comes through. This is the only way into the pharmacy. There weren't any windows behind us. That's both good and bad, because it means we're trapped.

I wonder if that's why the alien dragged Gaby and Niles in here.

As bait.

I glance back to the aisles of pills and medications. Bree and Gaby haven't come to join us yet, but I'm grateful for that. It's better if we're not all in the enemy's line of fire at the same time.

But what about Niles? If he wakes up now, he could start attacking us from behind our position. He could infect any one of us just as Gaby infected him.

Another stream of hooting growls and sing-song chattering draws my attention back to the door. They definitely know we're in here, otherwise they would have moved on by now.

So why haven't they made a move?

The alien conversation stops.

And then a *human* voice emerges. Bret's voice.

That sends a jolt through my system. He's dead. I saw him die.

Didn't I?

"We do not wish to harm you," Bret says. But he sounds wrong. His voice is utterly flat and inflectionless. Almost robotic.

"Lay down your weapons. No one else needs to die."

CHAPTER 40

"**B**ret?" I ask through the door.

There comes a pause.

"No."

I trade a confused look with my mother. "Then who is this?"

"My name is Primark Turian of the Ri'ka."

Ri'ka? I mouth to my mother. "You're not one of the flying ones?"

"I have wings. And I am a Kyra. The Ri'ka is one of our castes."

"What do you want?"

"Not to harm you, do not be afraid."

My mouth twists in a derisive sneer. "I saw one of you eating a man."

"He was already dead. Why let good meat go to waste?"

A chill goes down my spine. "He was dead, because you killed him!"

"He fired on us. I had no choice. It was... *ka'vari koom.* Death of the challenger."

"If you mean us no harm, then why did you take my daughter?"

"We needed test subjects. We did not harm her. She has become a Chimeran *K'sari*. The first of a royal blood line."

"And Bret? You brainwashed him!"

"All of his memories were left intact. We did not change his identity, only added to it, giving him a purpose that he previously lacked. You are the one who harmed him, not us. Now lay down your weapons, and open the door."

I hear a few thudding footsteps, but they're not receding or approaching. It sounds as if the four-legged ones are shuffling their feet impatiently.

"What will you do if we let you in?" I ask.

"We will take your daughter, and the one she infected. They require additional testing and should be monitored for their safety and yours."

"I can't let you take either of them."

A pause.

"I am sorry we could not reach a peaceful arrangement. I will try to prevent the *Horvals* from eating you, but they can be difficult to reason with."

My whole body grows cold with that threat, and a memory flashes through my mind's eye: one of the four-legged ones taking off that soldier's head in a single bite.

Time seems to slow to a crawl. My whole body feels electric. My hands are sweating on the cold metal frame of the alien weapon in my hands. Does it have enough shots left? For all I know it's just about to run out of charge.

Rather than see the doorknob turn, I hear an alien roar, followed by a hooting cry.

"Here they come!" I shout to my mother.

And then another sound issues, this one from deeper inside the pharmacy. It's a familiar snarling shriek. My head snaps to the source just in time to see my wife and Niles collide between two aisles of medication and pills. He's reaching for her with both hands, straining with snapping jaws for her throat. They fall into the nearest aisle, sending boxes and bottles of pills flying.

Gaby leaps onto his back, clawing at him with nails that are much longer and sharper than any human's.

Niles lets out another snarling shriek as my daughter flays his back open through his jacket. And then all three of them fall over together.

My feet are already moving in their direction when the door to the pharmacy bursts open, falling inward with a *bang.* A four-legged monster pushes through with a roar, widening the opening even further with its broad shoulders. My mother and I back away hurriedly. Her shotgun explodes with a deafening *BOOM* as she takes the first shot.

The creature staggers to one side as the blast hits it square in the shoulder. Then it rounds on us, giant red eyes wide and feral with fury. Time seems to freeze. Massive jaws of jutting, interlocking teeth yawn open just three feet from us.

Hot, fetid breath washes over us. Massive legs bend at the knee, and I realize that it's just about to pounce.

I pull the trigger of my plasma gun.

And nothing happens.

CHAPTER 41

Chuk-chuk. Boom! My mother shoots the beast full in the face just as it leaps into the air. We retreat into the aisles of junk food, and the monster falls short, landing with its chin at our feet.

I toss my plasma gun aside and grab the E9 off my vest just as the next four-legged alien comes charging through.

My mother is backing up fast, struggling to reload the shotgun with shells from her pocket.

Pulling the rifle up to my shoulder, I take aim for the slavering jaws of the second Behemoth. It charges, and the throat expands as the jaws open. The gullet of the creature is big enough to swallow me whole, and lined with short triangular teeth all the way down.

I pull the trigger and a roar of bullets tears into the monster's throat, spraying black blood in all directions.

It screams, but continues on with its momentum, crashing into me. Like a raging bull, it tries to gore me with the horns on top of its head. A dozen sharp spikes pierce me through my jacket and I both hear and feel my ribs snapping as it sends me flying clear over an aisle full of chips and candy bars. My arms and legs are churning as I fall. I come down hard, catching my chin on the edge of the pharmacy counter, and then my body explodes in blinding pain as the impact disturbs my freshly broken ribs. My whole side feels hot, like it's on fire, but there's no time to lick my wounds.

"Chris! Lookout!" my mother cries.

The aisle of junk food comes crashing down toward me, and I experience a flash of bitter irony as it falls. As a kid, my mother was always warning me that junk food would kill me.

But the heavy metal aisle hits the same counter that my chin did, and stops there. Potato chips and candy bars rain over me.

Chuk-chuk. Boom! Chuk-chuk. Boom!

An alien scream shatters the air, and I hear a heavy *thud,* as the second monster falls.

But this time it's not dead. It lies thrashing and kicking the shelving unit that's leaning over me like a tent. A crumpled metal shelf slices into me and rakes fire through my thigh.

Crawling out, I narrowly escape before the monster's thrashing can crush me against the side of the pharmacy counter.

Turning on the spot, I bring my rifle up and riddle the creature with bullets. They plink off armor plates, but make meaty *thups* in the seams.

After a few seconds, my rifle is empty, and the creature is dead. Pulling a spare magazine from my vest, I eject the empty one, backpedaling and wincing from the blinding pain in my side as I reload the rifle and turn to face the broken doorway. I'm half-expecting to see a third Behemoth come charging through. But either it's too smart for that, or it's not here.

My heart slams against my sternum. Blood leaks hotly from where the Behemoth gored me. But all I can think about is that there were six monster-sized doors in the lander. We killed three at the house, and two more here. Did someone else get the sixth? I'm still wondering about that as the fresh magazine clicks into place and I pull the charging handle with a resounding *click-click* to chamber the first cartridge.

Silence rings in the wake of that sound. I glance at my mother in the dark. My rifle doesn't have a flashlight attached like the plasma gun that I discarded, so all I can see is the barest hint of her features illuminated in the reflected glow of the tac-light on her shotgun.

"Where's the one we were talking to?" she whispers to me.

"Chris..." Bree's voice is shaking. Terrified.

Horror grips me. The last I saw, she and Gaby were struggling to hold off Niles. My whole body tenses up, and another wave of blinding pain washes over me from my broken ribs as I turn in the direction of her voice.

Bree stands rigidly behind the counter, her chin up to expose her throat. As I watch, a glistening line of blood appears, inching slowly toward her jugular vein. Bree cries out in pain, and I strain to reach her, crippled by my own wounds and screaming, "No!"

Bret's voice slithers out of darkness, sounding far too calm and reasonable: "Drop your weapons, or she dies."

CHAPTER 42

My rifle is aimed into darkness over Bree's right shoulder, exactly where I imagine an invisible alien would have to be holding her in order to cut her throat like that. But then I remember that the winged ones stand barely five feet high. It must be hidden perfectly behind Bree. There's no way to shoot it without also shooting her. She isn't bleeding too profusely, not yet, but the cut ended right before her carotid artery.

"Lower your weapons," Bret's voice instructs.

"Please," my mother sobs. "Don't. She has children."

"Weapons on the floor," the invisible alien insists.

My mind races for some way to avoid surrendering, but Gaby and Niles are both lying motionless on the floor. It must have stunned them while we weren't looking. Either that, or...

I try not to finish that thought.

The beam of the tac-light shivers, then falls away from Bree's face as my mother sets her shotgun down.

"Okay," I say, and turn my rifle on its side, realizing that this creature is still waiting for my response. "Don't hurt her."

I see Bree swallow, her eyes agleam, brimming with tears. "Don't," she pleads with me. Her head is still frozen in the same position, chin up, throat exposed, blood trickling down to her collarbone. "Don't let it take her. Shoot me."

I hesitate, and an irritated hiss fills the silence. Before I can reassure the alien holding my wife that I'm not going to shoot through her to get at it, I see Bree stagger forward with one hand clutching her throat, the other planted on the counter top for support.

My heart leaps inside my chest, dread slicing through me. But rather than a river of blood cascading between Bree's fingers, I see that it's still only a trickle. The Demon didn't kill her, even though it could have.

I sweep my rifle around in the dark, eyes straining for the unseeable, ears keening for the slightest sound.

The tac-light bobs back up as my mother retrieves the shotgun, and suddenly I can see again.

I pull the trigger, aiming through empty space to the end of the aisle.

The bullet cracks out, but there's no reaction. No alien cry of pain. Just the crunch of the bullet tearing through the far wall.

Adjusting my aim a few degrees to one side, I

try again. The bullet scatters boxes of medication on the shelves and plinks off the metal rack.

"I'll use the shotgun! Get down, Bree!" my mother says. She ducks down behind the counter.

"Don't!" I cry. "You could hit Gaby!"

But before my mother can either pull the trigger or acknowledge my concern, there comes a sharp crackling sound and a bright flash of light dazzles my eyes. I hear a crash and turn to see my mother lying on the ground.

I duck down beside her just as a second bolt tears out of darkness and lances over my head.

Aiming in the same direction, I squeeze off a brief torrent of fire. Bullets plink off racks of pills and scatter more boxes, but again, there's no reaction from my invisible enemy.

Realizing that I'm a sitting duck, I pull myself over the dead Behemoths. Their bulk provides shelter while I awkwardly position myself behind the overturned aisle of junk food.

"Bree, get out of there!" I cry.

Another crackling report shatters the silence with a bright flash of light, and I hear a second *thud* as my wife collapses on the floor.

Shit.

Pain pulses through my broken ribs like fireworks going off inside of me. I'm nauseated and dizzy from the injuries, but I grit my teeth to force the feelings aside. Can't pass out now. If I do, I'll never see Gaby again.

Gritting my teeth and flexing my hands on my rifle, I prepare to twist out of cover and spray the room with bullets in one final attempt to hit the Demon.

Before I can so much as twitch, a shrill cry comes from the direction of the shattered doorway. A canary yellow flash tears through, illuminated briefly by the beam of the tac-light still shining from my mother's shotgun. Doctor Turner leaps over the other dead Behemoth. Rather than a flashlight or a gun, she's holding a familiar red cylinder in both arms.

I watch as she holds out the nozzle and then sprays the room with a roar of white smoke.

Realizing what she's doing, and why, I ease out of cover, forcing my muscles to move against the agony in my ribs. My rifle is up and tracking.

There he is, the little fucker: standing right on top of the pharmacy counter, down at the far end by the door. I aim at the ghostly shadow and hold the trigger down. Bullets roar out in a steady stream, alternately crunching through the creature's armor and plinking off as they ricochet around.

Doctor Turner is still screaming as she drenches the thing in a thick coating of fire retardant.

I watch it sink to its knees under a hail of bullets and smoke. The air shimmers, and then comes a *pop* as something gives way. The creature face plants on the counter top and then lies still.

I release the trigger and stare fixedly at it, half-expecting it to get up, or for a second one to start shooting at us from the shadows.

Silence rages.

The smoke clears.

Doctor Turner sets down her fire extinguisher and pulls the flashlight I gave her from an external pocket. She flicks it on to study the creature.

"Is it dead?" she whispers.

I say nothing, keeping my aim steady on its dust-covered armor as I walk a stumbling path through empty shell casings and scattered junk food to get a closer look.

CHAPTER 43

I poke the alien in the back with the barrel of my rifle. One of its wings pops out of a bulky section of its armor and drapes the side of the counter top. Some of the powder from the fire extinguisher falls off, revealing matte black armor underneath.

"Hey!" I snap at it in a sharp whisper, and then jab it again. I remember these things have shields. That plus the armor makes me wonder if it's only pretending to be dead.

But again, the alien doesn't stir. Maybe it's not playing.

"Keep an eye on it," I say, glancing at Doctor Turner. She nods inside her suit. I shuffle back the other way, taking my time as I climb over the low wall to get to Bree. My side is on fire and I can feel my broken ribs grinding together. I have to force myself not to puke from the pain, and wonder how long I'm going to last before passing out from exhaustion and shock.

Bree is collapsed on the other side of the counter top. I hold myself up with one hand on the counter and reach down to shake her. When that doesn't rouse her, I call out, "I need the light!"

Doctor Turner comes over, and I check Bree's clothes for signs of entry wounds, laser burns, blood...

But the only injury she has is the cut across her throat which isn't actually very deep.

The Kyra wasn't lying. It didn't want to hurt us. Its weapon was set to stun.

I glance back at it, my brow tense with confusion. Even if it didn't directly try to kill us, it sent those Behemoths in, and I don't doubt that they would have torn us to shreds in a heartbeat.

My side is still pulsing with agony. But there's no time to deal with that now.

"Help me get her up," I say. "I need to go check on Gaby."

I move to the two dark shadows on the floor, and slowly crouch beside the smaller one. I clip the rifle to my vest so I can pick her up, then realize too late that it's not going to happen. Her weight combined with my injuries sends me staggering into one of the medicine racks. My thigh is on fire now, too, reminding me of the gash that the rack of junk food tore through my pajamas.

I manage to get Gaby over my shoulder on my good side, but I have to use both arms to hold her steady and not strain my broken ribs. It takes every ounce of will not to succumb to the wracking waves of pain.

"Hello?" a trembling voice calls from the doorway.

I turn with Gaby over my shoulder to see another flashlight beaming at us from the entrance of the pharmacy. It's Jessica.

"Are the kids okay?" I call to her.

"Y-yes. What..." Jessica trails off in muffled cursing. "Help Doctor Turner with Bree!" I call out to her. Crunching over boxes of pills, I carry Gaby back to where her mother is lying. "We need to get them out of here."

Jessica stumbles over the dead alien in the doorway to join Doctor Turner. They pocket their flashlights and manage to wrestle my wife up between the two of them. Grunting and panting, they carry her over the low door. I'm right behind them, but I'll never make it over with Gaby.

Doctor Turner realizes my predicament. She leaves Jessica holding Bree on her own, and comes to take Gaby from me. I sit on the top of the low door and carefully maneuver my legs over one at a time. Then I take Gaby back and Doctor Turner goes to help Jessica with my wife.

I spare a glance at my mother, who I haven't checked on yet. She's lying peacefully on a bed of diapers, wipes, and feminine products.

We don't have hands to spare, but I quietly vow to come back for her as soon as I can.

"Where is Niles?" Jessica asks between gasps for air as we carry Bree and Gaby across the hall to the next closest room.

I don't have the energy for a reply. The room we stumble into is a cafeteria. We lay my wife and daughter out on the tables, and I conduct another examination, checking for injuries while Doctor Turner shines the light.

"They both look fine," I say through a relieved sigh that makes me feel like I'm either going to throw up or pass out. I plant both palms on the nearest table to steady myself.

"But you're not," Doctor Turner says. "You're bleeding through your coat!"

"I'm okay," I mumble.

"You're going to bleed out if I don't do something."

"Where is Niles?" Jessica asks again.

"He's..."

An inhuman shriek splits the air, followed by the sound of pill boxes scattering. Adrenaline floods my system once more and I turn back the way we came with my rifle gripped tightly in both hands.

"Chris, wait!" Doctor Turner calls to me. Her flashlight bobs along in my wake, flickering off the walls and floor.

I reach the door to the cafeteria just in time to see Niles go streaking out of the pharmacy. He didn't see me. He's running for his life, heading straight for the emergency exit. I take aim at his back, then stop myself. I can't shoot him.

Running back into the pharmacy, I cast about

blindly for whatever that alien was using to stun us.

"Where is it?" I cry.

"Where is what?" Doctor Turner asks.

My eyes seize on a long-barreled black pistol, and I bend down with a gasp to snatch it off the floor. My finger finds the trigger quickly enough. Stumbling back out into the corridor, I take aim at Niles' dark, retreating form—

I pull the trigger with a crackling report. The bright blue-white flash of light dazzles my eyes, making it hard to see whether I hit him or not.

Doctor Turner's flashlight shines down to the end of the hall, and my vision clears in the same instant.

I'm just in time to see the emergency exit flying open and Niles dashing out into the snow.

I missed. I start limping after him, but the adrenaline is fading fast from my system, and I'm feeling cold and numb.

"Chris, stop!" Doctor Turner cries.

Her hurried footsteps chase after me, and she's just in time to catch me as I fall. I blink up at her helmet. Then my eyes slam shut.

The next time they open, it's because both her and Jessica are screaming at me, telling me to stay awake, but they sound muffled and far away. I can feel them dragging me.

Then it's lights out again.

DAY FOUR

CHAPTER 44

I wake up in a bed in the treatment room, feeling warm and surrounded by beeping machines. My curtain is only half-drawn. A light is on a few cubicles over. My ribs feel better, but still ache with every breath.

Bree appears standing over me, followed by Gaby—pale-faced and red-eyed, with sharp, bony features and four flexible stalks now clearly visible above her head.

"Daddy!" she cries in that husky voice she now has. The stalks above her head flatten slightly, like a dog's ears would.

I wrap an arm around Gaby and rub her bony back. Her vertebrae are more pronounced than I remember them. I'm unnerved by her appearance, but she doesn't seem to be sick anymore, and hearing her say *Daddy* reinforces a growing conviction that she's still my little girl.

Bree looks on with tears brimming in her eyes, biting her lower lip and smiling faintly.

Zach and my mother come shuffling over on my other side, looking worried. I pull my son in under my other arm and try on a crooked smile, but it comes out as a wince. My lips are cracked, so even smiling hurts.

My mother grips my arm in a tight, desperate grip and regards me quietly.

Working some moisture into my mouth, I jerk my chin to Bree and ask, "How long was I out?"

And with that, her face crumples and tears rain down her cheeks like a dam just broke. She piles on around the kids, being careful to mind my broken ribs, and buries her face in my neck, sobbing.

I smile and move my hand from Gaby's back to my wife's. "It's okay. I'm okay. We made it."

Even as I say that, I realize exactly who made it. Jessica and her two kids are looking on from beds across the room. Doctor Turner is there, too, blinking sleepily at us. She's getting up now, swinging legs over the side of her bed.

But there's no sign of Niles.

That realization brings with it a cold sobering weight that settles uneasily in my gut. Did he freeze to death out there? Or did he come back, delirious and frost-bitten, while I was recovering?

"Where is Niles?" I ask.

Bree withdraws, wiping tears and smiling grimly at me. Her smile fades as she shakes her head to acknowledge the question.

"We don't know. We never found him."

"How long has it been?"

"Almost an entire day. You nearly died."

That takes me by surprise. "By now you should know I'm not that easy to kill," I say with another crooked smile gracing my lips. But that facade crumbles fast. With Niles missing, it doesn't feel right to be smug.

Survivor's guilt rears its familiar head. I've lost people before. Squad mates. Those feelings all come rushing back now, hitting all the harder as I stare into Sean and Haley Pearson's faces. If we don't find Niles, they'll have lost a father.

"He must be lucid by now," I say. "We'll find him."

Bree nods quietly, and I try to sit up as Doctor Turner comes shuffling over.

"You're not going anywhere. Those ribs are still healing, and your stitches will tear if you go walking around before you've had a chance to heal."

"I *feel* better, though."

"That's the morphine talking. Lie still."

I recognize the warm, relaxing sensation for what it is just as she names the drug. Of course, they doped me up. Part of me wishes I'd had some say in the matter, but I also know how bad my injuries must have been for the doctor to provide that level of pain relief. I do as I'm told and watch as the doctor lifts my sheets to reveal nothing but a flimsy hospital gown underneath. I wonder who undressed me. Must have been a hell of a thing to pull off my clothes if I was unconscious. Even getting me up into this bed...

Doctor Turner lifts the gown to reveal a thick white roll of bandages running all the way around my torso. The bandages are patched with blood.

"We'll have to change those soon," she says.

"Hang on," I say, releasing Zach to ward off the doctor before she can come at me with a fresh roll of gauze. "I'm awake now. We need to leave before more of them can come here. They know where we are."

"It's been almost twelve hours," my mother says. "Wouldn't they have come by now? Maybe we got them all."

"Or maybe they're waiting for reinforcements from the valley."

"He's right," Bree says. "We need to go."

"Go where?" Jessica demands. "I'm not going anywhere until we find my husband."

"We can find another house to hide in," I suggest. "Or some business around here. I doubt anything is open right now. We just need to get away from the scene of the crime. We killed three of them here. If more come and they find those bodies..."

"Let's get you dressed," Bree says.

Doctor Turner is watching us uncertainly.

"What about your house?" I ask her.

She hesitates, then nods. "It's nearby."

"Safe?" I ask as Bree helps me to swing my

legs over the side of the bed.

"About as safe as anywhere," she says.

"Good." I look to Jessica, who's scowling darkly at me. "We'll look for Niles from there."

She looks like she's about to argue. The defiant gleam in Jessica's eyes makes me worry that she's just about to start a mutiny at gunpoint until we all go marching outside to find Niles.

Doctor Turner seems to realize what might be going through Jessica's head, and she hurries over to snatch the Glock away from her.

"You need your hands free to help your kids," she explains.

Jessica reacts belatedly with a scowl, but then turns away and starts snapping orders at her kids, telling them to put on their coats and boots. A knot of tension loosens inside my chest. Crisis averted. For now.

Ten minutes later, all nine of us go stumbling out into the cold with heavy bags of clothes, guns, and medical equipment. It's not dark yet, but I can see that it's just about to be. The sun is already dipping below the trees. If I was out for twelve hours, then I must have lost consciousness just before dawn.

I wonder if it's a coincidence that the majority of our encounters with the aliens have been at night. They arrived at night, too. Maybe they're nocturnal.

"Who's driving?" Doctor Turner asks as she helps me into one of the middle seats of the Pearsons' Suburban.

"I am," Jessica says.

"Come on, quickly," I say, gesturing for Gaby and Zach to hurry as they squeeze by me to the back seats. Then come Sean and Haley. Neither of them says a word to me as they take their seats, but they are watching my daughter with thinly-veiled terror. I'm not sure I blame them. She does look like something out of a kid's worst nightmares.

I'm still mulling over Sean and Haley's reaction to Gaby as the others finish packing the back of the Suburban. Bree squeezes past me and Sean Pearson in the aisle between middle seats to put Gaby on her lap in the back. My mother does the same with Zach. Then Doctor Turner jumps in on the passenger's side, still holding the Glock she took from Jessica earlier. I notice the way she's handling the gun, and can't help but recognize she's had some experience with firearms.

My eyebrows shoot up at that. I guess her rule about not using guns wasn't as firm as I thought. That, or maybe her dad taught her before she developed her anti-gun policy as an adult.

Jessica jumps in behind the wheel with a shotgun and balances it in her lap as she hits the ignition and puts on her seatbelt.

Lights snap on all over the dash and the big holo display between the front seats. Headlights blaze to life, illuminating the snowy world outside.

Jessica turns the wheel and hits the accelerator, and we go whirring out of the parking lot. Night falls, plunging Big Bear into a world of shadows and starlight as we go racing down the street to the main boulevard.

And then something unexpected happens. The streetlights come blazing to life, followed by the warm glow from businesses' holo signs and store fronts.

Power is back.

We hit the main boulevard just as three big black vehicles with sloping sides, small windows, and gun turrets on top go gliding by, hovering a few feet above the blacktop. Jessica slams on the brakes, and I smash my face into the seat in front of me. A dull ache erupts from my side, but it's not even enough to make me grimace. The morphine is still doing its job. Good stuff.

"What were those?" Jessica asks in a terrified whisper.

"Looked like enemy troop transports," I say. But they didn't seem big enough to carry any of the four-legged Behemoths. *Are they loaded up with Demons?* I wonder.

"Do you think they spotted us?" Bree whispers from the back.

Before I can venture a guess, one of the vehicles comes whirring back around and glides to a stop with dark blue headlights facing us.

"Come out with your hands up!" a deep,

booming voice exclaims.

My heart starts slamming against my sternum. Do they know what we did? Why else would they stop us?

"Oh no, oh no, oh no. What are we going to do?" Jessica whispers frantically. "What if we... what if we go back? I'm going to back up."

"Don't." My eyes are on the gun turret at the top of the hovering transport. It looks like it belongs on a tank or a mech. One shot from that gun would probably incinerate us all.

"Everybody get out. Slowly," I add. "And leave the guns in the car."

CHAPTER 45

We've been standing outside, shivering on the snow-covered street for at least a minute before a response comes from the hovering troop transport in front of us. I hear a sound like a door sliding open, and then see what look like humans in full suits of glossy black armor come marching out. Four of them, with matching black rifles.

A fire team? Are these our soldiers who have switched sides? I wonder. They'd have to be, because the armor isn't ours, and neither is this troop transport. We don't have the tech to defy gravity as effortlessly as that vehicle is doing.

These soldiers, whoever they are, are wearing helmets with tinted face plates, so there's no way for me to know for sure what they are. The number and position of their limbs checks out to be human. Their size, too. They're far too big to be Demons.

But they could also be hybrids like Gaby and Niles. I glance back at my daughter. She's hiding behind Bree's legs. Doctor Turner is standing close beside them, helping my daughter to stay out of sight. But I can still see a sliver of Gaby between Bree's legs. She's peeking out with one red eye. She doesn't even appear to be shivering. Her body temperature runs naturally hot, but shouldn't that make her even *more* susceptible to the cold? It makes me realize just how little we know about this new species that our daughter has become.

Looking away, I see one of the armored humanoids step to the fore and reach up to its helmet. It gives a twist and then pulls it off. Jessica sucks in a shallow breath. Haley Pearson makes a strangled sound. Zach mutters something about freaks.

But I bite my tongue as that bony, chalk-white face appears. Red, alien eyes squint at us through the glare of the Suburban's headlights. Four flexible stalks slowly erect themselves now that they're no longer being flattened by a helmet.

"Come over here," the leader tells us in a voice that is even deeper and huskier than Gaby's.

I hesitate briefly before starting across the odd fifteen feet of snow that separates us. I'm limping carefully. The morphine is still doing its job, but I can feel the stitches pulling, and I don't want to start bleeding out again.

"Stop," the man says. He holds up an armored hand, and drops the other to a bulky black pistol holstered at his side. "You're injured. What happened?"

My mind blanks. What can I say that won't implicate us in the recent encounters? They're going to find the bodies sooner or later. Did we leave any evidence that will point to us?

"Well?" the alien hybrid demands.

"Our daughter got infected," Bree says before I can reply. She steps up beside me with Gaby, and I notice several of the soldiers standing behind their leader stiffen with her appearance. Their aim wavers to her, and one of them even appears to rock back on its heels. These hybrids are surprised to see her. Why? I wonder.

"How did the child get infected?" the leader asks.

I realize we're getting back into dangerous territory. I seize on the only excuse I can think of that doesn't implicate us in killing the flying aliens. "We ran into another hybrid," I say.

"A Chimera," the leader replies, correcting me. "Go on."

"It bit her," I say, jerking a thumb to my daughter.

My mother sends me a sharp look, as if she's just realized what an elaborate lie I'm concocting. Technically, Gaby bit Niles, not the other way around. But none of that matters now.

"Was it a Dreg?" the Chimera asks.

"A what?" I reply, shaking my head.

"One of the ones who failed to ascend."

"Ascend..." I echo quietly. "That's what you call it?" I ask, pointing to the one I'm speaking with. "Becoming a hybrid is Ascending?"

"That's what the Kyra call it. Your daughter is lucky. The Kyra have screening tests for a reason. Not everyone is worthy of ascension. Clearly she was. Did any of the rest of you get bitten? Or scratched? Any signs of a fever?"

We each shake our heads, looking from one to another to verify that no one is feeling ill.

"I'll need to verify that." The Chimera produces a wand-shaped device from its belt. He points it at us, and a bright blue light blazes out from the tip of the wand. A beep sounds, and I blink the spots from my eyes to see the Chimera studying a glowing display floating in the air, projected behind the apparatus.

"Your temperatures are all normal, and there are no other signs of infection. That's good news. You need to come with us. I think we found the Dreg who attacked you."

Niles. A sinking feeling settles in the pit of my stomach.

"Is he okay?" Jessica asks suddenly.

I send her a sharp look, but she doesn't seem to notice. Thankfully, neither does the Chimeran soldier.

"No, he's not okay. Dregs are mindless animals, and they're dangerous, as you found out, because they remain infectious even after turning. We had to put him down."

"No!" Jessica cries. "You fucking monsters!" she adds as she rushes out at them. Three rifles snap up and the barrels converge on her chest.

"Stop!" the leader warns as his pistol clears the holster and comes into line with her as well.

She comes to her senses and stops short of actually reaching the Chimeras, but her fists are balled and her chest is heaving.

"You knew the Dreg?"

"He was my husband!" Jessica screams.

The Chimera looks to me, its red eyes flinty and full of suspicion. I can tell that he's trying to fit this new piece of information in with the rest of the story that I've told him. Is it a contradiction? Not necessarily, I decide. I can make this work.

"You said you ran into him. But the Dreg was her husband?"

"We didn't know it was him at the time."

"Ahh. I see. You met up after he turned...?"

"Yes," I lie, hoping that the Chimeras' enhanced physiology doesn't give them some kind of ability to tell when a person is lying.

But the alien hybrid gives up the interrogation and half turns to indicate his transport. "You need to come with us. It's not safe here. We've heard reports of Kyron Heretics operating in this area."

"Heretics?" I ask. Bree looks to me with eyebrows raised. Doctor Turner is frowning deeply, the wheels turning inside her head.

"What does that mean? Heretic?" I ask.

"That's need to know, I'm afraid. And I don't,

so I couldn't tell you if I wanted to. All I know is that they're outlaws among the Kyra. Now let's go. Hurry it up before we find out what they are the hard way."

"Where are you taking us?" Bree asks.

"To one of the safe zones. Are you from around here?"

I shake my head. "No. Just visiting a family cabin. We're from San Bernardino."

"You're lucky. LA was the hardest hit. One of the safe zones is smack in the middle of San Berdoo. If your home isn't in it, you can bunk with the other refugees in one of the communal facilities. Either way, it's not safe for you to be up here with Dregs and Heretics on the loose—and with a Chimeran child, of all things. My CO will be eager to meet her. We don't get a lot of ascended children. You're gonna have a bright future with the Guard, kiddo."

My mind is racing to catch up, piecing together terms that I've heard only once or twice before. Bret mentioned some of this before he went for that gun and I shot him. These guys have the bearing of soldiers from the Union Army, or of Marines from Space Force. But I can't imagine any of our guys laying down their arms peacefully—certainly not switching sides at the drop of a hat. Is this what has been happening since the enemy arrived? They've been working around the clock to turn our soldiers into *their* soldiers?

"Did you hear me, sir? I said it's not safe to—"

"What's your name?" I ask suddenly, as if learning that might somehow humanize him.

"Marine Sergeant Diedrick. You are?"

"Former Union Army Corporal Christopher Randall," I say. I'm trying to foster some type of kinship with these men. To make it clear that we all served, so I'm a friendly.

"Nice to meet you, Corporal Randall. Let's get your people in where it's warm, yes?"

"Yeah," I agree, and then lead the way, limping toward the alien transport. Glancing back, I see Bree holding both of our kids' hands. My mother trails behind them with Doctor Turner. Jessica and her kids are the last to follow. All three of them are crying, still mourning Niles' death.

I awkwardly climb a flight of three short steps into a cramped, bus-style interior with a low ceiling and an aisle running between the seats. Easing down into the nearest seat, I slide down to the window. Gaby comes to sit next to me and curls up against my uninjured side, clearly frightened. I wrap an arm around her shoulders and sit staring numbly ahead as the others come in. One difference from the average bus: ample leg room and racks for equipment along the walls and the backs of the seats. Bree and Zach come sit in the seats across the aisle from us. My mother and Doctor Turner slide in behind them. Jessica, Sean, and Haley crowd into the two seats behind mine. Then come the soldiers. I notice there isn't any space for a driver up front, nor for a gunner to man that turret on the roof.

The soldiers march by us in the aisle, their red eyes gleaming faintly behind their tinted black helmets.

The Sergeant offers a grim smile that curves his black lips and reveals sharp-looking white teeth. He nods to me as he walks by, and I twist around as far as my ribs will allow to watch as his men sit two rows behind us. They keep their eyes to the front, rifles balanced in their laps. They feel like the enemy, and I realize from their stiff postures and silent demeanors that they probably feel the same way about us.

Suppressing a shiver, I look away from them to the sergeant, who walks all the way to the back and sits down at some kind of control station with a rear-facing chair that swivels in the aisle. He sits and turns that chair to face the back of the vehicle, then reaches up to tap a curving, blank gray surface in front of him. The metal shimmers and becomes transparent, revealing a matching set of dim blue lights shining out the rear end of the transport.

We begin rolling backward, whooshing almost soundlessly down the snow-covered street, picking up speed. Streetlights flicker past the windows, shades of vermilion and copper peeling the shadows from my family's faces.

What I had assumed was the front of the vehicle was actually the back. Or maybe they can drive in both directions with equal ease. Looking back to my end of the vehicle I don't see a second control station, but I do spot a rail in the aisle that the sergeant's chair might be able to slide along in order to reach this end.

I twist around to watch the sergeant swiping and gesturing in the air, effortlessly summoning and minimizing alien versions of holoscreens. Every now and then the sergeant says something in a language that is both strikingly alien and vaguely familiar. It takes me a second to realize where I've heard it before.

It sounds like the chattering, sing-song language that the Demon was using to communicate with the Behemoths outside the Pharmacy.

I remember what Sergeant Diedrick said about Heretics operating in Big Bear. Were we attacked by some divergent group of alien outlaws?

I try to recall what that flying alien said to me when it was trying to get us to surrender. It called itself Primark Turian of the Riko... Rika? Ree-something, anyway. He said that Gaby is the first of a royal blood line. But what is that supposed to mean?

I swallow thickly, past a growing knot in my throat. It's been there ever since Sergeant Diedrick told us that they had to execute Niles because he was something called a *Dreg*.

These men, whoever they are now, are definitely not Union Soldiers anymore. It's only been four days since the Kyra arrived. That's not enough time for anyone to learn an alien language, much less how to operate their vehicles, and yet Sergeant Diedrick has managed to do both. His knowledge had to have been *implanted*, which means his attitudes and agenda probably were, too. These soldiers are all like Bret.

Brainwashed.

That makes me wonder if we can really trust them, or anything that they've told us. Maybe they know what we did. Maybe, this is just a sneaky way to arrest us.

Or maybe, there are no Heretics, and they were sent here to recover Gaby. I tighten my grip around her shoulders and grind my teeth, wishing I had found some way to smuggle a gun out of the Suburban.

Glancing over at Bree, she smiles tightly at me, and I notice her clutching her pocket.

There's a faint outline there.

A Glock.

My eyes widen, then crinkle in a smile. *I love you,* I mouth to her.

She mouths the same thing back, but there's a tightness around her eyes, and I realize that she's clutching that gun not to hide it, but because she's thinking she might have to use it.

I give my head a slight shake.

Don't.

She dips her chin. Relaxes slightly.

Gaby catches my eye as I look away, peering up at me, biting her lower lip. Something is worrying her, too.

"It's okay," I whisper. "We're safe now."

Lies come easily to a parent's lips.

"It's not that," she whispers back in her husky, alien voice.

I arch an eyebrow at my daughter.

Her crimson eyes dart around briefly, then she leans up to whisper in my ear:

"Can you hear them?"

"No. Hear what?" I ask.

Her cranial stalks flatten, then twitch, and I see two of them rotate to face behind us; the cones at the tips flare wide. Ears. That's what they are, I realize, confirming one of my early suspicions. And yet Gaby still has her human ears, too. She must have incredible hearing. I'm not surprised she's hearing things that I'm not.

"The voices," Gaby says.

"Are they talking about anything important?" I whisper back.

"It's not like that," she says.

"What do you mean?"

Gaby winces and her cranial stalks flatten completely. "They're all talking at the same time, and not to each other."

My brow furrows. Maybe they're on their comms, all talking to their loved ones at the same time?

But this isn't the first time Gaby was hearing

things. She heard Bret outside, and something she described as *sounds,* not talking.

Suspicion trickles through my gut, half-formed, but taking shape.

Gaby isn't hearing the soldiers talking inside their helmets.

She's hearing their *thoughts.*

Twisting around, I peer back at them over the Pearson kids' shoulders under the guise of looking out the forward display in front of Sergeant Diedrick. I see three glossy black helmets and three dimly-glaring pairs of alien eyes. Sergeant Diedrick's back is turned, but suddenly it feels like even he is watching me.

Are all Chimeras telepaths? If Gaby can read their thoughts, can they read mine?

If so, then they know exactly how many of the Demons I've killed. And how many of those four-legged Behemoths, too. The fact the sergeant didn't call me out on my lies tells me that we're in a whole hell of a lot more trouble than I thought.

Looking back to Bree, I eye the vague outline of the Glock in her jacket pocket. If I can find some excuse to go sit with her, maybe I could get my hands on it. The question is, can I shoot these four Chimeras before they can shoot me?

I look back down at Gaby and wonder if she's been silently following my train of thought.

Gaby, I think at her.

No response.

Gaby!

Not a blink.

"Gaby," I say aloud.

"Yes, Daddy?"

A world of tension bleeds out of me, and I sag against my seat.

I must be wrong about what Gaby can do. Maybe she really is hearing them talking through their helmets.

And maybe these soldiers really are escorting us to one of the "safe" zones.

I want to believe that. I really do. But something tells me there's no such thing as safe anymore, and that wherever we're headed, I'm going to need that gun. I'll be damned if they're going to turn me into a slave soldier.

Maybe the invasion is over, maybe they won, but I don't think it's that simple. The Kyra want us to help them fight their battles, and it looks like they're giving us the weapons and the gear to do it. Won't they be surprised when we turn those guns on them instead.

Vive la resistance.

GET THE SEQUEL FOR FREE

**New World Order
(The Kyron Invasion, Book 2)**

(Coming October 2021)

Pre-order it From Amazon Now

OR

Get a FREE digital copy if you post an honest review of this book on Amazon (https://geni.us/ki1review)

And then send it to me here (files.jaspertscott.com/invasion2free.htm).

Thank you in advance for your feedback! I read every review and use your comments to improve my work.

KEEP IN TOUCH

SUBSCRIBE to my Mailing List and get two FREE Books! (http://files.jaspertscott.com/mailinglist.html)

Follow me on Bookbub:

https://www.bookbub.com/authors/jasper-t-scott

Follow me on Amazon:

https://www.amazon.com/Jasper-T-Scott/e/B00B7A2CT4

Look me up on Facebook:

https://www.facebook.com/jaspertscott/

Check out my Website:

www.JasperTscott.com

Follow me on Twitter:

@JasperTscott

Or send me an e-mail:

JasperTscott@gmail.com

MORE BOOKS
BY JASPER T. SCOTT

Keep up with new releases and get two free books by signing up for his newsletter at www.jaspertscott.com

Note: as an Amazon Associate I earn a small commission from qualifying purchases.

The Cade Korbin Chronicles

The Bounty Hunter | Alien Artifacts | Paragon | The Omega Protocol

The Kyron Invasion

Arrival | New World Order | End Game

Ascension Wars

First Encounter | Occupied Earth | Fractured Earth | Second Encounter

Final Days

Final Days | Colony | Escape

Scott Standalones (No Sequels, No Cliffhangers)

Under Darkness | Into the Unknown | In Time for Revenge

Rogue Star

Rogue Star: Frozen Earth | Rogue Star: New Worlds

Broken Worlds

The Awakening | The Revenants | Civil War

New Frontiers Series (Standalone Prequels to Dark Space)

Excelsior | Mindscape | Exodus

Dark Space Series

Dark Space | The Invisible War | Origin | Revenge | Avilon | Armageddon

Dark Space Universe

Dark Space Universe | The Enemy Within | The Last Stand

ABOUT THE AUTHOR

Jasper Scott is a USA Today bestselling author of more than thirty sci-fi novels. With over a million copies sold, Jasper's work has been translated into various languages and published around the world.

He was born and raised in Canada by South African parents, with a British heritage on his mother's side and German on his father's. He now lives in an exotic locale with his wife, their two kids, and two Chihuahuas.

Made in the USA
Las Vegas, NV
01 November 2023

80080311R00215